AF589082

Bedside Companion to the Sea

Bedside Companion to the Sea

EDITED BY JANE MCMORLAND HUNTER
ILLUSTRATIONS BY ELEN WINATA

BATSFORD

First published in the United Kingdom
in 2026 by
Batsford
43 Great Ormond Street
London
WC1N 3HZ

An imprint of B. T. Batsford Holdings Limited

ISBN 978 1 83733 057 7

A CIP catalogue record for this book is available from the British Library.

10 9 8 7 6 5 4 3 2 1

Printed by Dream Colour, China
Reproduction by Rival Colour Ltd, UK

Illustrations by Elen Winata

This book can be ordered direct from the publisher at www.batsfordbooks.com, or try your local bookshop

Distributed throughout the UK and Europe by Abrams & Chronicle Books, 1st Floor, 22–24 Ely Place, London EC1N 6TE and 57 rue Gaston Tessier, 75166 Paris, France.

www.abramsandchronicle.co.uk
info@abramsandchronicle.co.uk

CONTENTS

To Mum and Dad, with happy memories of times at the seaside.

And also to Matilda, who would have hated it.

Acknowledgements

As always I want to thank Hatchards, at Piccadilly, St Pancras and Cheltenham, for looking after my books so well, and everyone at Hatchards Piccadilly in particular, for being so tolerant of the author/editor in their midst. Also, thanks to Alessia, Beth, Chris, Francis, Julia, Julie and Miranda for suggestions. Finally, thanks to my editors Nicola Newman and Magdalen Simões-Brown, and everyone at Batsford who helps with these anthologies.

About the editor

Jane McMorland Hunter has compiled anthologies for Batsford and the National Trust including collections on gardening, nature, friendship, London, England and the First World War. She has also worked as a gardener, potter and quilter, writes gardening, nature, cookery craft and children's books, and works at Hatchards Bookshop in Piccadilly. She was brought up near the seaside, but now lives happily in London with Matilda, a small grey tabby, in a house overflowing with books and a small garden overflowing with plants.

Introduction

I have lived in Britain all my life and although nowhere on this island is more than about 112km (70 miles) from the coast, I have always lived considerably closer than that and could not imagine a life lived far from the sea. My childhood was dominated by seaside trips where thick jerseys were the norm and windbreaks more important than parasols. I grew up jumping white horses in freezing waters, peering into rock pools, building elaborate castles and eating sandwiches gritty with sand. And I loved every moment of it. While researching this anthology, I discovered that mine was only one experience of the sea and my plan is to give the reader a taste of everything from adventure and excitement to beauty and gentle relaxation in works of fact and fiction, prose and poetry, adult and children's books. The entries range from the eighth century BCE to the present day and span the globe. Apart from complete poems, all extracts are accompanied by a listing of their original sources – indeed, I hope many readers will be inspired to seek out some of the entire works. For most of the prose entries, I have also given the date of when the work was first published. In some cases, this is important, as attitudes towards the sea have changed considerably during the timespan of these pieces and it is often as important to know when something was written as the actual opinions expressed within the piece.

Over the years the sea has been feared, worshipped, seen as a safe or perilous place to travel, regarded as a health cure and, most recently, as a source of recreation. Etiquette has changed too, with Victorian bathing machines giving way to a freer approach to swimming, and travel for summer beach-side holidays becoming both easier and more affordable. Many of the pieces involve travel of some type, with Phileas Fogg's well-known journey around the globe, as well as the real voyages of Nellie Bly, Joshua Slocum and others. There are journeys through ice and ships becalmed on placid seas and, of course, there are shipwrecks. There is even useful advice on how and when to travel from Rev Frank Tatchell. I have included all types of ships from pleasure crafts to slave and prison ships. Cargo vessels, workaday ferries, fishing smacks and submarines all have a place here, too.

Many people's introduction to the sea is at the beach or seaside and I have tried to include all holidays, with advice on 1930s British seaside attire to cultural and ethnic attitudes and biases. Then there are also the activities: surfing, sailing, swimming, fishing and beachcombing. Some rubbish such as driftwood, broken glass and china, can be rendered beautiful by the action of the sea over time. The more polluting plastics rarely age so charmingly.

Feelings range from passion to loathing but all writers seem to find it hard to explain the lure of the sea. Many of these extracts see their subjects leaving comfortable homes to embark on wild and often dangerous adventures on the high seas. For some it is the promise of discovery or treasure but for many it is something less tangible – perhaps the appeal of the unknown best sums it up.

I have also included the land which adjoins the sea – so often a changing area between high and low water. There are descriptions of sand dunes and estuaries, examples of the sea reclaiming the land and landmarks such as lighthouses. Islands are featured too, including one of my favourite pieces – Rachel Field's delightful and perceptive poem pointing out that you are never the same once you have slept on an island.

Much of the natural life of the sea is hidden below the surface. There are pieces here on fish, shells and plants and, of course, the monsters of the deep. From gigantic sea serpents to mermaids, mermen, selkies and sirens, the sea has a fantasy and mythology of its own. Ghosts and magic are also here, with a haunted cabin and vessels made of wizardwood. Sea-related subjects such as the Shipping Forecast, seasickness and white horses also have their places. Some of the locations and characters are well known – Neptune and Atlantis, Ishmael and Robinson Crusoe, Noah's Ark and the Titanic, Land's End and the Bay of Biscay and Byron's famous swim across the Hellespont – and others may, I hope, be new to readers.

When I began collecting the extracts, I envisaged a balance of weathers – perhaps with delightful summers on the water predominating. Instead, it seems storms, danger and hardship most inspire writers – as Joshua Slocum so aptly writes, 'But where, after all, would be the poetry of the sea were there no wild waves?'

Inevitably there were a great many pieces I could not include for reasons of space and copyright. Therefore I have worked on the slightly unrealistic premise that during the summer months, everyone has time to sit on or beside the sea and indulge in a little nautical reading. I have given recommended reading lists on the first day of each of the summer months: fiction, journeys and general non-fiction, listing books not included in the main selection. The lists are unbalanced and I am sure I shall have omitted many readers' favourites but they are all books I have enjoyed or found interesting.

Most of my anthologies do not come with a message or particular opinion. There is obviously a degree of personal bias but I try to present a reasonably balanced picture. While compiling this anthology one thing became clear to me – we have misused the sea. The calm blue surface may look clean and pristine but this can often disguise the environmental turmoil below. In 1896, Edward Step wrote 'The ocean does almost everything for man', and my final wish is that perhaps this collection will make people more aware of the marvels of the seas and so lead them to respect and look after them better.

JANUARY

In the Unknown Deeps

Sonnet LXXI

Written at Weymouth in Winter | Charlotte Smith (1749–1806)

The chill waves whiten in the sharp north-east;
    Cold, cold the night-blast comes, with sullen sound,
And black and gloomy, like my cheerless breast:
    Frowns the dark pier and lonely sea-view round.
Yet a few months – and on the peopled strand
    Pleasure shall all her varied forms display;
Nymphs lightly tread the bright reflecting sand,
    And proud sails whiten all the summer bay:
Then, from these winds that whistle keen and bleak,
    Music's delightful melodies shall float
O'er the blue waters; but 'tis mine to seek
    Rather, some unfrequented shade, remote
From sights and sounds of gaiety – I mourn
All that gave *me* delight – Ah! never to return!

The Need to Go to Sea

From *Moby-Dick, or the Whale, 1851* | Herman Melville (1819–1891)

Call me Ishmael. Some years ago – never mind how long precisely – having little or no money in my purse, and nothing particular to interest me on shore, I thought I would sail about a little and see the watery part of the world. It is a way I have of driving off the spleen and regulating the circulation. Whenever I find myself growing grim about the mouth; whenever it is a damp, drizzly November in my soul; whenever I find myself involuntarily pausing before coffin warehouses, and bringing up the rear of every funeral I meet; and especially whenever my hypos get such an upper hand of me, that it requires a strong moral principle to prevent me from deliberately stepping into the street, and methodically knocking people's hats off – then, I account it high time to get to sea as soon as I can. This is my substitute for pistol and ball. With a philosophical flourish Cato throws himself upon his sword; I quietly take to the ship. There is nothing surprising in this. If they but knew it, almost all men in their degree, some time or other, cherish very nearly the same feelings towards the ocean with me.

Mist surrounds the ship

Lemn Sissay (1967–)

Mist surrounds the ship
Icebergs draw near
The crew fall silent
And pray for it to clear

The Merchant Ships of India

From *The Travels, 1271–1295, published c. 1300*

The Book of Ser Marco Polo, the Venetian | Marco Polo (1254–1324)

Co-written by Rustichello da Pisa (fl. late 13th century)

Translated by Henry Yule, 1871 (1820–1889)

These ships, you must know, are of fir timber. They have but one deck, though each of them contains some 50 or 60 cabins, wherein the merchants abide greatly at their ease, every man having one to himself. The ship hath but one rudder, but it hath four masts; and sometimes they have two additional masts, which they ship and unship at pleasure.

[Moreover the larger of their vessels have some thirteen compartments or severances in the interior, made with planking strongly framed, in case mayhap the ship should spring a leak, either by running on a rock or by the blow of a hungry whale (as shall betide ofttimes, for when the ship in her course by night sends a ripple back alongside of the whale, the creature seeing the foam fancies there is something to eat afloat, and makes a rush forward, whereby it often shall stave in some part of the ship). In such case the water that enters the leak flows to the bilge, which is always kept clear; and the mariners, having ascertained where the damage is, empty the cargo from that compartment into those adjoining, for the planking is so well fitted that the water cannot pass from one compartment to another. They then stop the leak and replace the lading.]

The Formation of Sand-Dunes

From *Nature Rambles, 1930* | Edward Step (1855–1931)

The tall hills of loose sand that, on many of our seashores, shut out the violent winds and the view of the sea from the low-lying land behind, have been built up with the aid of plants. Blown in grain by grain at low-water, when the upper sand is dry, it piles up at first behind the shelter of spreading shore-plants, whose prostrate stems and branches secure it from blowing back to the water. We can watch the beginning of the sand-dune or its extension on any sandy shore when the wind is blowing in from the sea.

Impressions I

Oscar Wilde (1854–1900)

Les Silhouettes

The sea is flecked with bars of grey
The dull dead wind is out of tune,
And like a withered leaf the moon
Is blown across the stormy bay.

Etched clear upon the pallid sand
The black boat lies: a sailor boy
Clambers aboard in careless joy
With laughing face and gleaming hand.

And overheard the curlews cry,
Where through the dusky upland grass
The young brown-throated reapers pass,
Like silhouettes against the sky.

The Fear Line

From *Barbarian Days: A Surfing Life*, 2015

William Finnegan (1952–)

Surfing always had this horizon, this fear line, that made it different from other things, certainly from other sports I knew. You could do it with friends, but when the waves got big, or you got into trouble, there never seemed to be anyone around.

Everything out there was disturbingly interlaced with everything else. Waves were the playing field. They were the goal. They were the object of your deepest desire and adoration. At the same time, they were your adversary, your nemesis, even your mortal enemy. The surf was your refuge, your happy hiding place, but it was also a hostile wilderness – a dynamic, indifferent world. At thirteen, I had mostly stopped believing in God, but that was a new development, and it had left a hole in my world, a feeling that I'd been abandoned. The ocean was like an uncaring God, endlessly dangerous, power beyond measure.

The Seafarer

From *Codex Exoniensis: The Seafarer, lines 1–30* |

Anon, translated by Benjamin Thorpe (1782–1870)

I of myself can
a true tale relate,
my fortunes recount,
how I, in days of toil,
a time of hardship
oft suffer'd,
bitter breast-cares
have endur'd,
prov'd in *the* ship
strange mishaps many.
The fell rolling of *the* waves
has me there oft drench'd:
an anxious night-watch,
at *the* vessel's prow,
when on the cliffs it strikes,
pierc'd with cold
were my feet,
bound with frost,
with cold bonds.
There cares sigh'd
hot around *my* heart,
hunger tore *me* within,
the sea-wolf's rage.
That *the* man knows not,
to whom on land
all falls out most joyfully,
how I miserable and sad,
on *the* ice-cold sea
a winter pass'd,
with exile traces.

The Shivering Sand

From *The Moonstone, 1868* | Wilkie Collins (1824–1899)

9 January

The sand-hills here run down to the sea, and end in two spits of rock jutting out opposite each other, till you lose sight of them in the water. One is called the North Spit, and one the South. Between the two, shifting backwards and forwards at certain seasons of the year, lies the most horrible quicksand on the shores of Yorkshire. At the turn of the tide, something goes on in the unknown deeps below, which sets the whole face of the quicksand shivering and trembling in a manner most remarkable to see, and which has given to it, among the people in our parts, the name of the Shivering Sand. A great bank, half a mile out, nigh the mouth of the bay, breaks the force of the main ocean coming in from the offing. Winter and summer, when the tide flows over the quicksand, the sea seems to leave the waves behind it on the bank, and rolls its waters in smoothly with a heave, and covers the sand in silence. A lonesome and a horrid retreat, I can tell you! No boat ever ventures into this bay. No children from our fishing-village, called Cobb's Hole, ever come here to play. The very birds of the air, as it seems to me, give the Shivering Sand a wide berth.

Under the Surface

Part I | Frances Ridley Havergal (1836–1879)

I

On the surface, foam and roar,
  Restless heave and passionate dash,
Shingle rattle along the shore,
  Gathering boom and thundering crash.

Under the surface, soft green light,
  A hush of peace and an endless calm,
Winds and waves from a choral height,
  Falling sweet as a far-off psalm.

On the surface, swell and swirl,
  Tossing weed and drifting waif,
Broken spars that the mad waves whirl,
  Where wreck-watching rocks they chafe.

Under the surface, loveliest forms,
  Feathery fronds with crimson curl,
Treasures too deep for the raid of storms,
  Delicate coral and hidden pearl.

II

On the surface, lilies white,
  A painted skiff with a singing crew,
Sky-reflections soft and bright,
  Tremulous crimson, gold and blue.

Under the surface, life in death,
  Slimy tangle and oozy moans,
Creeping things with watery breath,
  Blackening roots and whitening bones.

On the surface a shining reach,
    A crystal couch for the moonbeams' rest,
Starry ripples along the beach,
    Sunset songs from the breezy west.

Under the surface, glooms and fears,
    Treacherous currents swift and strong,
Deafening rush in the drowning ears:
    Have ye rightly read my song?

A Happy Thing

From *Twelve Years a Slave, 1853* | Solomon Northup (1807/8–c. 1863)

Scarcely were we out of sight of land before we were overtaken by a violent storm. The brig rolled and plunged until we feared she would go down. Some were sea-sick, others on their knees praying, while some were fast holding to each other, paralyzed with fear. The sea-sickness rendered the place of our confinement loathsome and disgusting. It would have been a happy thing for most of us – it would have saved the agony of many hundred lashes, and miserable deaths at last – had the compassionate sea snatched us that day from the clutches of remorseless men.

Sea-Fever

John Masefield (1878–1967)

I must go down to the seas again, to the lonely sea and the sky,
And all I ask is a tall ship and a star to steer her by,
And the wheel's kick and the wind's song and the white sail's
shaking,
And a grey mist on the sea's face and a grey dawn breaking.

I must go down to the seas again, for the call of the running tide
Is a wild call and a clear call that may not be denied;
And all I ask is a windy day with the white clouds flying,
And the flung spray and the blown spume, and the sea-gulls crying.

I must go down to the seas again, to the vagrant gypsy life,
To the gull's way and the whale's way where the wind's like a whetted
knife;
And all I ask is a merry yarn from a laughing fellow-rover,
And a quiet sleep and a sweet dream when the long trick's over.

The Treasure-Ship

From *The Treasure-Ship, 1914* | Saki / H. H. Munroe (1870–1916)

The great galleon lay in semi-retirement under the sand and weed and water of the northern bay where the fortune of war and weather had long ago ensconced it. Three and a quarter centuries had passed since the day when it had taken the high seas as an important unit of a fighting squadron – precisely which squadron the learned were not agreed. The galleon had brought nothing into the world, but it had, according to tradition and report, taken much out of it. But how much? There again the learned were in disagreement. Some were as generous in their estimate as an income-tax assessor, others applied a species of higher criticism to the submerged treasure chests, and debased their contents to the currency of goblin gold.

The Wintry Ocean

From *The Ascent of Man, III, 1889* | Mathilde Blind (1841–1896)

Sinking, swelling roared the wintry ocean,
  Pitch-black chasms struck with flying blaze,
As the cloud-winged storm-sky's sheer commotion
  Showed the blank Moon's mute Medusa face
  White o'er wastes of water – surges crashing
  Over surges in the formless gloom,
And a mastless hulk, with great seas washing
  Her scourged flanks, pitched toppling to her doom.

Through the crash of wave on wave gigantic,
  Through the thunder of the hurricane,
My wild heart in breaking shrilled with frantic
  Exultation – 'Chaos come again!
  Yea, let earth be split and cloven asunder
  With man's still accumulating curse –
Life is but a momentary blunder
  In the cycle of the universe.'

The Lifeboat

From *The Open Boat, 1897* | Stephen Crane (1871–1900)

A seat in this boat was not unlike a seat upon a bucking bronco, and, by the same token, a bronco is not much smaller. The craft pranced and reared, and plunged like an animal. As each wave came, and she rose for it, she seemed like a horse making at a fence outrageously high. The manner of her scramble over these walls of water is a mystic thing, and, moreover, at the top of them were ordinarily these problems in white water, the foam racing down from the summit of each wave, requiring a new leap, and a leap from the air. Then, after scornfully bumping a crest, she would slide, and race, and splash down a long incline, and arrive bobbing and nodding in front of the next menace.

A singular disadvantage of the sea lies in the fact that after successfully surmounting one wave you discover that there is another behind it just as important and just as nervously anxious to do something effective in the way of swamping boats. In a ten-foot dinghy one can get an idea of the resources of the sea in the line of waves that is not probable to the average experience which is never at sea in a dinghy. As each slaty wall of water approached, it shut all else from the view of the men in the boat, and it was not difficult to imagine that this particular wave was the final outburst of the ocean, the last effort of the grim water. There was a terrible grace in the move of the waves, and they came in silence, save for the snarling of the crests.

Lighthouses

From *The Sea, 1861* | Jules Michelet (1798–1874)

Translated by W. H. D. Adams (1828–1891)

16 January

Who can tell how many lives and how many ships are saved by the lighthouses? Not only does their radiance, when beheld in the awful tumult of tempestuous nights which disturbs even the most intrepid – not only does it point out the path, but it sustains the courageous soul, and prevents the spirit from giving way. It is a great moral support which, in the hour of supreme peril, exclaims: 'Strive! strive! one effort more! The wind and the Sea may be against you; but you are not alone. Humanity yonder watches over you.'

The ancients, who in their voyages closely hugged the shore and never lost sight of it, had even more need than ourselves to light up its dangerous places. The Etruscans, it is said, began by maintaining watch-fires on the sacred stones. Their pharos was an alter and a temple, a column, a tower. The Celts followed their example; some very important *dôlmens* are extant, situated exactly at the most favourable points for the full display of their fires. The Romans illuminated the entire circuit of the Mediterranean, from promontory to promontory.

The Atlantides

Henry David Thoreau (1817–1862)

The smothered streams of love, which flow
More bright than Phlegethon, more low,
Island us ever, like the sea,
In an Atlantic mystery.
Our fabled shores none ever reach,
No mariner has found our beach,
Scarcely our mirage now is seen,
And neighboring waves with floating green,
Yet still the oldest charts contain
Some dotted outline of our main;
In ancient times midsummer days
Unto the western islands' gaze,
To Teneriffe and the Azores,
Have shown our faint and cloud-like shores.

But sink not yet, ye desolate isles,
Anon your coast with commerce smiles,
And richer freights ye'll furnish far
Than Africa or Malabar.
Be fair, be fertile evermore,
Ye rumored but untrodden shore,
Princes and monarchs will contend
Who first unto your land shall send,
And pawn the jewels of the crown
To call your distant soil their own.

Sea Ice

From *On Top of the World, 2005* | Bernadine Evaristo (1959–)

We travelled across the frozen desert and out onto the sea ice which resembled frosted glass. It was scary at first. Far below I could hear the hollow rumble of water. When the ice was flat, the dogs raced ahead, tongues panting, releasing themselves on the job. It was a vision of flying, smelly excrement and jets of urine which formed beautiful, fluorescent-yellow flowers in the luminous snow. Sometimes the snow was so deep, the dogs almost slowed to a full stop, or we came upon frozen waves which rose up in large, jagged lumps where the tide had pushed up against the snow and solidified. The sledge ran over them and landed with a spine-shattering bump.

Sculpted icebergs a hundred feet high were always somewhere to be seen on the horizon. Calved from glaciers years ago, they sailed slowly downstream in summer, getting trapped in ice in winter before the melting water released them again. I never got used to the crystal-clear visibility which made everything appear nearer than it actually was. Icebergs half a day away looked like I could sprint there in a mere twenty minutes. On sunny days the ice was so bright it was blue.

The Parting of the Red Sea

Exodus, 14: 15-22

The King James Bible, 1611

19 January

15: And the Lord said unto Moses, 'Wherefore criest thou unto me?'
Speak unto the children of Israel, that they go forward.
16: But lift thou up thy rod, and stretch out thine hand over the
sea, and divide it: and the children of Israel shall go on dry ground
through the midst of the sea.
17: And I, behold, I will harden the hearts of the Egyptians, and they
shall follow them: and I will get me honour upon Pharaoh, and upon
all his host, upon his chariots, and upon his horsemen.
18: And the Egyptians shall know that I am the Lord, when I have
gotten me honour upon Pharaoh, upon his chariots, and upon his
horsemen.
19: And the angel of God, which went before the camp of Israel,
removed and went behind them; and the pillar of the cloud went
from before their face, and stood behind them.
20: And it came between the camp of the Egyptians and the camp of
Israel, and it was a cloud and darkness to them, but it gave light by
night to these: so that the one came not near the other all the night.
21: And Moses stretched out his hand over the sea; and the
Lord caused the sea to go back by a strong east wind all that night,
and made the sea dry land, and the waters were divided.
22: And the children of Israel went into the midst of the sea upon
the dry ground: and the waters were a wall unto them on their right
hand, and on their left.

Neptune

From *The Aeneid, 29–19 BCE* | Virgil (70–19 BCE)

Translated by John Dryden (1631–1700)

Book I, lines 176–204

Meantime imperial *Neptune* heard the Sound
Of raging Billows breaking on the Ground;
Displeas'd, and fearing for his Wat'ry Reign,
He reard his awful Head above the Main:
Serene in Majesty, then rowl'd his Eyes
Around the Space of Earth, and Seas, and Skies.
He saw the *Trojan* Fleet dispers'd, distress'd
By stormy Winds and wintry Heav'n oppress'd.
Full well the God his Sister's envy knew,
And what her Aims, and what her Arts pursue:
He summon'd *Eurus* and the Western blast,
And first an angry glance on both he cast:
Then thus rebuk'd; Audacious Winds! from whence
This bold Attempt, this Rebel Insolence?
Is it for you to ravage Seas and Land,
Unauthoriz'd by my supreme Command?
To raise such Mountains on the troubl'd Main?
Whom I - But first 'tis fit, the Billows to restrain,
And then you shall be taught obedience to my Reign.
Hence, to your Lord my Royal Mandate bear,
The Realms of Ocean and the Fields of Air
Are mine, not his; by fatal Lot to me
The liquid Empire fell, and Trident of the Sea.
His pow'r to hollow Caverns is confin'd.
There let him reign, the Jailor of the Wind;
With hoarse Commands his breathing Subjects call,
And boast and bluster in his empty Hall.
He spoke: And while he spoke he smooth'd the Sea,
Dispell'd the Darkness and restor'd the Day.

The Mysteries of the Ocean

From *The Pirate, published 1821, dated 1822*

Sir Walter Scott (1771–1832)

The ocean also had its mysteries, the effect of which was aided by the dim twilight, through which it was imperfectly seen for more than half the year. Its bottomless depths and secret caves contained, according to the account of Sweyn and others, skilled in legendary lore, such wonders as modern navigators reject with disdain. In the quiet moonlight bay, where the waves came rippling to the shore, upon a bed of smooth sand intermingled with shells, the mermaid was still seen to glide along the waters, and, mingling her voice with the sighing breeze, was often heard to sing of subterranean wonders, or to chant prophecies of future events. The kraken, that hugest of living things, was still supposed to cumber the recesses of the Northern Ocean; and often, when some fog-bank covered the sea at a distance, the eye of the experienced boatman saw the horns of the monstrous leviathan welking and waving amidst the wreaths of mist, and bore away with all press of oar and sail, lest the sudden suction, occasioned by the sinking of the monstrous mass to the bottom, should drag within the grasp of its multifarious feelers his own frail skiff. The sea-snake was also known, which, arising out of the depths of ocean, stretches to the skies his enormous neck, covered with a mane like that of a war-horse, and with its broad glittering eyes, raised mast-head high, looks out, as it seems, for plunder or for victims.

I'd Like To Be a Lighthouse

Rachel Field (1894–1942)

I'd like to be a lighthouse
  All scrubbed and painted white.
I'd like to be a lighthouse
  And stay awake all night
To keep my eye on everything
  That sails my patch of sea;
I'd like to be a lighthouse
  With the ships all watching me.

Wrecks on a Sunday

From *The Vicar of Morwenstow: Being a Life of Robert Stepehn Hawker, 1876* | S. Baring-Gould (1834–1924)

In former times, when a ship was being driven on the rocks on Sunday, whilst divine service was going on, news was sent to the parson, who announced the fact from the pulpit, or reading-desk, whereupon ensued a rapid clearance of the church. The story is told of a parson at Poughill, near Morwenstow, who, on hearing the news, proceeded down the nave in his surplice as far as the font; and the people, supposing there was to be a christening, did not stir. But when he was near the door he shouted: 'My Christian brethren, there's a ship wrecked in the cove: let us all start fair!' and, flinging off his surplice, led the way to the scene of spoliation.

'I do not see why it is,' said a Cornish clerk one day, 'why there be prayers in the Buke o' Common Prayer for rain and for fine weather, and thanksgivings for them and for peace, and there's no prayer for wrecks, nor thanksgiving for a really gude one when it is come.'

The Voice of the Sea

From *Anne's House of Dreams, 1917* | L. M. Montgomery (1874–1942)

The Four Winds light was built on a spur of red sand-stone cliff jutting out into the gulf. On one side, across the channel, stretched the silvery sand shore of the bar; on the other, extended a long, curving beach of red cliffs, rising steeply from the pebbled coves. It was a shore that knew the magic and mystery of storm and star. There is a great solitude about such a shore. The woods are never solitary – they are full of whispering, beckoning, friendly life. But the sea is a mighty soul, forever moaning of some great, unshareable sorrow, which shuts it up into itself for all eternity. We can never pierce its infinite mystery – we may only wander, awed and spellbound, on the outer fringe of it. The woods call to us with a hundred voices, but the sea has one only – a mighty voice that drowns our souls in its majestic music. The woods are human, but the sea is of the company of the archangels.

The World Below the Brine

Walt Whitman (1819–1892)

The world below the brine,
Forests at the bottom of the sea, the branches and leaves,
Sea-lettuce, vast lichens, strange flowers and seeds, the thick tangle,
openings, and pink turf,
Different colors, pale gray and green, purple, white, and gold, the
play of light through the water,
Dumb swimmers there among the rocks, coral, gluten, grass, rushes,
and the aliment of the swimmers,
Sluggish existences grazing there suspended, or slowly crawling close
to the bottom,
The sperm-whale at the surface blowing air and spray, or disporting
with his flukes,
The leaden-eyed shark, the walrus, the turtle, the hairy sea-leopard,
and the sting-ray,
Passions there, wars, pursuits, tribes, sight in those ocean-depths,
breathing that thick-breathing air, as so many do,
The change thence to the sight here, and to the subtle air breathed by
beings like us who walk this sphere,
The change onward from ours to that of beings who walk other spheres.

Security

From *Sea Wolf, 1904* | Jack London (1876–1916)

26 January

The danger lay in the heavy fog which blanketed the bay, and of which, as a landsman, I had little apprehension. In fact, I remember the placid exaltation with which I took up my position on the forward upper deck, directly beneath the pilot-house, and allowed the mystery of the fog to lay hold of my imagination. A fresh breeze was blowing, and for a time I was alone in the moist obscurity – yet not alone, for I was dimly conscious of the presence of the pilot, and of what I took to be the captain, in the glass house above my head.

I remember thinking how comfortable it was, this division of labour which made it unnecessary for me to study fogs, winds, tides, and navigation, in order to visit my friend who lived across an arm of the sea. It was good that men should be specialists, I mused. The peculiar knowledge of the pilot and captain sufficed for many thousands of people who knew no more of the sea and navigation than I knew.

Tides

Jenny Joseph (1931–2018)

There are some coasts
Where the sea comes in spectacularly
Throwing itself up gullies, challenging cliffs,
Filling the harbours with great swirls and flourish,
A theatrical event that people gather for
Curtain up twice daily. You need to know
The hour of its starting, you have to be on guard.

There are other places
Places where you do not really notice
The gradual stretch of the fertile silk of water
No gurgling or dashings here, no froth no pounding
Only at some point the echo may sound different
And looking by chance one sees 'Oh the tide is in.'

27 January

The Phenomena of Nature

From *Domestic Manners of the Americans, 1832* |

Fanny Trollope (1779–1863)

28 January

In truth, to those who have pleasure in contemplating the phenomena of nature, a sea voyage may endure many weeks without wearying. Perhaps some may think that the first glance of ocean and of sky shew all they have to offer; nay, even that that first glance may suggest more of dreariness than sublimity; but to me, their variety appeared endless, and their beauty unfailing. The attempt to describe scenery, even where the objects are prominent and tangible, is very rarely successful; but where the effect is so subtile and so varying, it must be vain. The impression, nevertheless, is perhaps deeper than any other; I think it possible I may forget the sensations with which I watched the long course of the gigantic Mississippi; the Ohio and the Potomac may mingle and be confounded with other streams in my memory, I may even recall with difficulty the blue outline of the Alleghany mountains, but never, while I remember any thing, can I forget the first and last hour of light on the Atlantic.

Sea Jealousy

Ford Madox Ford (1873–1939)

Cast not your looks upon the wan grey sea,
Waste not your voice upon the wind:
Let not your footsteps sink upon the sand,
Hold no sea-treasure in your hand,
And let no sea-shell in your ear
Nor any sea-thought in your mind
Murmur a mystery.

Turn your soft eyes upon mine eyes that long,
Let your sweet lips on mine be sealed;
Fold soft sweet hands between your sweet soft breasts
And, as a weary sea-mew rests
Upon the sea,
Utterly, utterly yield
Your being up to me,
And all around, grey seascape and the sound
Of droned sea song.

The Great Whirlpool of Maelström

From *A Descent into the Maelström, 1841*

Edgar Allan Poe (1809–1849)

Here the vast bed of the waters, seamed and scarred into a thousand conflicting channels, burst suddenly into frenzied convulsion – heaving, boiling, hissing – gyrating in gigantic and innumerable vortices, and all whirling and plunging on to the eastward with a rapidity which water never elsewhere assumes except in precipitous descents.

In a few minutes more, there came over the scene another radical alteration. The general surface grew somewhat more smooth, and the whirlpools, one by one, disappeared, while prodigious streaks of foam became apparent where none had been seen before. These streaks, at length, spreading out to a great distance, and entering into combination, took unto themselves the gyratory motion of the subsided vortices, and seemed to form the germ of another more vast. Suddenly – very suddenly – this assumed a distinct and definite existence, in a circle of more than half a mile in diameter. The edge of the whirl was represented by a broad belt of gleaming spray; but no particle of this slipped into the mouth of the terrific funnel, whose interior, as far as the eye could fathom it, was a smooth, shining, and jet-black wall of water, inclined to the horizon at an angle of some forty-five degrees, speeding dizzily round and round with a swaying and sweltering motion, and sending forth to the winds an appalling voice, half shriek, half roar, such as not even the mighty cataract of Niagara ever lifts up in its agony to Heaven.

Weather at Sea

From *The Pocket Encyclopaedia of Natural Phenomena, 1827* |
Thomas Furley Forster (1761–1825)

Porpuses, when they sport about ships, and chase one another as if in play, and indeed their being numerous on the surface of the sea at any time, is rather a stormy sign. The same may be said of dolphins and grampuses. That the cause of these motions is some electrical change in the air seems probable. Wilsford, in his *Secrets of Nature*, tells us: Porpoises, or sea hogs, when observed to sport and chase one another about ships, expect then some stormy weather.

Dolphins, in fair and calm weather, pursuing one another as one of their waterish pastimes, foreshews wind, and from that part whence they fetch their frisks; but if they play thus when the seas are rough and troubled, it is a sign of fair and calm weather to ensue.

Cuttles, with their many legs swimming on the top of the water, and striving to be above the waves, do presage a storm.

Sea Urchins thrusting themselves into the mud, or striving to cover their bodies with sand, foreshews a storm.

Cockles, and most shell fish, are observed against a tempest to have gravel sticking hard unto their shells, as a providence of nature to stay or poise themselves, and to help to weigh them down, if raised from the bottom by surges.

Fishes in general, both in salt and fresh waters, are observed to sport most, and bite more eagerly, against rain than at any other time.

FEBRUARY

The Map of an Island

The Winds of Fate

Ella Wheeler Wilcox (1850–1919)

One ship drives east and another drives west
With the self-same winds that blow;
    'Tis the set of the sails
    And not the gales
That tells them the way to go.

Like the winds of the sea are the winds of fate
As we voyage along through life;
    'Tis the set of the soul
    That decides its goal
And not the calm or the strife.

From Barnacles to Birds

From *Survey of Cornwall, 1602* | Richard Carew (1555–1620)

It is held, that the Barnacle breedeth under water on such ships sides, as have beene verie long at Sea, hanging there by the Bill, untill his full growth dismisse him to be a perfect fowle: and for proofe hereof, many little things like birds, are ordinarily found in such places, but I cannot heare any man speake of having seene them ripe.

The Life of a Ship

From *Ship of Magic, 1998* | Robin Hobb (1952–)

Night after night, Althea sprawled upon the wooden deck and dreamed with her ship. Even by day, she lay there, her cheek pressed firmly to the plank, musing on her future. She became attuned to the *Vivacia*, from the shuddering of her wooden body as she strained through a sudden change in course, to the peaceful sounds the wood made when the wind drove her on a steady and true course. The shouts of the sailors, the light thunder of their feet on her decks were only slightly more significant than the cries of the gulls who sometimes alighted on her. At such times it seemed to Althea that she became the ship, aware of the small men who clambered up her masts only as a great whale might be aware of the barnacles that clung upon it. There was so much more to the ship than the folk that worked her. Althea had no human words to express the fine differences she now sensed in wind and current. There was pleasure in working with a good steersman, and annoyance in the one who was always making minute and unnecessary adjustments, but it was a surface thing compared to what went on between the ship and the water. This concept that the life of a ship might be larger than what went on between her and her captain was a major revelation to Althea. In the space of a handful of nights, her whole concept of what a ship was underwent a sea-change.

At Carbis Bay

From *Intermezzo: Pastoral* | Arthur Symons (1865–1945)

Out of the night of the sea,
Out of the turbulent night,
A sharp and hurrying wind
Scourges the waters white:
The terror by night.

Out of the doubtful dark,
Out of the night of the land,
What is it breathes and broods
Hoveringly at hand?
The menace of land.

Out of the night of heaven,
Out of the delicate sky,
Pale and serene the stars
In their silence reply:
The peace of the sky.

The Long Waves

From *Lorna Doone, 1869* | R. D. Blackmore (1825–1900)

But during those two months of fog (for we had it all the winter), the saddest and the heaviest thing was to stand beside the sea. To be upon the beach yourself, and see the long waves coming in; to know that they are long waves, but only see a piece of them; and to hear them lifting roundly, swelling over smooth green rocks, plashing down in the hollow corners, but bearing on all the same as ever, soft and sleek and sorrowful, till their little noise is over.

Ice Floes at Greenland

From *Michel the Giant: An African in Greenland, 1981*

Tété-Michel Kpomassie (1941–)

Translated by James Kirkup (1918–2009)

Towards one o'clock in the afternoon, we spotted the first ice floes.

These were ice blocks of varying shapes and sizes, drifting here and there as the waves took them. The smallest looked like swimming swans, and some were like crouching camels rocking gently from side to side. Some were white, others green or blue. A brilliant sun, cold as steel, glittered on them and transformed the sea into a fairy-tale world: a vast ice-blue expanse strewn with great chunks of crystal. A dazzling glitter seethed and multiplied.

Half an hour later, these blocks were the size of anthills, and the much larger submerged parts formed enormous azure masses in the glaucous depths as they passed us. A little later on, they had reached the height of hills: these were the fabled icebergs, transported by the polar current that flows along the coast. Soon we could see hundreds of them, and their size never ceased to astonish me.

Meanwhile the smaller masses were becoming more and more densely packed. By evening, we could see only one vast sheet of ice spread all across the sea, with white mountains rising here and there. Creeping through this pack-ice, the ship left a narrow channel in her wake that quickly filled again with slabs of ice.

Sea Longing

Sara Teasdale (1884–1933)

A thousand miles beyond this sun-steeped wall
  Somewhere the waves creep cool along the sand,
  The ebbing tide forsakes the listless land
With the old murmur, long and musical;
The windy waves mount up and curve and fall,
  And round the rocks the foam blows up like snow, –
  Tho' I am inland far, I hear and know,
For I was born the sea's eternal thrall.
I would that I were there and over me
  The cold insistence of the tide would roll,
  Quenching this burning thing men call the soul, –
Then with the ebbing I should drift and be
  Less than the smallest shell along the shoal,
Less than the sea-gulls calling to the sea.

Diaries

From *Essays: Of Travel, 1625* | Francis Bacon (1561–1626)

It is a strange thing, that in sea voyages, where there is nothing to be seen, but sky and sea, men should make diaries; but in land-travel, wherein so much is to be observed, for the most part they omit it.

A Ghost in the Captain's Cabin

From *Bullion! 1911* | William Hope Hodgson (1877–1918)

This is a most peculiar yarn. It was a pitchy night in the South Pacific. I was the second mate of one of the fast clipper-ships running between London and Melbourne at the time of the big gold finds up at Bendigo. There was a fresh breeze blowing, and I was walking hard up and down the weather side of the poop-deck, to keep myself warm, when the captain came out of the companionway and joined me.

'Mr James, do you believe in ghosts?' he asked suddenly, after several minutes of silence.

'Well, sir,' I replied, 'I always keep an open mind; so I can't say I'm a proper disbeliever, though I think most ghost yarns can be explained.'

'Well,' he said in a queer voice, 'someone keeps whispering in my cabin at nights. It's making me feel funny to be there.'

Coast

Oluwaseun Olayiwola (1996–)

Calm, he said, in another language
I had become proficient in pretending
I understood. The beach was still
the beach: picturesque, cold
this time of year when everyone preferred
the closeness of coffee shops. *Need it be that serious? Yes*,
he said, the waves moaning how they're
moon-trained all year regardless of season,
folding, unfolding, unconcerned with us,
little interruptions in the way of things.

Jack Recovers

From *Mr. Midshipman Easy, 1836* | Frederick Marryat (1792–1848)

When Jack Easy had gained the deck, he found the sun shining gaily, a soft air blowing from the shore, and the whole of the rigging and every part of the ship loaded with the shirts, trousers, and jackets of the seamen, which had been wetted during the heavy gale, and were now hanging up to dry. The captain and first lieutenant were standing on the gangway in converse, and the majority of the officers were with their quadrants and sextants ascertaining the latitude at noon. The decks were white and clean, the sweepers had just laid by their brooms, and the men were busy coiling down the ropes.

The Influence of the Sea

From *Sea Life in Literature, 1925* | Sir Henry Newbolt (1862–1938)

A nation living in an island, and especially in an island so small as Great Britain, could not possibly escape the influence of the sea. Many millions of Russians or of Chinese pass their lives in communities so far inland that neither physically nor intellectually have they ever realised the existence of coasts or sundering oceans. An English child may not yet have seen the sea, but he cannot long have attained the power to read before becoming aware that the sea is his boundary, his safeguard, the only highroad of his food supply and his foreign travel. Whether or not it is an influence in his own personal life, it comes to him unavoidably as an element in the national life, a fact of practical and historical importance. And if he reads our English Literature he will soon find out that it has given experience, tradition, and impulse to the imaginative wishes of his country for many generations. In short, whether we are landsmen or seamen ourselves, sea life is essentially a part of national life, part of its daily course, part of its record, part of its imaginative experience

On the Sea

John Keats (1795–1821)

It keeps eternal whisperings around
Desolate shores, and with its mighty swell
Gluts twice ten thousand caverns, till the spell
Of Hecate leaves them their old shadowy sound.
Often 'tis in such gentle temper found
That scarcely will the very smallest shell
Be moved for days from whence it sometime fell,
When last the winds of Heaven were unbound.
Oh ye! who have your eye-balls vexed and tired,
Feast them upon the wideness of the Sea –
Oh ye! whose ears are dinn'd with uproar rude,
Or fed too much with cloying melody –
Sit ye near some old cavern's mouth, and brood
Until ye start, as if the sea-nymphs quired!

Dangers and Difficulties

From *The Principal Navigations, Voyages, Traffiques and Discoveries of the English Nation, 1589–1590, enlarged 1598–1600* | Richard Hakluyt (1552/3–1616)

Preface to the second edition, 1598

Into what dangers and difficulties they plunged themselves, I tremble to recount. For first they were to expose themselves unto the rigour of the stern and uncouth northern seas, then they were to sail by the ragged and perilous coast of Norway, to frequent the uncharted shores of Finmark, to double the dreadful and misty North Cape, and as it were to open an unlock the sevenfold mouth of Dvina. Unto what drifts of snow and mountains of ice even in June, July, and August, unto what hideous over-falls, uncertain currents, dark mists and fogs, and divers other fearful inconveniences they were subject and in danger of, I wish you rather learn out of the voyages of Sir Hugh Willoughby, Stephen Burrough, Arthur Pet and the rest.

The Sea Voyage

From *Beowulf, lines 205–228*

Anon, translated by John Duncan Spaeth (1868–1954)

15 February

Beowulf chose from the band of the Jutes
Heroes brave, the best he could find;
He with fourteen followers hardy
Went to embark: he was wise in seamanship,
Showed them the landmarks, leading the way.

Soon they descried their craft in the water,
At the foot of the cliff. Then climbed aboard
The chosen troop; the tide was churning
Sea against sand: they stowed away
In the hold of the ship their shining armor,
War-gear and weapons; the warriors launched
Their well-braced boat on her welcome voyage.

Swift o'er the waves with a wind that favored,
Foam on her breast, like a bird she flew;
A day and night they drove to seaward,
Cut the waves with the curving prow,
Till the seamen that sailed her sighted the land,
Shining cliffs and coast-wise hills,
Headlands bold. The harbor opened,
Their cruise was ended. Then quickly the sailors
The crew of Weder-folk clambered ashore;
Moored their craft with clank of chain-mail
And goodly war-gear. God they thanked
That their way was smooth o'er the surging waves.

The Prison Ship

From *His Natural Life, 1870–1872, later For the Term of His Natural Life, 1874* | Marcus Clarke (1846–1881)

Save for the man at the wheel and the guard at the quarter-railing, he was alone on the deck. A few birds flew round about the vessel, and seemed to pass under her stern windows only to appear again at her bows. A lazy albatross, with the white water flashing from his wings, rose with a dabbling sound to leeward, and in the place where he had been glided the hideous fin of a silently-swimming shark. The seams of the well-scrubbed deck were sticky with melted pitch, and the brass plate of the compass-case sparkled in the sun like a jewel. There was no breeze, and as the clumsy ship rolled and lurched on the heaving sea, her idle sails flapped against her masts with a regularly recurring noise, and her bowsprit would seem to rise higher with the water's swell, to dip again with a jerk that made each rope tremble and tauten. On the forecastle, some half-dozen soldiers, in all varieties of undress, were playing at cards, smoking, or watching the fishing-lines hanging over the catheads.

So far the appearance of the vessel differed in no wise from that of an ordinary transport. But in the waist a curious sight presented itself. It was as though one had built a cattle-pen there. At the foot of the foremast, and at the quarter-deck, a strong barricade, loop-holed and furnished with doors for ingress and egress, ran across the deck from bulwark to bulwark. Outside this cattle-pen an armed sentry stood on guard; inside, standing, sitting, or walking monotonously, within range of the shining barrels in the arm chest on the poop, were some sixty men and boys, dressed in uniform grey. The men and boys were prisoners of the Crown, and the cattle-pen was their exercise ground. Their prison was down the main hatchway, on the 'tween decks, and the barricade, continued down, made its side walls.

The Mediterranean

From *The Pillars of Hercules, 1995* | Paul Theroux (1941–)

17 February

'The grand object of traveling is to see the shores of the Mediterranean,' Dr Johnson said. 'On these shores were the four great Empires of the world; the Assyrian, the Persian, the Grecian, and the Roman. All our religion, almost all our law, almost all our arts, almost all that sets us above savages, has come to us from the shores of the Mediterranean.'

'Our' of course is as questionable as 'savages', but you get the idea. It was not until the second century B.C. that the Romans sailed through the Pillars of Hercules. The reason for this late, if not timid, penetration of the straits was not the current, nor was it the inconvenient westerlies that blow through this narrow opening of the inland sea; it was the Mediterranean notion that nothing lay beyond the pillars except the Isles of the Hesperides and the lost continent of Atlantis, and hellish seas.

The Brook that Ran into the Sea

Verses 5–10 | Lucy Larcom (1824–1893)

'My own mysterious life I love,
  Its shadow and its shine;
And all sweet voices that above
  Make melody with mine.

'But most I love the mighty voice
  Which calls me, draws me so,
That every ripple lisps, "Rejoice!"
  As with a laugh I go.

'My drop of freshness to the Sea
  In music trickles on;
Nor grander could my welcome be
  Were I an Amazon.

'And if his moaning waves can feel
  My sweetness near the shore,
Even to his heart the thrill may steal: –
  What could I wish for more?

'The largest soul to take love in
  Knows how to give love best;
So peacefully my tinkling din
  Dies on the great Sea's breast.

'One heart encircles all that live,
  And blesses great and small;
And meet it is that each should give
  His little to the All.'

The Lighthouse Keeper

From *The Echo of a Mutiny, 1912* | R. Austin Freeman (1862–1943)

Three long years had he spent in this dreary solitude, so repugnant to his active, restless nature: three blank, interminable years, with nothing to look back on but the endless succession of summer calms, stormy nights and the chilly fogs of winter, when the unseen steamers hooted from the void and the fog-horn bellowed its hoarse warning.

Why had he come to this God-forgotten spot? and why did he stay, when the wide world called to him? And then memory painted him a picture on which his mind's eye had often looked before and which once again arose before him, shutting out the vision of the calm sea and the distant land. It was a brightly-coloured picture. It showed a cloudless sky brooding over the deep blue tropic sea; and in the middle of the picture, see-sawing gently on the quiet swell, a white-painted barque.

Her sails were clewed up untidily, her swinging yards jerked at the slack braces and her untended wheel revolved to and fro to the oscillations of the rudder.

She was not a derelict, for more than a dozen men were on her deck; but the men were all drunk and mostly asleep, and there was never an officer among them.

Then he saw the interior of one of her cabins. The chart-rack, the tell-tale compass and the chronometers marked it as the captain's cabin. In it were four men, and two of them lay dead on the deck. Of the other two, one was a small, cunning-faced man, who was, at the moment, kneeling beside one of the corpses to wipe a knife upon its coat. The fourth man was himself.

Again, he saw the two murderers stealing off in a quarter-boat, as the barque with her drunken crew drifted towards the spouting surf of a river-bar. He saw the ship melt away in the surf like an icicle in the sunshine; and, later, two shipwrecked mariners, picked up in an open boat and set ashore at an American port.

That was why he was here. Because he was a murderer.

On the Rocks!

From *The Interesting Narrative 1789* | Olaudah Equiano (c. 1745–1797)

At twelve o'clock the watch was changed; and, as I had always the charge of the captain's watch, I then went upon deck. At half after one in the morning the man at the helm saw something under the lee-beam that the sea washed against, and he immediately called to me that there was a grampus, and desired me to look at it. Accordingly I stood up and observed it for some time; but, when I saw the sea wash up against it again and again, I said it was not a fish but a rock. Being soon certain of this, I went down to the captain, and, with some confusion, told him the danger we were in, and desired him to come upon deck immediately. He said it was very well, and I went up again. As soon as I was upon deck the wind, which had been pretty high, having abated a little, the vessel began to be carried sideways towards the rock, by means of the current. Still the captain did not appear. I therefore went to him again, and told him the vessel was then near a large rock, and desired he would come up with speed. He said he would, and I returned to the deck. When I was upon the deck again I saw we were not above a pistol shot from the rock, and I heard the noise of the breakers all around us. I was exceedingly alarmed at this; and the captain having not yet come on the deck I lost all patience; and, growing quite enraged, I ran down to him again, and asked him why he did not come up, and what he could mean by all this? 'The breakers,' said I, 'are round us, and the vessel is almost on the rock.' With that he came on the deck with me, and we tried to put the vessel about, and get her out of the current, but all to no purpose, the wind being very small. We then called all hands up immediately; and after a little we got up one end of a cable, and fastened it to the anchor. By this time the surf was foaming round us, and made a dreadful noise on the breakers, and the very moment we let the anchor go the vessel struck against the rocks. One swell now succeeded another, as it were one wave calling on its fellow: the roaring of the billows increased, and, with one single heave of the swells, the sloop was pierced and transfixed among the rocks!

The Storme

Lines 25–50 | John Donne (1572–1631)

Then like two mighty Kings, which dwelling farre
Asunder, meet against a third to warre,
The South and West winds joyn'd, and, as they blew,
Waves like a rolling trench before them threw.
Sooner than you read this line, did the gale,
Like shot, not fear'd till felt, our sailes assaile;
And what at first was call'd a gust, the same
Hath now a stormes, anon a tempests name.
Jonas, I pitty thee, and curse those men,
Who when the storm rag'd most, did wake thee then;
Sleepe is paines easiest salve, and doth fulfill
All offices of death, except to kill.
But when I wakt, I saw, that I saw not.
I, and the Sunne, which should teach mee'had forgot
East, West, day, night, and I could onely say,
If'the world had lasted, now it had been day.
Thousands our noyses were, yet wee'mongst all
Could none by his right name, but thunder call:
Lightning was all our light, and it rain'd more
Than if the Sunne had drunk the sea before.
Some coffin'd in their cabbins lye, 'equally
Griev'd that they are not dead, and yet must dye.
And as sin-burd'ned souls from graves will creepe,
At the last day, some forth their cabbins peepe:
And tremblingly'ask what newes, and doe heare so,
Like jealous husbands, what they would not know.

The Floss Estuary

From *Mill on the Floss, 1860* | George Eliot (1819–1880)

A wide plain, where the broadening Floss hurries on between its green banks to the sea, and the loving tide, rushing to meet it, checks its passage with an impetuous embrace. On this mighty tide the black ships – laden with the fresh-scented fir-planks, with rounded sacks of oil-bearing seed, or with the dark glitter of coal – are borne along to the town of St Ogg's, which shows its aged, fluted red roofs and the broad gables of its wharves between the low wooded hill and the river-brink, tingeing the water with a soft purple hue under the transient glance of this February sun. Far away on each hand stretch the rich pastures, and the patches of dark earth made ready for the seed of broad-leaved green crops, or touched already with the tint of the tender-bladed autumn-sown corn. There is a remnant still of last year's golden clusters of beehive-ricks rising at intervals beyond the hedgerows; and everywhere the hedgerows are studded with trees; the distant ships seem to be lifting their masts and stretching their red-brown sails close among the branches of the spreading ash.

Winter Seascape

John Betjeman (1906–1984)

The sea runs back against itself
    With scarcely time for breaking wave
To cannonade a slatey shelf
    And thunder under in a cave

Before the next can fully burst.
    The headwind, blowing harder still,
Smooths it to what it was at first -
    A slowly rolling water-hill.

Against the breeze the breakers haste,
    Against the tide their ridges run
And all the sea's a dappled waste
    Criss-crossing underneath the sun.

Far down the beach the ripples drag
    Blown backward, rearing from the shore,
And wailing gull and shrieking shag
    Alone can pierce the ocean roar.

Unheard, a mongrel hound gives tongue,
    Unheard are shouts of little boys:
What chance has any inland lung
    Against this multi-water noise?

Here where the cliffs alone prevail
    I stand exultant, neutral, free,
And from the cushion of the gale
    Behold a huge consoling sea.

The Map

From *Treasure Island, 1883* | Robert Louis Stevenson (1850–1894)

The paper had been sealed in several places with a thimble by way of seal; the very thimble, perhaps, that I had found in the captain's pocket. The doctor opened the seals with great care, and there fell out the map of an island, with latitude and longitude, soundings, names of hills and bays and inlets, and every particular that would be needed to bring a ship to a safe anchorage upon its shores. It was about nine miles long and five across, shaped, you might say, like a fat dragon standing up, and had two fine land-locked harbours, and a hill in the centre part marked 'The Spy-glass'. There were several additions of a later date, but above all, three crosses of red ink – two on the north part of the island, one in the southwest – and beside this last, in the same red ink, and in a small, neat hand, very different from the captain's tottery characters, these words: 'Bulk of treasure here.'

Over on the back the same hand had written this further information:

'Tall tree, Spy-glass shoulder, bearing a point to the N. of N.N.E.

'Skeleton Island E.S.E. and by E.

'Ten feet.

'The bar silver is in the north cache; you can find it by the trend of the east hummock, ten fathoms south of the black crag with the face on it.

'The arms are easy found, in the sand-hill, N. point of north inlet cape, bearing E. and a quarter N.

'J.F.'

That was all; but brief as it was, and to me incomprehensible, it filled the squire and Dr. Livesey with delight.

Moods

James Weldon Johnson (1871–1938)

I love the sea when it is windswept
The ships ploughing up the foam
The sailor man loudly swearing
From sheer excess of joy,
The shrill cry of a solitary sea bird,
And the smell of the sharp, salt spray.

I love the melancholy beach
Under the shimmering magic of the moon.
When just above the ocean's rim
One lone star marks a path for me;
And the waves are moaning to the shore
Their monotone love melody.

25 February

Surviving the Bay of Biscay

From *Four Friends and Death, 1935*

Christopher St John Sprigg, aka Christopher Caudwell (1907–1937)

The small yacht floated motionless, mirrored in the calm waters of Vigo Harbour. Her split headsail, tattered pennant, and stove-in dinghy were mute evidence of the storms that had battered the ketch in the Bay of Biscay, three days out from Falmouth.

O That I Could Also Go!

From *Narrative of the Life of Frederick Douglass, 1845* |

Frederick Douglass (1818–1895)

27 February

Our house stood within a few rods of the Chesapeake Bay, whose broad bosom was ever white with sails from every quarter of the habitable globe. Those beautiful vessels, robed in purest white, so delightful to the eye of freemen, were to me so many shrouded ghosts, to terrify and torment me with thoughts of my wretched condition. I have often, in the deep stillness of a summer's Sabbath, stood all alone upon the lofty banks of that noble bay, and traced, with saddened heart and tearful eye, the countless number of sails moving off to the mighty ocean. The sight of these always affected me powerfully. My thoughts would compel utterance; and there, with no audience but the Almighty, I would pour out my soul's complaint, in my rude way, with an apostrophe to the moving multitude of ships:

'You are loosed from your moorings, and are free; I am fast in my chains, and am a slave! You move merrily before the gentle gale, and I sadly before the bloody whip! You are freedom's swift-winged angels, that fly round the world; I am confined in bands of iron! O that I were free! O, that I were on one of your gallant decks, and under your protecting wing! Alas! betwixt me and you, the turbid waters roll. Go on, go on. O that I could also go!'

Chamber Music XXXV

James Joyce (1882–1941)

All day I hear the noise of waters
  Making moan,
Sad as the sea-bird is when, going
  Forth alone,
He hears the winds cry to the waters'
  Monotone.

The grey winds, the cold winds are blowing
  Where I go.
I hear the noise of many waters
  Far below.
All day, all night, I hear them flowing
  To and fro.

One Misfortune Succeeds Another

From *The Female Soldier: The Surprising Life and Adventures of Hannah Snell, 1750* | Hannah Snell (1723–1792)

As it often happens for the wise and noble Purposes of Heaven, that one Misfortune succeeds another, as close as the Waves on the Sea-shore; so the *Swallow* set sail in Company with the *Vigilant* Man of War, in Order to join the Admiral's Squadron; and the next Night after their Departure, another violent Storm happened, in which the *Swallow* not only lost sight of the *Vigilant*, but also sprung her Main-mast, lost most of her Rigging, and was so much damaged in her Hold, that all the Sailors and Marines were obliged to take their several Turns at the Pump, which is by far a harder Piece of Labour, than those who have never tried it are apt to imagine. Such a Series of Calamities succeeding each other so fast, and so unexpectedly, were, in all Appearance, sufficient to daunt the strongest Resolution, and cool the Courage of the bravest young Sailor that ever trod the Deck of a Ship. But some Minds are cast, if I may so speak, in so happy a Mould, that Danger and Difficulties instead of depressing, raise them above themselves, enlarge their Views, and animate them to stem the Tide of Adversity, which they rarely fail to surmount by Steadiness and Perseverance. To this favourite Class of Mortals our Heroine belonged, since on this Occasion she not only willingly took her Turn at the Pump of a sinking Vessel, but also performed the several Offices of a common Sailor, and in both Qualities behaved with such Judgment and Intrepidity, that, next under God, she was looked upon by the Ship's Company as a Kind of Deliverer, and an Instrument of their Preservation.

MARCH

The Bold Swimmer

The Sailor

From *Martin Eden, 1909* | Jack London (1876–1916)

The one opened the door with a latch-key and went in, followed by a young fellow who awkwardly removed his cap. He wore rough clothes that smacked of the sea, and he was manifestly out of place in the spacious hall in which he found himself. He did not know what to do with his cap, and was stuffing it into his coat pocket when the other took it from him. The act was done quietly and naturally, and the awkward young fellow appreciated it. 'He understands,' was his thought. 'He'll see me through all right.'

He walked at the other's heels with a swing to his shoulders, and his legs spread unwittingly, as if the level floors were tilting up and sinking down to the heave and lunge of the sea. The wide rooms seemed too narrow for his rolling gait, and to himself he was in terror lest his broad shoulders should collide with the doorways or sweep the bric-a-brac from the low mantel. He recoiled from side to side between the various objects and multiplied the hazards that in reality lodged only in his mind. Between a grand piano and a centre-table piled high with books was space for a half a dozen to walk abreast, yet he essayed it with trepidation. His heavy arms hung loosely at his sides. He did not know what to do with those arms and hands, and when, to his excited vision, one arm seemed liable to brush against the books on the table, he lurched away like a frightened horse, barely missing the piano stool. He watched the easy walk of the other in front of him, and for the first time realized that his walk was different from that of other men. He experienced a momentary pang of shame that he should walk so uncouthly. The sweat burst through the skin of his forehead in tiny beads, and he paused and mopped his bronzed face with his handkerchief.

Cargoes

John Masefield (1878–1967)

Quinquireme of Nineveh from distant Ophir,
Rowing home to haven in sunny Palestine,
With a cargo of ivory,
And apes and peacocks,
Sandalwood, cedarwood, and sweet white wine.

Stately Spanish galleon coming from the Isthmus,
Dipping through the tropics by the palm-green shores,
With a cargo of diamonds,
Emeralds, amythysts,
Topazes, and cinnamon, and gold moidores.

Dirty British coaster with a salt-caked smoke stack,
Butting through the channel in the mad March days,
With a cargo of Tyne coal,
Road-rails, pig-lead,
Firewood, iron-ware, and cheap tin trays.

A Dismal Hurricane

From *The Female Soldier: The Surprising Life and Adventures of Hannah Snell, 1750* | Hannah Snell (1723–1792)

Disguised as James Gray, Hannah Snell enlists and joins Admiral Boscawen's fleet on board the *Swallow* sloop:

On their first setting sail, they enjoyed as fine weather, and as fair Winds as could possibly be wished for, to convey a Ship safely and expeditiously from one Harbour to another. But no sooner were they arrived in the Bay of *Biscay* than the Scene was altered; their favourable Weather converted into a dismal Hurricane, and their smooth placed Ocean, changed into Billows, which threaten'd them with immediate Death, by this Moment raising them to the Clouds, and in the next plunging them, as it were, to the Centre of the Earth. The Danger may be easily estimated, from the Circumstance, for the *Swallow* was as strong and well built a Vessel, as any belonging to his Majesty's Navy of her Burden: yet such was the Stress of Weather, that she sprung her Main-mast, and lost not only the Gib-Boom, but also two Top-masts. After they had for several Days been beat about in this imminent Danger, they with great Difficulty arrived in the Port of *Lisbon*, which was great Joy to them, after having suffered so much in the Bay of *Biscay*, where every Moment they had been in danger of being swallowed up in the vast Abyss. In this Port, which to them was like a safe Asylum, or Sanctuary, to a Man pursued by a hungry and enraged Lyon, they continued three Weeks; because the Vessel was so damaged, that the Number of Hands employed in refitting her could not do it sooner.

Water-Front Streets

Langston Hughes (1901–1967)

The spring is not so beautiful there –
  But dream ships sail away
To where the spring is wondrous rare
  And life is gay.

The spring is not so beautiful there –
  But lads put out to sea
Who carry beauties in their hearts
  And dreams, like me.

The Lands End

From *Through England on a Side-Saddle, written 1702, extracts published 1812, published in full 1888* |

Celia Fiennes (1662–1741)

5 March

The Lands End terminates in a poynt or peak of great rocks which runs a good way into the sea, I clamber'd over them as farre as safety permitted me; there are abundance of rocks and sholes of stones stand up in the sea, a mile off some, and soe here and there some quite to the shore, which they name by severall names of Knights and Ladies roled up in mantles from some old tradition or fiction the poets advance, description of the amours of some great persons; but these many rocks and stones which lookes like the Needles in the Isle of Wight makes it hazardous for shipps to double the poynt especially in stormy weather; here at the Lands End they are but a little way off of France, 2 days saile at farthest convey them to Haure De Grace in France, but the peace being but newly entred into with the French I was not willing to venture, at least by myself, into a Forreign Kingdom, and being then at the end of the land, my horses leggs could not carry me through th deep and so return'd againe to Pensands 10 mile more, and soe came in view of both the seas and saw the Lizard Point and Pensands, the Mount in Cornwall which looked very fine in the broad day the sunn shineing on the rocke in the sea.

The Need to Cross the Channel

From *The Scarlet Pimpernel, 1905* | Baroness Orczy (1865–1947)

[Sir Andrew] 'I am sorry to say we cannot cross over to-night.'

'Not cross over to-night?' she [Lady Blakeney] repeated in amazement. 'But we must, Sir Andrew, we must! There can be no question of cannot, and whatever it may cost, we must get a vessel to-night.'

But the young man shook his head sadly.

'I am afraid it is not a question of cost, Lady Blakeney. There is a nasty storm blowing from France, the wind is dead against us, we cannot possibly sail until it has changed.'

Marguerite became deadly pale. She had not foreseen this. Nature herself was playing her a horrible, cruel trick. Percy was in danger, and she could not go to him, because the wind happened to blow from the coast of France.

'But we must go! – we must!' she repeated with strange, persistent energy, 'you know, we must go! – can't you find a way?'

'I have been down to the shore already,' he said, 'and had a talk to one or two skippers. It is quite impossible to set sail to-night, so every sailor assured me. No one,' he added, looking significantly at Marguerite, '*no one* could possibly put out of Dover to-night.'

Marguerite at once understood what he meant. *No one* included Chauvelin as well as herself.

Castaway

Verses 1–4 | William Cowper (1731–1800)

Obscurest night involv'd the sky,
        Th' Atlantic billows roar'd,
When such a destin'd wretch as I,
        Wash'd headlong from on board,
Of friends, of hope, of all bereft,
His floating home for ever left.

No braver chief could Albion boast
        Than he with whom he went,
Nor ever ship left Albion's coast,
        With warmer wishes sent.
He lov'd them both, but both in vain,
Nor him beheld, nor her again.

Not long beneath the whelming brine,
        Expert to swim, he lay;
Nor soon he felt his strength decline,
        Or courage die away;
But wag'd with death a lasting strife,
Supported by despair of life.

He shouted: nor his friends had fail'd
        To check the vessel's course,
But so the furious blast prevail'd,
        That, pitiless perforce,
They left their outcast mate behind,
And scudded still before the wind.

The Power of the Sea

From *The Sea, 1861* | Jules Michelet (1798–1874)

Translated by W. H. D. Adams (1828–1891)

It is opaque and dull; it weighs heavily. He who risks his life within it, feels that it lifts him up. Thus it assists, we confess, the bold swimmer, but it also masters him; he feels like a feeble child, supported by a powerful hand which can as easily shatter him to atoms.

The Secret

Katherine Mansfield (1888–1923)

In the profoundest ocean
There is a rainbow shell,
It is always there, shining most stilly
Under the greatest storm waves
And under the happy little waves
That the old Greek called 'ripples of laughter'
And you listen, the rainbow shell
Sings – in the profoundest ocean.
It is always there, singing most silently!

Ships and Art

From *The Harbours of England, 1856* | John Ruskin (1819–1900)

Shipping, therefore, in its perfection, never can become the subject of noble art; and that just because to represent it in its perfection would tax the powers of art to the utmost. If a great painter could rest in drawing a ship, as he can rest in drawing a piece of drapery, we might sometimes see vessels introduced by the noblest workmen, and treated by them with as much delight as they would show in scattering lustre over an embroidered dress, or knitting the links of a coat of mail. But ships cannot be drawn at times of rest. More complicated in their anatomy than the human frame itself, so far as that frame is outwardly discernible; liable to all kinds of strange accidental variety in position and movement, yet in each position subject to imperative laws which can only be followed by unerring knowledge; and involving, in the roundings and foldings of sail and hull, delicacies of drawing greater than exist in any other inorganic object, except perhaps a snow wreath, – they present, irrespective of sea or sky, or anything else around them, difficulties which could only be vanquished by draughtsmanship quite accomplished enough to render even the subtlest lines of the human face and form. But the artist who has once attained such skill as this will not devote it to the drawing of ships. He who can paint the face of St. Paul will not elaborate the parting timbers of the vessel in which he is wrecked; and he who can represent the astonishment of the apostles at the miraculous draught will not be solicitous about accurately showing that their boat is overloaded.

10 March

Captain Reece

W. S. Gilbert (1836–1911)

Of all the ships upon the blue,
No ship contained a better crew
Than that of worthy Captain Reece,
Commanding of *The Mantelpice*.

He was adored by all his men,
For worthy Captain Reece, R.N.,
Did all that lay within him to
Promote the comfort of his crew.

If ever they were dull or sad,
Their captain danced to them like mad,
Or told, to make the time pass by,
Droll legends of his infancy.

A feather bed had every man,
Warm slippers and hot-water can,
Brown windsor from the captain's store,
A valet, too, to every four.

Did they with thirst in summer burn,
Lo, seltzogenes at every turn,
And on all very sultry days
Cream ices handed round on trays.

Then currant wine and ginger pops
Stood handily on all the 'tops';
And also, with amusement rife,
A 'Zoetrope, or Wheel of Life.'

Permission to Hide

From *Twelve Years a Slave, 1853* | Solomon Northup (c. 1807–post 1857)

Vessels run up the Rio Teche to Centreville. While there, I was bold enough one day to present myself before the captain of a steamer, and beg permission to hide myself among the freight. I was emboldened to risk the hazard of such a step, from overhearing a conversation, in the course of which I ascertained he was a native of the North. I did not relate to him the particulars of my history, but only expressed an ardent desire to escape from slavery to a free State. He pitied me, but said it would be impossible to avoid the vigilant custom house officers in New-Orleans, and that detection would subject him to punishment, and his vessel to confiscation. My earnest entreaties evidently excited his sympathies, and doubtless he would have yielded to them, could he have done so with any kind of safety. I was compelled to smother the sudden flame that lighted up my bosom with sweet hopes of liberation, and turn my steps once more towards the increasing darkness of despair.

Beautiful, Proud Sea

Sara Teasdale (1884–1933)

Careless forever, beautiful proud sea,
You laugh in happy thunder all alone,
You fold upon yourself, you dance your dance
Impartially on drift-weed, sand or stone.

You make us believe that we can outlive death,
You make us for an instance, for your sake,
Burn, like stretched silver of a wave,
Not breaking, but about to break.

The Cobb

From *The French Lieutenant's Woman, 1969*

John Fowles (1926–2005)

The Cobb has invited what familiarity breeds for at least seven hundred years, and the real Lymers will never see much more to it than a long claw of old grey wall that flexes itself against the sea. In fact, since it lies well apart from the main town, a tiny Piraeus to a microscopic Athens, they seem almost to turn their backs on it. Certainly it has cost them enough in repairs through the centuries to justify a certain resentment. But to a less tax-paying, or more discriminating, eye it is quite simply the most beautiful sea-rampart on the south coast of England. And not only because it is, as the guidebooks say, redolent of seven hundred years of English history, because ships sailed to meet the Armada from it, because Monmouth landed beside it ... but finally because it is a superb fragment of folk-art.

Primitive yet complex, elephantine but delicate; as full of subtle curves and volumes as a Henry Moore or a Michelangelo; and pure, clean, salt, a paragon of mass. I exaggerate? Perhaps, but I can be put to the test, for the Cobb has changed very little since the year of which I write; though the town of Lyme has, and the test is not fair if you look back towards land.

When to Sail

From *The Happy Traveller: A Book for Poor Men, 1923* |

Rev Frank Tatchell (Vicar of Midhurst 1906–1935)

Make your voyage at the best season of the year; because, however good a sailor a man may be, day after day of dirty weather soon palls. April to October are the bad monsoon months in the China Sea, and June to October in the Indian Ocean. Typhoons occur round Japan in May and in September, the hurricane months in the South Sea Islands are December, January and February, and, for going round Cape Horn, all months are bad except January and February. The Red Sea is always hot and stuffy. At the North end the wind blows from the North and at the South end from the South. The middle is always smooth and often a flat calm. Here collects the red scum from which the sea has its name. It is called plankton and is a vegetable fish-food.

The Age of the Sea

From *The Mirror of the Sea, 1906* | Joseph Conrad (1857–1924)

It seems to me that no man born and truthful to himself could declare that he ever saw the sea looking young as the earth looks young in spring. But some of us, regarding the ocean with understanding and affection, have seen it looking old, as if the immemorial ages had been stirred up from the undisturbed bottom of ooze. For it is a gale of wind that makes the sea look old.

From a distance of years, looking at the remembered aspects of the storms lived through, it is that impression which disengages itself clearly from the great body of impressions left by many years of intimate contact.

If you would know the age of the earth, look upon the sea in a storm. The greyness of the whole immense surface, the wind furrows upon the faces of the waves, the great masses of foam, tossed about and waving, like matted white locks, give to the sea in a gale an appearance of hoary age, lustreless, dull, without gleams, as though it had been created before light itself.

The Mermaid

Part I and II | Alfred, Lord Tennyson (1809–1892)

I.

Who would be
A mermaid fair,
Singing alone,
Combing her hair
Under the sea,
In a golden curl
With a comb of pearl,
On a throne?

II.

I would be a mermaid fair;
I would sing to myself the whole of the day;
With a comb of pearl I would comb my hair;
And still as I comb'd I would sing and say,
'Who is it loves me? who loves not me?'
I would comb my hair till my ringlets would fall
Low adown, low adown,
From under my starry sea-bud crown
Low adown and around,
And I should look like a fountain of gold
Springing alone
With a shrill inner sound,
Over the throne
In the midst of the hall;
Till that great sea-snake under the sea
From his coiled sleeps in the central deeps
Would slowly trail himself sevenfold
Round the hall where I sate, and look in at the gate
With his large calm eyes for the love of me.
And all the mermen under the sea
Would feel their immortality
Die in their hearts for the love of me.

Sanditon

From *Sanditon, 1817* | Jane Austen (1775–1817)

'I do not mean to take exception to *any* place in particular,' answered Mr. Heywood. 'I only think our coast is too full of them altogether. But had we not better try to get you–'

'Our coast too full!' repeated Mr. Parker. 'On that point perhaps we may not totally disagree. At least there are *enough.* Our coast is abundant enough. It demands no more. Everybody's taste and everybody's finances may be suited. And those good people who are trying to add to the number are, in my opinion, excessively absurd and must soon find themselves the dupes of their own fallacious calculations. Such a place as Sanditon, sir, I may say was wanted, was called for. Nature had marked it out, had spoken in most intelligible characters. The finest, purest sea breeze on the coast – acknowledged to be so – excellent bathing – fine hard sand – deep water ten yards from the shore – no mud – no weeds – no slimy rocks. Never was there a place more palpably designed by nature for the resort of the invalid – the very spot which thousands seemed in need of! The most desirable distance from London! One complete, measured mile nearer than Eastbourne. Only conceive, sir, the advantage of saving a whole mile in a long journey.'

Exiled

Edna St Vincent Millay (1892–1950)

19 March

Searching my heart for its true sorrow,
This is the thing I find to be:
That I am weary of words and people,
Sick of the city, wanting the sea;

Wanting the sticky, salty sweetness
Of the strong wind and shattered spray;
Wanting the loud sound and the soft sound
Of the big surf that breaks all day.

Always before about my dooryard,
Marking the reach of the winter sea,
Rooted in sand and dragging drift-wood,
Straggled the purple wild sweet-pea;

Always I climbed the wave at morning,
Shook the sand from my shoes at night,
That now am caught beneath great buildings,
Stricken with noise, confused with light.

If I could hear the green piles groaning
Under the windy wooden piers,
See once again the bobbing barrels,
And the black sticks that fence the weirs,

If I could see the weedy mussels
Crusting the wrecked and rotting hulls,
Hear once again the hungry crying
Overhead, of the wheeling gulls,

Feel once again the shanty straining
    Under the turning of the tide,
Fear once again the rising freshet,
    Dread the bell in the fog outside, –

    I should be happy, – that was happy
    All day long on the coast of Maine!
I have a need to hold and handle
    Shells and anchors and ships again!

    I should be happy, that am happy
    Never at all since I came here.
I am too long away from water.
    I have a need of water near.

An Enormous Thing

From *Vingt mille lieues sous les mers, 1870*

Twenty Thousand Leagues under the Sea, 1876

Jules Verne (1828–1905)

Translated by Henry Frith (1840–1917)

For some time many vessels had encountered 'an enormous thing', long, spindle-shaped, phosphorescent at times – very much larger and swifter than a whale.

The facts relating to this apparition, as recorded in various 'logs', agreed sufficiently respecting the formation of the object – or being – in question, the unheard-of celerity of its movements, its wonderful power of motion, the peculiar life with which it seemed endowed. If it were a whale species, it exceeded in bulk all that science had hitherto classified.

A Parable

Mathilde Blind (1841–1896)

Between the sandhills and the sea
  A narrow strip of silver sand,
  Whereon a little maid doth stand,
Who picks up shells continually
Between the sandhills and the sea.

Far as her wondering eyes can reach
  A Vastness, heaving grey in grey
  To the frayed edges where the day
Furls his red standard on the breach,
Between the skyline and the beach.

The waters of the flowing tide
  Cast up the sea-pink shells and weed;
  She toys with shells, and doth not heed
The ocean, which on every side
Is closing round her vast and wide.

It creeps her way as if in play,
  Pink shells at her pink feet to cast;
  But now the wild waves hold her fast,
And bear her off and melt away
A Vastness heaving grey in grey.

A Rather Heavy Sea

From *American Notes, 1842* | Charles Dickens (1812–1870)

22 March

It is the third morning. I am awakened out of my sleep by a dismal shriek from my wife, who demands to know whether there's any danger. I rouse myself, and look out of bed. The water-jug is plunging and leaping like a lively dolphin; all the smaller articles are afloat, except my shoes, which are stranded on a carpet-bag, high and dry, like a couple of coal-barges. Suddenly I see them spring into the air, and behold the looking-glass, which is nailed to the wall, sticking fast upon the ceiling. At the same time the door entirely disappears, and a new one is opened in the floor. Then I begin to comprehend that the state-room is standing on its head.

Before it is possible to make any arrangement at all compatible with this novel state of things, the ship rights. Before one can say 'Thank Heaven!' she wrongs again. Before one can cry she *is* wrong, she seems to have started forward, and to be a creature actually running of its own accord, with broken knees and failing legs, through every variety of hole and pitfall, and stumbling constantly. Before one can so much as wonder, she takes a high leap into the air. Before she has well done that, she takes a deep dive into the water. Before she has gained the surface, she throws a summerset. The instant she is on her legs, she rushes backward. And so she goes on staggering, heaving, wrestling, leaping, diving, jumping, pitching, throbbing, rolling, and rocking: and going through all these movements, sometimes by turns, and sometimes altogether: until one feels disposed to roar for mercy.

A steward passes. 'Steward!' 'Sir?' 'What *is* the matter? what *do* you call this?' 'Rather a heavy sea on, sir, and a head-wind.'

Farewell and Adieu

From *Poor Jack, 1840* | Captain Frederick Marryat (1792–1848)

Verses 1–3

"Farewell and adieu to you, Spanish ladies,
Farewell and adieu to you, ladies of Spain;
For we have received orders
For to sail to old England,
But we hope in a short time to see you again.

We'll rant and we'll roar, like true British sailors,
We'll rant and we'll roar across the salt seas;
Until we strike soundings
In the Channel of old England
(From Ushant to Scilly 'tis thirty-five leagues).

Then we hove our ship to, with the wind at sou'west, my boys,
Then we hove our ship to, for to strike soundings clear;
Then we filled the maintopsail
And bore right away, my boys,
And straight up the Channel of old England did steer.

Vague and Broken Impressions

From *Father and Son, 1907* | Edmund Gosse (1849–1928)

Looking back, I cannot see a cloud on the terrestrial horizon – I see nothing but a blaze of sunshine; descents of slippery grass to moons of snow-white shingle, cold to the bare flesh; red promontories running out into a sea that was like sapphire; and our happy clan climbing, bathing, boating, lounging, chattering, all the hot day through. Once more I have to record the fact, which I think is not without interest, that precisely as my life ceases to be solitary, it ceases to be distinct. I have no difficulty in recalling, with the minuteness of a photograph, scenes in which my Father and I were the sole actors within the four walls of a room, but of the glorious life among wild boys on the margin of the sea I have nothing but vague and broken impressions, delicious and illusive.

Eternal Father, Strong to Save

William Whiting (1825–1878)

Eternal Father, strong to save,
whose arm hath bound the restless wave,
who bidd'st the mighty ocean deep
its own appointed limits keep;
  O hear us when we cry to Thee,
  for those in peril on the sea!

O Christ, whose voice the waters heard
and hushed their raging at Thy word,
who walkedst on the foaming deep,
and calm amidst its rage didst sleep;
  O hear us when we cry to thee,
  for those in peril on the sea!

O Holy Spirit, who didst brood
upon the chaos dark and rude,
and bid its angry tumult cease,
and give, for wild confusion, peace;
  O hear us when we cry to Thee,
  for those in peril on the sea!

O Trinity of love and power,
our brethren shield in danger's hour;
from rock and tempest, fire and foe,
protect them wheresoe'er they go;
  thus evermore shall rise to thee
  glad hymns of praise from land and sea.

A Dangerous Paradise

From *The Arabian Nights: The First Voyage of Sinbad the Sailor, 1775*

Translated by Sir Richard Burton, 1885 (1821–1890)

26 March

I embarked, with a company of merchants, on board a ship bound for Bassorah. There we again embarked and sailed many days and nights, and we passed from isle to isle and sea to sea and shore to shore, buying and selling and bartering everywhere the ship touched, and continued our course till we came to an island as it were a garth of the gardens of Paradise. Here the captain cast anchor and making fast to the shore, put out the landing planks. So all on board landed and made furnaces and lighting fires therein, busied themselves in various ways, some cooking and some washing, whilst other some walked about the island for solace, and the crew fell to eating and drinking and playing and sporting. I was one of the walkers but, as we were thus engaged, behold the master who was standing on the gunwale cried out to us at the top of his voice, saying, "Ho there! passengers, run for your lives and hasten back to the ship and leave your gear and save yourselves from destruction, Allah preserve you! For this island whereon ye stand is no true island, but a great fish stationary a-middlemost of the sea, whereon the sand hath settled and trees have sprung up of old time, so that it is become like unto an island; but, when ye lighted fires on it, it felt the heat and moved; and in a moment it will sink with you into the sea and ye will all be drowned. So leave your gear and seek your safety ere ye die!"

Over the Great Windy Waters

From *Amours de Voyage* | Arthur Hugh Clough (1819–1861)

Canto I

Over the great windy waters, and over the clear-crested summits,
  Unto the sun and the sky, and unto the perfecter earth,
Come, let us go, – to a land wherein gods of the old time wandered,
  Where every breath even now changes to ether divine.
Come, let us go; though withal a voice whisper, 'The world that we
    live in,
  Whithersoever we turn, still is the same narrow crib;
'Tis but to prove limitation, and measure a cord, that we travel;
  Let who would 'scape and be free go to his chamber and think;
'Tis but to change idle fancies for memories wilfully falser;
  'Tis but to go and have been.' – Come, little bark! let us go.

Keys in the West-Indies

From *A General History of the Pyrates, from the first Rise and Settlement in the Island of Providence, to the present Time. With the remarkable Actions and Adventures of the two female Pyrates Mary Read and Anne Bonny*, 1724 |

Captain Charles Johnson, Identity unknown. Thought by some to be a pseudonym for Daniel Defoe (c. 1660–1731) or the journalist and printer Nathaniel Mist (d. 1737)

28 March

It may here perhaps be no unnecessary Digression, to explain upon what they call Keys in the *West-Indies*: These are small sandy Islands, appearing a little above the Surf of the Water, with only a few Bushes or Weeds upon them, but abound (those most at any Distance from the Main) with Turtle, amphibious Animals, that always chuse the quietest and most unfrequented Place, for laying their Eggs, which are to a vast Number in the Seasons, and would seldom be seen, but for this, (except by Pyrates:) Then Vessels from *Jamaica* and the other Governments make Voyages, called Turtling, for supplying the People, a common and approved Food with them. I am apt to think these *Keys*, especially those nigh Islands, to have been once contiguous with them, and separated by Earthquakes (frequently there) or Inundations, because some of them that have been within continual View, as those nigh *Jamaica*, are observed within our Time, to be entirely wasted away and lost, and others daily wasting. There are not only of the Use above taken Notice of to Pyrates; but it is commonly believed were always in buccaneering pyratical Times, the hiding Places for their Riches, and often Times a Shelter for themselves, till their Friends on the Main, had found Means to obtain Indemnity for their Crimes.

Upon the shore

Verses 1–4 | Robert Bridges (1844–1930)

Who has not walked upon the shore,
And who does not the morning know,
The day the angry gale is o'er,
The hour the wind has ceased to blow?

The horses of the strong southwest
Are pastured round his tropic tent,
Careless how long the ocean's breast
Sob on and sigh for passion spent.

The frightened birds, that fled inland
To house in rock and tower and tree,
Are gathering on the peaceful strand,
To tempt again the sunny sea;

Whereon the timid ships steal out
And laugh to find their foe asleep,
That lately scattered them about,
And drave them to the fold like sheep.

The Sea Roughened

From *Villette, 1853* | Charlotte Brontë (1816–1855)

As dark night drew on, the sea roughened: larger waves swayed strong against the vessel's side. It was strange to reflect that blackness and water were round us, and to feel the ship ploughing straight on her pathless way, despite noise, billow, and rising gale. Articles of furniture began to fall about, and it became needful to lash them to their places.

An Illusion

From *Mansfield Park, 1814* | Jane Austen (1775–1817)

The day was uncommonly lovely. It was really March; but it was April in its mild air, brisk soft wind, and bright sun, occasionally clouded for a minute; and everything looked so beautiful under the influence of such a sky, the effects of the shadows pursuing each other on the ships at Spithead and the island beyond, with the ever-varying hues of the sea, now at high water, dancing in its glee and dashing against the ramparts with so fine a sound, produced altogether such a combination of charms for Fanny, as made her gradually almost careless of the circumstances under which she felt them.

APRIL

A Ship at Anchor

At Sea

From *The Modern Traveller IV* | Hilaire Belloc (1870–1953)

At sea the days go slipping past,
Monotonous from first to last –
A trip like any other one
In vessels going south. The sun
   Grew higher and more fiery.
We lay and drank, and swore, and played
At Trick-my-neighbour in the shade;
And you may guess how every sight,
However trivial or slight,
   Was noted in my diary.
I have it here – the usual things –
A serpent (not the sort with wings)
   Came rising from the sea:
In length (as far as we could guess)
A quarter of a mile or less.
The weather was extremely clear
The creature dangerously near
   And plain as it would be.
It had a bifurcated tail,
And in its mouth it held a whale.
Just north, I find, of Cape de Verd
We caught a very curious bird
   With horns upon its head;
And – not, as one might well suppose,
Web-footed or with jointed toes –
   But having hoofs instead.
As no one present seemed to know
Its use or name, I let it go.

The Response of the Sea

From *The Beauties of Scenery, 1943* | Vaughan Cornish (1862–1948)

Those who dwell upon the shore learn to recognize how swift and perfect is the response of the sea to the changing tone and colour of the sky. In fine weather the sparkling surface reflects the brightness of the sun in a thousand changing points of light; then if the heavens are clouded the sea takes on a sombre tone. Thus the tone and colour of the water respond to the round of the day and the variety of weather, though lacking the longer period of response in which the vegetation of the forest records the seasons of the year.

Glanmore Sonnets VII

Seamus Heaney (1939–2013)

Dogger, Rockall, Malin, Irish Sea:
Green, swift upsurges, North Atlantic flux
Conjured by that strong gale-warning voice
Collapse into a sibilant penumbra.
Midnight and closedown. Sirens of the tundra,
Of eel-road, seal-road, keel-road, whale-road, raise
Their wind-compounded keen behind the baize
And drive the trawlers to the lee of Wicklow.
L'Étoile, Le Guillemot, La Belle Hélène
Nursed their bright names this morning in the bay
That toiled like mortar. It was marvellous
And actual, I said out loud, 'A haven',
The word deepening, clearing, like the sky
Elsewhere on Minches, Cromarty, The Faroes.

The Shipping Forecast

Weather Shipping finally became known as the Shipping Forecast in 1954.

1. Viking
2. North Utsire
3. South Utsire
4. Forties
5. Cromarty
6. Forth
7. Tyne
8. Dogger
9. Fisher
10. German Bight
11. Humber
12. Thames
13. Dover
14. Wight
15. Portland
16. Plymouth
17. Biscay
18. Trafalgar
19. FitzRoy
20. Sole
21. Lundy
22. Fastnet
23. Irish Sea
24. Shannon
25. Rockall
26. Malin
27. Hebrides
28. Bailey
29. Fair Isle
30. Faeroes
31. Southeast Iceland

In 2002 Finisterre was renamed FitzRoy in recognition of Vice-Admiral FitzRoy, founder of the Met Office and originator of the original storm warning service.

Sea-sickness

From *Three Men in a Boat: To say nothing of the Dog!* 1889 |

Jerome K. Jerome (1859–1927)

It is a curious fact, but nobody ever is sea-sick – on land. At sea, you come across plenty of people very bad indeed, whole boat-loads of them; but I never met a man yet, on land, who had ever known at all what it was to be sea-sick. Where the thousands upon thousands of bad sailors that swarm in every ship hide themselves when they are on land is a mystery.

If most men were like a fellow I saw on the Yarmouth boat one day, I could account for the seeming enigma easily enough. It was just off Southend Pier, I recollect, and he was leaning out through one of the port-holes in a very dangerous position. I went up to him to try and save him.

'Hi! come further in,' I said, shaking him by the shoulder. 'You'll be overboard.'

'Oh my! I wish I was,' was the only answer I could get; and there I had to leave him.

Three weeks afterwards, I met him in the coffee-room of a Bath hotel, talking about his voyages, and explaining, with enthusiasm, how he loved the sea.

'Good sailor!' he replied in answer to a mild young man's envious query; 'well, I did feel a little queer *once*, I confess. It was off Cape Horn. The vessel was wrecked the next morning.'

I said:

'Weren't you a little shaky by Southend Pier one day, and wanted to be thrown overboard?'

'Southend Pier!' he replied, with a puzzled expression.

'Yes; going down to Yarmouth, last Friday three weeks.'

'Oh, ah – yes,' he answered, brightening up; 'I remember now. I did have a headache that afternoon. It was the pickles, you know. They were the most disgraceful pickles I ever tasted in a respectable boat. Did *you* have any?'

For myself, I have discovered an excellent preventive against sea-sickness, in balancing myself. You stand in the centre of the deck, and, as the ship heaves and pitches, you move your body about, so as to keep it always straight. When the front of the ship rises, you lean forward, till the deck almost touches your nose; and when its back end gets up, you lean backwards. This is all very well for an hour or two; but you can't balance yourself for a week.

The Dhow

From *A Voyage by Dhow, 2001* | Norman Lewis (1908–2003)

It was a hot and airless evening. The burnished breast of the harbour curved gently with a sinuous movement from the depths and, in places, a vagrant breeze frosted its surface with changing designs. Momentarily the great triangular sail filled with wind, and strained billowing at the mast. Then just as suddenly it drained out and hung down loosely. We moved so slowly that looking at distant objects we seemed to be stationary. Only a gentle straining of timbers assured us that we were under way, and in the water thin streams of iridescence spread out and curled into rings over the gently heaving wake as the ship's sides disturbed the oiliness of the surface. Even the gull perched on the mast remained standing trance-like on one leg, and, as night drew close, stirred only to put its head under its wing.

Merman

Verses I and II | Alfred, Lord Tennyson (1809–1892)

I.

Who would be
A merman bold,
Sitting alone,
Singing alone
Under the sea,
With a crown of gold,
On a throne?

II.

I would be a merman bold,
I would sit and sing the whole of the day;
I would fill the sea-halls with a voice of power;
But at night I would roam abroad and play
With the mermaids in and out of the rocks,
Dressing their hair with the white sea-flower;
And holding them back by their flowing locks
I would kiss them often under the sea,
And kiss them again till they kiss'd me
Laughingly, laughingly;
And then we would wander away, away
To the pale-green sea-groves straight and high,
Chasing each other merrily.

Suitable Crew

From *The Voyages of Dr Dolittle, 1922* | Hugh Lofting (1886–1947)

8 April

The mussel-man took us off a little way down the river and showed us the neatest, prettiest, little vessel that ever was built. She was called *The Curlew*. Joe said he would sell her to us cheap. But the trouble was that the boat needed three people, while we were only two.

'Of course I shall be taking Chee-Chee,' said the Doctor. 'But although he is very quick and clever, he is not as strong as a man. We really ought to have another person to sail a boat as big as that.'

'I know of a good sailor, Doctor,' said Joe – 'a first-class seaman who would be glad of the job.'

'No, thank you, Joe,' said Doctor Dolittle. 'I don't want any seamen. I couldn't afford to hire them. And then they hamper me so, seamen do, when I'm at sea. They're always wanting to do things the proper way; and I like to do them *my* way. Now let me see: who could we take with us?'

'There's Matthew Mugg, the cat's-meat-man,' I said.

'No, he wouldn't do. Matthew's a very nice fellow, but he talks too much – mostly about his rheumatism. You have to be frightfully particular whom you take with you on long voyages.'

'How about Luke the Hermit?' I asked.

'That's a good idea – splendid – if he'll come. Let's go and ask him right away.'

A Sea Dirge

Verses 1–6 | Lewis Carroll (1832–1898)

There are certain things – a spider, a ghost,
The income-tax, gout, an umbrella for three –
That I hate, but the thing that I hate the most
Is a thing they call the Sea.

Pour some salt water over the floor –
Ugly I'm sure you'll allow it to be:
Suppose it extended a mile or more,
That's very like the Sea.

Beat a dog till it howls outright –
Cruel, but all very well for a spree;
Suppose that one did so day and night,
That would be like the Sea.

I had a vision of nursery-maids;
Tens of thousands passed by me –
All leading children with wooden spades,
And this was by the Sea.

Who invented those spades of wood?
Who was it cut them out of the tree?
None, I think, but an idiot could –
Or one that loved the Sea.

It is pleasant and dreamy, no doubt, to float
With 'thoughts as boundless, and souls as free'!
But, suppose you are very unwell in a boat,
How do you like the Sea?

Buried by the Sea

From *Lost England: The Story of our Submerged Coasts, 1902* |
Beckles Willson (1869–1942)

10 April

For hundreds of miles on the English coasts are buried once prosperous towns and villages and mighty forests, where once roamed the red deer, inclosed in lordly parks, and assuaging their thirst in lakes long since vanished. The line of anchorage for ships off Selsey in Sussex is still, by mariners ignorant of the term's origin, called 'the Park'. For in Henry VIII's reign it was full of noble stags and does, and for poaching in these royal preserves a bishop once fiercely excommunicated certain unhappy deer-stealers.

Then, when we fall back on old chronicles and old traditions, we are confronted with even more impressive evidence of loss by action of the sea.

In Yorkshire alone there are no fewer than twelve buried towns and villages. In Suffolk there are at least four. At many places on the coast to-day the remains of submerged forests are visible at low water. Such a forest may be seen plainly off the coast in the Wirrall district of Cheshire.

The Word of an Engineer

Verses 1–3 | James Weldon Johnson (1871–1938)

'She's built of steel
From deck to keel,
And bolted strong and tight;
In scorn she'll sail
The fiercest gale,
And pierce the darkest night.

'The builder's art
Has proved each part
Throughout her breadth and length;
Deep in the hulk,
Of her mighty bulk,
Ten thousand Titans' strength.'

The tempest howls,
The Ice Wolf prowls,
The winds they shift and veer,
But calm I sleep,
And faith I keep
In the word of an engineer.

The Ship

From *The Modern Traveller, poem IV* | Hilaire Belloc (1870–1953)

The ship was dropping down the stream,
The Isle of Dogs was just abeam,
And Sin and Blood and I
Saw Greenwich Hospital go past,
And gave a look – (for them the last) –
Towards the London sky!
Ah! nowhere have I ever seen
A sky so pure and so serene!

Did we at length, perhaps, regret
Our strange adventurous lot?
And were our eyes a trifle wet
With tears that we repressed, and yet
Which started blinding hot?
Perhaps – and yet, I do not know,
For when we came to go below,
We cheerfully admitted
That though there was a smell of paint
(And though a very just complaint
Had to be lodged against the food),
The cabin furniture was good
And comfortably fitted.
And even out beyond the Nore
We did not ask to go ashore.

Waves

From *The Beauties of Scenery, 1943* | Vaughan Cornish (1862–1948)

Beyond a foreground of deep sea waves, massive in form and strong in tone and colour, the distant shore, etherialized by atmosphere, seems like Elysium, the happy land where only soft zephyrs from the ocean blow.

Sailing out on the broad sea beyond the sight of land, the waves become the main feature of scenery. When, in stormy weather, the crests of the waves rise above the sky line, the sea assumes a 'mountainous' appearance, in the sense which the word bore when the term first came into use. This included the lesser eminences which we now call hills, i.e. those attaining to hundreds, not thousands, of feet. The actual height of storm waves is usually between forty and fifty feet, but when the crests rise well above the sky line the height appears much greater. This effect is enhanced in the squalls of rain which occur during a storm, the screening effect of the rain-drops increasing the apparent distance of the horizon between which and the vessel is a sea of moving hills and valleys.

The Storm

Adelaide Procter (1825–1864)

The tempest rages wild and high,
The waves lift up their voice and cry
Fierce answers to the angry sky, –
Miserere Domine.

Through the black night and driving rain
A ship is struggling, all in vain,
To live upon the stormy main; –
Miserere Domine.

The thunders roar, the lightnings glare,
Vain is it now to strive or dare;
A cry goes up of great despair, –
Miserere Domine.

The stormy voices of the main,
The moaning winds and pelting rain
Beat on the nursery window-pane: –
Miserere Domine.

Warm curtained was the little bed,
Soft pillowed was the little head;
'The storm will wake the child,' they said: –
Miserere Domine.

Cowering among his pillows white
He prays, his blue eyes dim with fright,
'Father, save those at sea to-night!' –
Miserere Domine.

The morning shone all clear and gay
On a ship at anchor in the bay,
And on a little child at play, –
Gloria tibi Domine!

In the Water

From *Every Man for Himself, 1996* | Beryl Bainbridge (1932–2010)

As the ship staggered and tipped, a great volume of water flowed over the submerged bows and tossed me like a cork to the roof. … My fingers touched some kind of bolt near the ventilation grille, and I grabbed it tight. I filled my lungs with air and fixed my eyes on the blurred horizon, determined to hang on until I was sure I could float free rather than be swilled back and forth in a maelstrom. I wouldn't waste my strength in swimming, not yet, for I knew the ship was now my enemy and if I wasn't vigilant would drag me with her to the grave. I waited for the next slithering dip and when it came and the waves rushed in and swept me higher, I released my grip and let myself be carried away, over the tangle of ropes and wires and davits, clear of the rails and out into the darkness. I heard the angry roaring of the dying ship, the deafening cacophony as she stood on end and all her guts tore loose. I choked on soot and cringed beneath the sparks dancing like fire-flies as the forward funnel broke and smashed the sea in two. … I was sucked under, as I knew I would be, down, down, and still I waited, waited until the pull slackened – then I struck out with all my strength.

I don't know how long I swam under that lidded sea – time had stopped with my breath – and just as it seemed as if my lungs would burst the blackness paled and I kicked to the surface. I had thought I was entering paradise, for I was alive and about to breathe again.

The Convergence of the Twain

(Lines on the loss of the *Titanic*) | Thomas Hardy (1840–1928)

Verses I–V

I

In a solitude of the sea
Deep from human vanity,
And the Pride of Life that planned her, stilly couches she.

II

Steel chambers, late the pyres
Of her salamandrine fires,
Cold currents thrid, and turn to rhythmic tidal lyres.

III

Over the mirrors meant
To glass the opulent
The sea-worm crawls – grotesque, slimed, dumb, indifferent.

IV

Jewels in joy designed
To ravish the sensuous mind
Lie lightless, all their sparkles bleared and black and blind.

V

Dim moon-eyed fishes near
Gaze at the gilded gear
And query: 'What does this vaingloriousness down here?' …

Key West

From *A Narrative of the Life and Travels of Mrs. Nancy Prince, 1850* | Nancy Prince (1799–post 1856)

After leaving Jamaica, the vessel was tacked to a south-west course. I asked the Captain what this meant. He said he must take the current, as there was no wind. Without any ceremony, I told him it was not the case, and told the passengers that he had deceived us. There were two English men that were born on the island, that had never been on the water; before the third day passed, they asked the Captain why they had not seen Hayti. He told them they passed when they were asleep. I told them it was not true, he was steering south south-west. The passengers in the steerage got alarmed, and every one was asking the Captain what this meant. The ninth day we made land. 'By –,' said the Captain, 'this is Key West; come, passengers, let us have a vote to run over the neck, and I will go ashore and bring aboard fruit and turtle.' They all agreed but myself. He soon dropped anchor. The officers from the shore came on board and congratulated him on keeping his appointment, thus proving that my suspicions were well founded. The Captain went ashore with these men, and soon came back, called for the passengers, and asked for their vote for him to remain until the next day, saying that he could, by this delay, make five or six hundred dollars, as there had been a vessel wrecked there lately. They all agreed but myself. The vessel was soon at the side of the wharf. In one hour there were twenty slaves at work to unload her; every inducement was made to persuade me to go ashore, or set my feet on the wharf. A law had just been passed there that every free colored person coming there, should be put in custody on their going ashore; there were five colored persons on board; none dared to go ashore, however uncomfortable we might be in the vessel, or however we might desire to refresh ourselves by a change of scene. We remained at Key West four days.

Wind and Sea

Mary Coleridge (1861–1907)

The Wind and the Sea are sisters,
They moan for evermore,
One in the pine-tree branches
And one against the shore,
One for the land behind her,
One for the land before.

The Wind is the Sea's young brother,
The selfsame voice have they,
Sunlight and moonlight kiss them,
And then they kiss and play.
Sometimes they hate each other,
And then they fight all day.

'What silly stuff you scribble!'
My fair love said to me.
'As if such things as those are,
Could ever strive or agree.
They are neither brothers nor sisters,
But just the Wind and the Sea!'

Atlantis

From *Timaeus, c. 360 BCE* | Plato (c. 428/3–348/7 BCE)

Translated by A. E. Taylor, 1929 (1869–1945)

[There] came a time of extraordinary earthquakes and inundations. In one terrible day and night of storm, your warriors were swallowed in a body by the earth, and Atlantis likewise sank into the sea and vanished. This is why the Ocean in that part to this day cannot be navigated or explored, owing to the great depth of the mud caused by the subsiding of the island.

. . . . . .

The Story of Atlantis by A. E. Taylor

It is as certain as such a thing can be that the whole story of Atlantis, including the statement that Solon had met with tales about the island in Egypt is one of Plato's imaginative fictions.

A Wizardwood Ship

From *Ship of Magic, 1998* | Robin Hobb (1952–)

Two men look at the ship:

'This has not been here thirty years,' the younger voice asserted. 'A ship pulled out and left on a beach for thirty years would be wormholed and barnacled over.'

'Unless it's made from wizardwood,' responded the older voice. 'Liveships don't rot, Mingsley. Nor do barnacles or tubeworms find them appetizing. That is but one of the reasons the ships are so expensive and so desirable. They endure for generations, with little of the hull maintenance an ordinary ship requires. Out on the seas, they take care of themselves. They'll yell to a steersman if they see hazards in their paths. Some of them near sail themselves. What other vessel can warn you that a cargo has shifted, or that you've overloaded them? A wizardwood ship on the sea is a wonder to behold!'

Casabianca

Felicia Hemans (1793–1835)

The boy stood on the burning deck
  Whence all but him had fled;
The flame that lit the battle's wreck
  Shone round him o'er the dead.

Yet beautiful and bright he stood,
  As born to rule the storm;
A creature of heroic blood,
  A proud, though child-like form.

The flames roll'd on – he would not go
  Without his Father's word;
That Father, faint in death below,
  His voice no longer heard.

He call'd aloud: – 'Say, Father, say
  If yet my task is done?'
He knew not that the chieftain lay
  Unconscious of his son.

'Speak, Father!' once again he cried
  'If I may yet be gone!
And' – but the booming shots replied,
  And fast the flames roll'd on.

Upon his brow he felt their breath,
  And in his waving hair,
And look'd from that lone post of death,
  In still yet brave despair.

And shouted but once more aloud,
  'My Father, must I stay?'
While o'er him fast, through sail and shroud,
  The wreathing fires made way,

They wrapt the ship in splendour wild,
  They caught the flag on high,
And streamed above the gallant child,
  Like banners in the sky.

There came a burst of thunder sound –
  The boy – oh! where was he?
Ask of the winds that far around
  With fragments strewed the sea!

With mast, and helm, and pennon fair,
  That well had borne their part –
But the noblest thing which perished there
  Was that young faithful heart!

Advice

From *Robinson Crusoe, 1719* | Daniel Defoe (1660–1731)

22 April

Daniel is given advice after his first voyage:

'Young man,' says he, 'you ought never to go to sea any more; you ought to take this for a plain and visible token that you are not to be a seafaring man.' – 'Why, sir,' said I, 'will you go to sea no more?' – 'That is another case,' said he; 'it is my calling, and therefore my duty; but as you made this voyage on trial, you see what a taste Heaven has given you of what you are to expect if you persist. Perhaps this has all befallen us on your account, like Jonah in the ship of Tarshish. Pray,' continues he, 'what are you; and on what account did you go to sea?' Upon that I told him some of my story; at the end of which he burst out into a strange kind of passion: 'What had I done,' says he, 'that such an unhappy wretch should come into my ship? I would not set my foot in the same ship with thee again for a thousand pounds.' This indeed was, as I said, an excursion of his spirits, which were yet agitated by the sense of his loss, and was farther than he could have authority to go. However, he afterwards talked very gravely to me, exhorting me to go back to my father, and not tempt Providence to my ruin, telling me I might see a visible hand of Heaven against me. 'And, young man,' said he, 'depend upon it, if you do not go back, wherever you go, you will meet with nothing but disasters and disappointments, till your father's words are fulfilled upon you.'

We parted soon after; for I made him little answer, and I saw him no more; which way he went I knew not. As for me, having some money in my pocket, I travelled to London by land; and there, as well as on the road, had many struggles with myself what course of life I should take, and whether I should go home or to sea.

Familiarity

Rachel Field (1894–1942)

Those who live by the sea
Too familiar grow
With the changing ways of it,
And its magic ebb and flow.
Nothing they see or care to know
Save when will the tide be high or low.

Though green waves glitter
With white flung spray,
By their kitchen fires
They bend all day.
They turn their backs on the selfsame sea
That can make the heart leap up in me!

My Own Opinions

From *Sailing Alone around the World, 1900* | Joshua Slocum

(1844–disappeared after sailing south from Martha's Vineyard 1909)

24 April

A photographer on the outer pier at East Boston got a picture of her as she swept by, her flag at the peak throwing its folds clear. A thrilling pulse beat high in me. My step was light on deck in the crisp air. I felt that there could be no turning back, and that I was engaging in an adventure the meaning of which I thoroughly understood. I had taken little advice from any one, for I had a right to my own opinions in matters pertaining to the sea. That the best of sailors might do worse than even I alone was borne in upon me not a league from Boston docks, where a great steamship, fully manned, officered, and piloted, lay stranded and broken. This was the *Venetian*. She was broken completely in two over a ledge. So in the first hour of my lone voyage I had proof that the *Spray* could at least do better than this full-handed steamship, for I was already farther on my voyage than she. 'Take warning, *Spray,* and have a care,' I uttered aloud to my bark, passing fairylike silently down the bay.

The Plan

From *The Cruise of the Snark, 1911* | Jack London (1876–1916)

It began in the swimming pool at Glen Ellen. Between swims it was our wont to come out and lie in the sand and let our skins breathe the warm air and soak in the sunshine. Roscoe was a yachtsman. I had followed the sea a bit. It was inevitable that we should talk about boats. We talked about small boats, and the seaworthiness of small boats. We instanced Captain Slocum and his three years' voyage around the world in the *Spray.* We asserted that we were not afraid to go around the world in a small boat, say forty feet long. We asserted furthermore that we would like to do it. We asserted finally that there was nothing in this world we'd like better than a chance to do it.

'Let us do it,' we said … in fun. Then I asked Charmian privily if she'd really care to do it, and she said that it was too good to be true.

Not Waving but Drowning

Stevie Smith (1902–1971)

Nobody heard him, the dead man,
But still he lay moaning:
I was much further out than you thought
And not waving but drowning.

Poor chap, he always loved larking
And now he's dead
It must have been too cold for him his heart gave way,
They said.

Oh, no no no, it was too cold always
(Still the dead one lay moaning)
I was much too far out all my life
And not waving but drowning.

The Sound of the Sea

From *The Sea, 1861* | Jules Michelet (1798–1874)

Translated by W. H. D. Adams (1828–1891)

Long before the Sea meets our gaze we hear, and we divine our vicinity to the awful despot. At first a distant, dull, monotonous sound salutes the ear. By degrees all other sounds yield to and are absorbed in this. Soon we remark the solemn alteration, the invariable return of the same note, a strong bass, which increasingly rolls and roars – more regular even than that oscillation of the pendulum which marks for us the minutes. But here the balance lacks the monotony of mechanical appliances. We perceive, or think we perceive, in it the trembling intonation of life. And, in truth, at the hour of the flow, when wave mounts upon wave, immense and electrical, there mingles in the stormy roll of the waters the rattle of the shells and of the thousand different creatures which they bring up from the depths. Then comes the ebb, and a hoarse murmur makes us understand that the tide is carrying back this world of living things to the Ocean's bosom.

Safe Harbour

From *The Aeneid, 29–19 BCE* | Virgil (70–19 BCE)

Translated by John Dryden (1631–1700)

Book I lines 218–242

28 April

Within a long Recess there lies a Bay,
An Island shades it from the rolling Sea,
And forms a Port secure for Ships to ride.
Broke by the jutting Land on either side:
In double Streams the briny Waters glide.
Betwixt two rows of Rocks, a Sylvan Scene
Appears above, and Groves for ever green:
A Grott is form'd beneath, with Mossy Seats,
To rest the *Nereids*, and exclude the Heats.
Down thro' the Cranies of the living Walls
The Crystal Streams descend in murm'ring Falls.
No Haulsers need to bind the Vessels here,
Nor bearded Anchors, for no Storms they fear.
Sev'n Ships within this happy Harbour meet,
The thin Remainders of the scatter'd Fleet.

The Big Water

From *Breaking the Maafa Chain, 2019* | Anni Domingo (1950–)

Salimatu had never seen the 'big water', the ocean, before and here was water as far as her eyes could see. As they sat in the canoe, the water raced towards them, attacking, roaring, hungry. Just as she thought it would swallow them alive, it backed away slithering and sliding, hissing, only to come rushing back with greater power. It was like an animal with two heads that went both ways. Water splashed her face, she licked her lips and her eyes widened with surprise. It tasted of salt. On the long journey to Abomey she had learnt that salt was important, not just for cooking but for buying and selling. Did the white man have so much salt they could put it in all this water? Another wave hit the canoe and she let go of the side. Her gloved hand plunged into the furious ocean.

The Shell

Mary Webb (1881–1927)

What has the sea swept up?
A Viking oar, long mouldered in the peace
Of grey oblivion? Some dim-burning bowl
Of unmixed gold, from far-off island feasts?
Ropes of old pearls? Masses of ambergris?
Something of elfdom from the ghastly isles
Where white-hot rocks pierce through the flying spindrift?
Or a pale sea-queen, close wound in a net of spells?

Nothing of these. Nothing of antique splendours
That have a weariness about their names:
But – fresh and new, in frail transparency,
Pink as a baby's nail, silky and veined
As a flower petal – this casket of the sea,
One shell.

MAY

Neptune's Empire

A Great Fish

Jonah, 1:17–2:10

The King James Bible, 1611

Chapter 1
17 Now the LORD had prepared a great fish to swallow up Jonah.
And Jonah was in the belly of the fish three days and three nights.

Chapter 2
1 Then Jonah prayed unto the LORD his God out of the fish's belly,
2 and said,

'I cried by reason of mine affliction unto the LORD,
and he heard me;
out of the belly of hell cried I,
and thou heardest my voice.
3 For thou hadst cast me into the deep,
in the midst of the seas;
and the floods compassed me about:
all thy billows and thy waves passed over me.
4 Then I said, "I am cast out of thy sight;
yet I will look again toward thy holy temple."
5 The waters compassed me about, even to the soul:
the depth closed me round about,
the weeds were wrapped about my head.
6 I went down to the bottoms of the mountains;
the earth with her bars was about me for ever:
yet hast thou brought up my life from corruption,
O LORD my God.
7 When my soul fainted within me
I remembered the LORD:
and my prayer came in unto thee, into thine holy temple.

8 They that observe lying vanities forsake their own mercy.
9 But I will sacrifice unto thee with the voice of thanksgiving;
I will pay that that I have vowed.
Salvation is of the LORD.'
10 And the LORD spake unto the fish, and it vomited out Jonah upon
the dry land.

The Estuary

Verses 1–2 | Patricia Beer (1919–1999)

A light elegant wall waves down
The riverside, for tidiness
Or decoration – this water
Needs little keeping in – but turns
The corner to face the ocean
And thickens to a bastion.

No one can really taste or smell
Where the salt starts but at one point
The first building looks out to sea
And the two sides of the river
Are forced apart by cold light
And wind and different grasses.

Four Winds Harbour

From *Anne's House of Dreams, 1917* | L. M. Montgomery (1874–1942)

Anne never forgot the loveliness of the view that broke upon them when they had driven over the hill behind the village. Her new home could not yet be seen; but before her lay Four Winds Harbour like a great, shining mirror of rose and silver. Far down, she saw its entrance between the bar of sand dunes on one side and a steep, high, grim, red sandstone cliff on the other. Beyond the bar the sea, calm and austere, dreamed in the afterlight. The little fishing village, nestled in the cove where the sand-dunes met the harbour shore, looked like a great opal in the haze. The sky over them was like a jewelled cup from which the dusk was pouring; the air was crisp with the compelling tang of the sea, and the whole landscape was infused with the subtleties of a sea evening. A few dim sails drifted along the darkening, fir-clad harbour shores. A bell was ringing from the tower of a little white church on the far side; mellowly and dreamily sweet, the chime floated across the water blent with the moan of the sea. The great revolving light on the cliff at the channel flashed warm and golden against the clear northern sky, a trembling, quivering star of good hope. Far out along the horizon was the crinkled grey ribbon of a passing steamer's smoke.

My First Experience of the Ocean

From *The Promised Land, 1912* | Mary Antin (1881–1949)

4 May

We were conducted through the gate of departure, and after some hours of bewildering manœuvres, described in great detail in the report to my uncle, we found ourselves – we five frightened pilgrims from Polotzk – on the deck of a great big steamship afloat on the strange big waters of the ocean.

For sixteen days the ship was our world. My letter dwells solemnly on the details of the life at sea, as if afraid to cheat my uncle of the smallest circumstance. It does not shrink from describing the torments of seasickness; it notes every change in the weather. A rough night is described, when the ship pitched and rolled so that people were thrown from their berths; days and nights when we crawled through dense fogs, our foghorn drawing answering warnings from invisible ships. The perils of the sea were not minimized in the imaginations of us inexperienced voyagers. The captain and his officers ate their dinners, smoked their pipes and slept soundly in their turns, while we frightened emigrants turned our faces to the wall and awaited our watery graves.

All this while the seasickness lasted. Then came happy hours on deck, with fugitive sunshine, birds atop the crested waves, band music and dancing and fun. I explored the ship, made friends with officers and crew, or pursued my thoughts in quiet nooks. It was my first experience of the ocean, and I was profoundly moved.

A Hymn in Praise of Neptune

Thomas Campion (1567–1620)

Of Neptune's empire let us sing,
At whose command the waves obey,
To whom the rivers tribute pay,
        Down the high mountains sliding;
To whom the scaly nation yields
Homage for the crystal fields
                Wherein they dwell;
And every sea-god pays a gem,
Yearly out of his watery cell,
To deck the great Neptune's diadem.

The Tritons dancing in a ring
Before his palace gates, do make
The water with their echoes quake,
        Like the great thunder sounding:
The sea-nymphs chant their accents shrill;
        And the Sirens, taught to kill
                With their sweet voice,
Make every echoing rock reply
Unto their gentle murmuring noise
The praise of Neptune's empery.

Fishing in the Red Sea

From *A Voyage by Dhow, 2001* | Norman Lewis (1908–2003)

The more than leisurely progress of the dhow came as a surprise. Occasionally a breeze tightened the sails, but by the end of the first full day at sea we were to learn that we had covered only ten miles, and by the next morning we were in a flat calm. It was a situation accepted almost with jubilation both by the male passengers and several members of the crew. Many of the passengers had brought fishing tackle along, in readiness for forced inactivity, and now they baited their hooks and lowered them into the sea. Within minutes the first catch had been landed. The shores of the Red Sea were devoid of human population, and the fishing boats of Aden needed to go no further than the Gulf. Thus the Red Sea abounded in fish.

Different Seas

From *The Rime of the Ancient Mariner* |

Samuel Taylor Coleridge (1772–1834)

Part I lines 21-28

'The ship was cheered, the harbour cleared,
Merrily did we drop
Below the kirk, below the hill,
Below the lighthouse top.

The Sun came up upon the left,
Out of the sea came he!
And he shone bright, and on the right
Went down into the sea.

Part I lines 41-54

And now the STORM-BLAST came, and he
Was tyrannous and strong:
He struck with his o'ertaking wings,
And chased us south along.

With sloping masts and dipping prow,
As who pursued with yell and blow
Still treads the shadow of his foe,
And forward bends his head,
The ship drove fast, loud roared the blast,
And southward aye we fled.

And now there came both mist and snow,
And it grew wondrous cold:
And ice, mast-high, came floating by,
As green as emerald.

Ladies Island

From *'Life on the Sea Islands', Atlantic Monthly,* Part I, May 1864 |
Charlotte Forten Grimké (1837–1914)

We rowed across to Ladies Island, which adjoins St. Helena, through the splendors of a grand Southern sunset. The gorgeous clouds of crimson and gold were reflected as in a mirror in the smooth, clear waters below. As we glided along, the rich tones of the negro boatmen broke upon the evening stillness, - sweet, strange, and solemn.

Written after Swimming from Sestos to Abydos

George Gordon, Lord Byron (1788–1824)

If, in the month of dark December,
 Leander, who was nightly wont
(What maid will not the tale remember?)
 To cross thy stream, broad Hellespont!

If, when the wintry tempest roar'd,
 He sped to Hero, nothing loth,
And thus of old thy current pour'd,
 Fair Venus! how I pity both!

For *me*, degenerate modern wretch,
 Though in the genial month of May,
My dripping limbs I faintly stretch,
 And think I've done a feat to-day.

But since he cross'd the rapid tide,
 According to the doubtful story,
To woo, – and – Lord knows what beside,
 And swam for Love, as I for Glory;

'Twere hard to say who fared the best:
 Sad mortals! thus the Gods still plague you!
He lost his labour, I my jest;
 For he was drown'd, and I've the ague.

May 9 1810

Lovely Scenery

From *The Murder on the Golf Links, 1907* | Matthias McDonnell Bodkin (1850–1933)

10 May

The western sky was a sea of crimson and gold, in which floated a huge black cloud, shaped like a sea monster with the blazing sun in its jaws. The placid surface of the sea gave back the beauty of the sky, and in the clear, still air familiar objects took on a new beauty. Their way lay over the crisp velvet of the seaside turf, embroidered with wild flowers, to the Thornvale Hotel in the valley a mile away.

'How beautiful!' the girl whispered half to herself, and caught her breath with a queer little sigh.

Mr Beck looked down and saw that the blue eyes were very bright with tears. She met his look and smiled a wan little smile.

'Lovely scenery always makes me sad,' she explained feebly.

The Duchess' Desperate Means of Escape

From *Tales of a Traveller, 1824* | Washington Irving (1783–1859)

The Marquis said:

'One dark unruly night, she issued secretly out of a small postern gate of the castle, which the enemy had neglected to guard. She was followed by her female attendants, a few domestics, and some gallant cavaliers who still remained faithful to her fortunes. Her object was to gain a small port about two leagues distant, where she had privately provided a vessel for her escape in case of emergency.

'The little band of fugitives were obliged to perform the distance on foot. When they arrived at the port the wind was high and stormy, the tide contrary, the vessel anchored far off in the road, and no means of getting on board, but by a fishing shallop that lay tossing like a cockle shell on the edge of the surf. The Duchess determined to risk the attempt. The seamen endeavored to dissuade her, but the imminence of her danger on shore, and the magnanimity of her spirit urged her on. She had to be borne to the shallop in the arms of a mariner. Such was the violence of the wind and waves, that he faltered, lost his foothold, and let his precious burden fall into the sea.

'The Duchess was nearly drowned; but partly through her own struggles, partly by the exertions of the seamen, she got to land. As soon as she had a little recovered strength, she insisted on renewing the attempt. The storm, however, had by this time become so violent as to set all efforts at defiance. To delay, was to be discovered and taken prisoner. As the only resource left, she procured horses; mounted with her female attendants *en croupe* behind the gallant gentlemen who accompanied her; and scoured the country to seek some temporary asylum.'

Beacon

Oluwaseun Olayiwola (1996–)

In the end, the lighthouse,
we had walked to
was never the point, being
only what we were
to the sea: blank moons
inside us, waxed,
astonished, slipped
like exposed oysters
down our throats.
That force. Those frozen
purple lips releasing
struggles of breath—fogging.
We climbed a ladder to the top
because there were no stairs

Crossing the Atlantic

From *Personal Narrative of Travels to the Equinoctial Regions of America during the years 1799–1804, published in thirty volumes 1807–1834* | Alexander von Humboldt (1769–1859)

Translated by Thomasina Ross (1795–1875), published in three volumes 1851

Volume I

We in vain reflect on the great facility with which, from the improved state of navigation, we traverse the Atlantic, which compared to the Pacific is but a larger arm of the sea.

Goodwin Sands

From *The Merchant of Venice, Act III,* scene i |

William Shakespeare (1564–1616)

SOLANIO Now, what news on the Rialto?

SALARINO Why, yet it lives there uncheck'd that Antonio hath a ship of rich lading wreck'd on the narrow seas; the Goodwins I think they call the place; a very dangerous flat and fatal, where the carcasses of many a tall ship lie buried, as they say, if my gossip Report be an honest woman of her word.

The Cunard Line

From *'Historical Sketches of the Jubilee Singers', Part II, Fisk University News: The Jubilee Singers, October 1911* |

Ella Shepherd (1851–1914)

The Jubilee Singers plan a visit to England 1873:
An evidence of civic and social prejudice was shown through the refusal of one after another of the ocean steamship lines to take us as cabin passenger. Finally the Cunard Line received us on the good ship 'Batavia'. The kindness of the captain and crew we shall never forget.

. . . . . .

Second Campaign Abroad 1875:
On May 15th our reorganized company of eleven members, with Mr. White and Miss Gilbert, our loved chaperone, again sailed for England. It was gratifying to find that more than one steamship line which had before refused us passage, now offered it to us at reduced rates, but we turned to the Cunard ship 'Algeria'.

Islands

Rachel Field (1894–1942)

All the islands have run away
From the land which is their mother;
Out where the lighthouse guards the bay
They race with one another.

Rocky or wooded, humped and small,
Edged whitely round with spray,
What should we do if the islands all
Ran back to land some day?

How would the ships know where to steer?
Where would the sea-gulls fly?
How flat the sea would look, and queer,
How lonely under the sky!

Flora and Fauna

From *England: A Natural History, 2024* | John Lewis-Stempel (1967–)

The flora and fauna of the shore is subject to the extremes of saline inundation, then desiccation by the sun; it is an extreme environment, whether rocky shore or sandy beach. For the naturalist, the sloping habitat of rock shore, sandy shore is ranged in horizontal bands according to the lengths of time the land is left exposed by the ebb tide. From dry land to sea these zones, with their typical animals and plants, are:

Splash zone: sea slater (closely related to the woodlouse, and capable of leggy movement at 1mph), black lichen, small winkle, sandhopper.

Upper shore: barnacle, limpet, shore crab, lugworm.

Mid shore: bladder wrack, mussel, sand mason worm, dog whelk.

Lower shore: sea mat (moss animals), blenny, edible winkle, dahlia sea anemone, shrimp, cockle.

Sublittoral zone: edible sea urchin, oar weed, edible crab, lobster, starfish, razor shell, blue rayed limpet.

Naturally, nature itself is not so boundary conscious. I've found shore crabs in the lower shore and sea urchins mid shore.

The boat is chafing

John Davidson (1857–1909)

The boat is chafing at our long delay,
    And we must leave too soon
The spicy sea-pinks and the inborne spray,
    The tawny sands, the moon.

Keep us, O Thetis, in our western flight!
    Watch from thy pearly throne
Our vessel, plunging deeper into night
    To reach a land unknown.

Above the Sea's Horizon

From *Sea and Sardinia, 1921* | D. H. Lawrence (1885–1930)

Ah, the lovely morning! Away behind us the sun was just coming above the sea's horizon, and the sky all golden, all a joyous, fire-heated gold, and the sea was glassy bright, the wind gone still, the waves sunk into long, low undulations, the foam of the wake was pale ice-blue in the yellow air. Sweet, sweet wide morning on the sea, with the sun coming, swimming up, and a tall sailing bark, with her flat fore-ladder of sails delicately across the light, and a far-far steamer on the electric vivid morning horizon.

The lovely dawn: the lovely pure, wide morning in the mid-sea, so golden-aired and delighted, with the sea like sequins shaking, and the sky far, far, far above, unfathomably clear. How glad to be on a ship! What a golden hour for the heart of man! Ah if one could sail for ever, on a small quiet, lonely ship, from land to land and isle to isle, and saunter through the spaces of this lovely world, always through the spaces of this lovely world. Sweet it would be sometimes to come to the opaque earth, to block oneself against the stiff land, to annul the vibration of one's flight against the inertia of our *terra firma!* but life itself would be in the flight, the tremble of space. Ah the trembling of never-ended space, as one moves in flight! Space, and the frail vibration of space, the glad lonely wringing of the heart. Not to be clogged to the land any more.

The Horses of the Sea

Christina Rossetti (1830–1894)

The horses of the sea
    Rear a foaming crest,
But the horses of the land
    Serve us the best.

The horses of the land
    Munch corn and clover,
While the foaming sea-horses
    Toss and turn over.

Useful Advice on Sailing to the Far East

From *The Happy Traveller: A Book for Poor Men, 1923* |

Rev Frank Tatchell (Vicar of Midhurst 1906–1935)

Choose the newest boat of the line by which you are going. The cost is the same and everything is fresh and clean. But the second trip of a new boat is to be preferred to her maiden voyage, as by ten the ship's servants will have shaken down into their places.

. . . . . .

Select a cabin which will be on the cool side of the ship in the evening: the port (or left) side going South and the starboard side going North.

. . . . . .

Comfort at sea is doubly welcome, and those who can afford it get good value foor the cost of a first- or second-class ticket; but a poor man, who is ready to give and take, can get along quite well in the steerage.

. . . . . .

Most ships have libraries aboard, usually very poor stuff, so it is well to take a bundle of books, which you can pass on when you have read them.

. . . . . .

Spend much time in the bows of the boat, where you have the freshest of air and an unbounded horizon.

. . . . . .

A last, but important, piece of advice is not to eat too much. The meals on boards ship are on a scale far exceeding what most of us are used to at home, and there is little scope for exercise unless you have had the happy thought to take a skipping-rope with you.

The Old Ships

Lines 1–14 | James Elroy Flecker (1884–1915)

I have seen old ships sail like swans asleep
Beyond the village which men still call Tyre,
With leaden age o'ercargoed, dipping deep
For Famagusta and the hidden sun
That rings black Cyprus with a lake of fire;
And all those ships were certainly so old
Who knows how oft with squat and noisy gun,
Questing brown slaves or Syrian oranges,
The pirate Genoese
Hell-raked them till they rolled
Blood, water, fruit and corpses up the hold.
But now through friendly seas they softly run,
Painted the mid-sea blue or shore-sea green,
Still patterned with the vine and grapes in gold.

The Benefits of Brighton

From *Pride and Prejudice, 1813* | Jane Austen (1775–1817)

'If one could but go to Brighton!' observed Mrs. Bennet.

'Oh yes! – if one could but go to Brighton! But papa is so disagreeable.'

'A little sea-bathing would set me up for ever.'

'And my aunt Philips is sure it would do *me* a great deal of good,' added Kitty.

The Jumblies

Verses I-II | Edward Lear (1812–1888)

They went to sea in a Sieve, they did,
  In a Sieve they went to sea:
In spite of all their friends could say,
On a winter's morn, on a stormy day,
  In a Sieve they went to sea!
And when the Sieve turned round and round,
And every one cried, 'You'll all be drowned!'
They called aloud, 'Our Sieve ain't big,
But we don't care a button! we don't care a fig!
  In a Sieve we'll go to sea!'
   Far and few, far and few,
    Are the lands where the Jumblies live;
   Their heads are green, and their hands are blue,
    And they went to sea in a Sieve.

They sailed away in a Sieve, they did,
  In a Sieve they sailed so fast,
With only a beautiful pea-green veil
Tied with a riband by way of a sail,
  To a small tobacco-pipe mast;
And every one said, who saw them go,
'O won't they be soon upset, you know!
For the sky is dark, and the voyage is long,
And happen what may, it's extremely wrong
  In a Sieve to sail so fast!'
   Far and few, far and few,
    Are the lands where the Jumblies live;
  Their heads are green, and their hands are blue,
    And they went to sea in a Sieve.

The Sight of the Sea

From *Castle in the Sand, 2013* | Attillah Springer

At a bend in the road, you turn right at the University of Cape Coast and the sight of the sea is startling. Not just the sun shining silver on its surface. The row of coconuts makes me feel like I've fallen asleep and woken up back in Trinidad, on the road to Manzanilla. And I remember all those times I have stood on the other side of the Atlantic, watching the same sun shining silver on the sea's surface imagining what the coast in Africa looked like.

The Continent of Europe

From *Villette, 1853* | Charlotte Brontë (1816–1855)

Deep was the pleasure I drank in with the sea-breeze; divine the delight I drew from the heaving Channel waves, from the sea-birds on their ridges, from the white sails on their dark distance, from the quiet yet beclouded sky, overhanging all. In my reverie, methought I saw the continent of Europe, like a wide dream-land, far away. Sunshine lay on it, making the long coast one line of gold; tiniest tracery of clustered town and snow-gleaming tower, of woods deep massed, of heights serrated, of smooth pasturage and veiny stream, embossed the metal-bright prospect.

Running Away to Sea

From *Martin Rattler, 1858* | R. M. Ballantyne (1825–1894)

One day Bob took Martin by the arm, and said, 'I say, Rattler, come with me to Bilton, and have some fun among the shipping.'

'Well, I don't mind if I do,' said Martin. 'I'm just in the mood for a ramble, and I'm not expected home till bed-time.'

In little more than an hour the two boys were wandering about the dock-yards of the sea-port town, and deeply engaged in examining the complicated rigging of the ships. While thus occupied, the clanking of a windlass and the merry, 'Yo heave ho! and away she goes,' of the sailors, attracted their attention.

'Hallo! there goes the *Firefly*, bound for the South Seas,' cried Bob Croaker; 'come, let's see her start. I say, Martin, isn't your friend, Barney O'Flannagan, on board?'

'Yes, he is. He tries to get me to go out every voyage, and I wish I could. Come quickly; I want to say good-bye to him before he starts.'

'Why don't you run away, Rattler?' inquired Bob, as they hurried round the docks to where the vessel was warping out.

'Because I don't need to. My aunt has given me leave to go if I like; but she says it would break her heart if I do; and I would rather be screwed down to a desk for ever than do that, Bob Croaker.'

The vessel, upon the deck of which the two boys now leaped, was a large, heavy-built barque. Her sails were hanging loose, and the captain was giving orders to the men, who had their attention divided between their duties on board and their mothers, wives, and sisters, who still lingered to take a last farewell.

'Now, then, those who don't want to go to sea had better go ashore,' roared the captain.

There was an immediate rush to the side.

Song from the Ship

From *Death's Jest-Book,* Act I, scene i | Thomas Lovell Beddoes (1803–1849)

To sea, to sea! The calm is o'er;
The wanton water leaps in sport,
And rattles down the pebbly shore;
The dolphin wheels, the sea-cows snort,
And unseen Mermaids' pearly song
Comes bubbling up, the weeds among.
Fling broad the sail, dip deep the oar:
To sea, to sea! the calm is o'er.

To sea, to sea! our wide-winged bark
Shall billowy cleave its sunny way,
And with its shadow, fleet and dark,
Break the caved Tritons' azure day,
Like mighty eagle soaring light
O'er antelopes on Alpine height.
The anchor heaves, the ship swings free,
The sails swell full. To sea, to sea!

The First Lifeboat

From *Stories of the Lifeboat, 1894* | Frank Mundell (1870–1932)

To Lionel Lukin, a coachbuilder of Long Acre, London, belongs the honour of inventing the lifeboat. As early as the year 1784 he designed and fitted a boat, which was intended 'to save the lives of mariners wrecked on the coast.' It had a projecting gunwale of cork, and air-tight lockers or enclosures under the seats. These gave the boat great buoyancy, but it was liable to be disabled by having the sides stove in. Though Lukin was encouraged in his efforts by the Prince of Wales – afterwards George the Fourth – his invention did not meet with the approval of those in power at the Admiralty, and Lukin's only lifeboat which came into use was a coble that he fitted up for the Rev. Dr. Shairp of Bamborough. For many years this was the only lifeboat on the coast, and it is said to have saved many lives.

The Song of the Wreck

Verses I-II | Charles Dickens (1812–1870)

The wind blew high, the waters raved,
A ship drove on the land,
A hundred human creatures saved
Kneel'd down upon the sand.
Threescore were drown'd, threescore were thrown
Upon the black rocks wild,
And thus among them, left alone,
They found one helpless child.

II

A seaman rough, to shipwreck bred,
Stood out from all the rest,
And gently laid the lonely head
Upon his honest breast.
And travelling o'er the desert wide
It was a solemn joy,
To see them, ever side by side,
The sailor and the boy.

Dolphins

From *The Pocket Encyclopaedia of Natural Phenomena, 1827* |
Thomas Furley Forster (1761–1825)

Dolphins, as well as Porpuses, when they come about a ship, and sport and gambol on the surface of the water, betoken a storm; hence they are regarded as unlucky omens for sailors. According to ancient fable they formerly offered themselves in times of storm to convey shipwrecked mariners to the shore; but this is, of course, a story of a mere human invention.

JUNE

A Visit to the Seaside

Seaside Reading: Fiction

These are the novels which, for various reasons, didn't get into the anthology. They are all perfect seaside reading. You will find survival, seaside holidays, pirates, murder and love.

Patrick O'Brian, *Master and Commander,* and the following twenty books in the Aubrey/Maturin series, 1969–2004.
Set aside a couple of weeks, or a couple of months, or however long it takes, and read the whole series. You will be immersed in early nineteenth-century naval life, accurate in historical time until Patrick O'Brian realises he runs the risk of running out of history. The charming author apologies and from then on the stories are accurate in spirit, if not in chronological order. More than any other books, this series inspired my love of the sea. I cannot recommend them highly enough – even if you think you are not interested in naval fiction.

Alessandro Baricco, *Ocean Sea, 1993,* translated into English, 1999
Agatha Christie, *Evil Under the Sun, 1941*
(There is a murder on a beach but what earns the book its place on this list is Hercule Poirot's wonderfully unenthusiastic description of the movement of the sea.)
Daphne du Maurier, *The Loving Spirit, 1931*
Frenchman's Creek, 1941
C. S. Forester, The Hornblower series, 1937-1967
William Golding, *Rites of Passage, 1980*
Alastair MacLean, *HMS Ulysses, 1955*
Gabriel García Márquez, *The Story of a Shipwrecked Sailor, 1970, translated 1986*
Philip Marsden, *The Main Cages, 2002*
Nicholas Monsarrat, *The Cruel Sea, 1951*
Yann Martel, *The Life of Pi, 2001*
Joseph O'Connor, *Star of the Sea, 2002*
Charlotte Rogan, *The Lifeboat, 2012*
R. C. Sherriff, *The Fortnight in September, 1931*
Emma Stonex, *The Lamplighters, 2021*

Along the Sea Wall

Juanita Cox

The sun shafts the shore
Parched tongues of cracked-clay
Plead in sibilant whisper:
'Lil' moisture nah … Lil' moisture nah …'
In cruel tease the ocean tosses a wave
And a shoal of silver fish that flail in the heat of living
As the sea with sleight of magician's hand
Leaves them stranded.

Cast Off!

From *The Innocents Abroad, 1869* | Mark Twain (1835–1910)

The vessel was appointed to sail on a certain Saturday early in June.

A little after noon on that distinguished Saturday I reached the ship and went on board. All was bustle and confusion. [I have seen that remark before somewhere.] The pier was crowded with carriages and men; passengers were arriving and hurrying on board; the vessel's decks were encumbered with trunks and valises; groups of excursionists, arrayed in unattractive traveling costumes, were moping about in a drizzling rain and looking as droopy and woebegone as so many molting chickens. The gallant flag was up, but it was under the spell, too, and hung limp and disheartened by the mast. Altogether, it was the bluest, bluest spectacle! It was a pleasure excursion – there was no gainsaying that, because the program said so – it was so nominated in the bond – but it surely hadn't the general aspect of one.

Finally, above the banging, and rumbling, and shouting, and hissing of steam rang the order to 'cast off!' – a sudden rush to the gangways – a scampering ashore of visitors – a revolution of the wheels, and we were off – the picnic was begun! Two very mild cheers went up from the dripping crowd on the pier; we answered them gently from the slippery decks; the flag made an effort to wave, and failed; the 'battery of guns' spake not – the ammunition was out.

Impressions de Voyage

Oscar Wilde (1854–1900)

The sea was sapphire coloured, and the sky
    Burned like a heated opal through air,
    We hoisted sail; the wind was blowing fair
For the blue lands that to the Eastward lie.
From the steep prow I marked with quickening eye
    Zakynthos, every olive grove and creek,
    Ithaca's cliff, Lycaon's snowy peak,
And all the flower-strewn hills of Arcady.
The flapping of the sail against the mast,
    The ripple of the water on the side,
    The ripple of girls' laughter at the stern,
The only sounds: – when 'gan the West to burn,
    And a red sun upon the seas to ride,
    I stood upon the soil of Greece at last!

Dawn

From *The Waves, 1931* | Virginia Woolf (1882–1941)

5 June

The sun had not yet risen. The sea was indistinguishable from the sky, except that the sea was slightly creased as if a cloth had wrinkles in it. Gradually as the sky whitened a dark line lay on the horizon dividing the sea from the sky and the grey cloth became barred with thick strokes moving, one after another, beneath the surface, following each other, pursuing each other, perpetually.

As they neared the shore each bar rose, heaped itself, broke and swept a thin veil of white water across the sand. The wave paused, and then drew out again, sighing like a sleeper whose breath comes and goes unconsciously. Gradually the dark bar on the horizon became clear as if the sediment in an old wine-bottle had sunk and left the glass green. Behind it, too, the sky cleared as if the white sediment there had sunk, or as if the arm of a woman couched beneath the horizon had raised a lamp and flat bars of white, green and yellow spread across the sky like the blades of a fan. Then she raised her lamp higher and the air seemed to become fibrous and to tear away from the green surface flickering and flaming in red and yellow fibres like the smoky fire that roars from a bonfire. Gradually the fibres of the burning bonfire were fused into one haze, one incandescence which lifted the weight of the woollen grey sky on top of it and turned it to a million atoms of soft blue. The surface of the sea slowly became transparent and lay rippling and sparkling until the dark stripes were almost rubbed out. Slowly the arm that held the lamp raised it higher and then higher until a broad flame became visible; an arc of fire burnt on the rim of the horizon, and all round it the sea blazed gold.

A Cavern

From *A Journey to the Western Isles of Scotland, 1775* |

Samuel Johnson (1709–1784)

We were then told of a cavern by the sea-side, remarkable for the powerful reverberation of sounds. After dinner we took a boat, to explore this curious cavity.

. . . . . .

The sea was smooth. We never left the shore, and came without any disaster to the cavern, which we found rugged and misshapen, about one hundred and eighty feet long, thirty wide in the broadest part, and in the loftiest, as we guessed, about thirty high. It was now dry, but at high water the sea rises in it near six feet. Here I saw what I had never seen before, limpets and mussels in their natural state. But, as a new testimony to the veracity of common fame, here was no echo to be heard.

We then walked through a natural arch in the rock, which might have pleased us by its novelty, had the stones, which incumbered our feet, given us leisure to consider it. We were shown the gummy seed of the kelp, that fastens itself to a stone, from which it grows into a strong stalk.

The Meditation of the Old Fisherman

W. B. Yeats (1865–1939)

You waves, though you dance by my feet like children at play,
Though you glow and you glance, though you purr and you dart;
In the Junes that were warmer than these are, the waves were more gay,
When I was a boy with never a crack in my heart.

The herring are not in the tides as they were of old;
My sorrow! for many a creak gave the creel in the-cart
That carried the take to Sligo town to be sold,
When I was a boy with never a crack in my heart.

And ah, you proud maiden, you are not so fair when his oar
Is heard on the water, as they were, the proud and apart,
Who paced in the eve by the nets on the pebbly shore,
When I was a boy with never a crack in my heart.

The Sea-breeze and the Buoy

From *The Water Babies, 1863* | Charles Kingsley (1819–1875)

The sea-breeze came in freshly with the tide and blew the fog away; and the little waves danced for joy around the buoy, and the old buoy danced with them. The shadows of the clouds ran races over the bright blue bay, and yet never caught each other up; and the breakers plunged merrily upon the wide white sands, and jumped up over the rocks, to see what the green fields inside were like, and tumbled down and broke themselves all to pieces, and never minded it a bit, but mended themselves and jumped up again. And the terns hovered over Tom like huge white dragon-flies with black heads, and the gulls laughed like girls at play, and the sea-pies, with their red bills and legs, flew to and fro from shore to shore, and whistled sweet and wild.

Desirable Villa Residences

From *The Sea Lady*, 1902 | H. G. Wells (1866–1946)

The villa residences to the east of Sandgate Castle, you must understand, are particularly lucky in having gardens that run right down to the beach. There is no intervening esplanade or road or path such as cuts off ninety-nine out of the hundred of houses that face the sea. As you look down on them from the western end of the Leas, you see them crowding the very margin. And as a great number of high groins stand out from the shore along this piece of coast, the beach is practically cut off and made private except at very low water, when people can get around the ends of the groins. These houses are consequently highly desirable during the bathing season, and it is the custom of many of their occupiers to let them furnished during the summer to persons of fashion and affluence.

The Open Pacific

From *Voyage of the Beagle, 1831–1836* | Charles Darwin (1809–1882)

June 10th – In the morning we made the best of our way into the open Pacific. The western coast generally consists of low, rounded, quite barren hills of granite and greenstone. Sir J. Narborough called one part South Desolation, because it is 'so desolate a land to behold'; and well indeed might he say so. Outside the main islands, there are numberless scattered rocks on which the long swell of the open ocean incessantly rages. We passed out between the East and West Furies; and a little farther northward there are so many breakers that the sea is called the Milky Way. One sight of such a coast is enough to make a landsman dream for a week about shipwrecks, peril, and death; and with this sight we bade farewell for ever to Tierra del Fuego.

A Closer View

From *Kidnapped, 1886* | Robert Louis Stevenson (1850–1894)

I wished a nearer view of the sea and ships. You are to remember I had lived all my life in the inland hills, and just two days before had my first sight of the firth lying like a blue floor, and the sailed ships moving on the face of it, no bigger than toys.

. . . . . .

Just then we came to the top of the hill, and looked down on the Ferry and the Hope. The Firth of Forth (as is very well known) narrows at this point to the width of a good-sized river, which makes a convenient ferry going north, and turns the upper reach into a landlocked haven for all manner of ships. Right in the midst of the narrows lies an islet with some ruins; on the south shore they have built a pier for the service of the Ferry; and at the end of the pier, on the other side of the road, and backed against a pretty garden of holly-trees and hawthorns, I could see the building which they called the Hawes Inn.

The town of Queensferry lies farther west, and the neighbourhood of the inn looked pretty lonely at that time of day, for the boat had just gone north with passengers. A skiff, however, lay beside the pier, with some seamen sleeping on the thwarts; this, as Ransome told me, was the brig's boat waiting for the captain; and about half a mile off, and all alone in the anchorage, he showed me the *Covenant* herself. There was a sea-going bustle on board; yards were swinging into place; and as the wind blew from that quarter, I could hear the song of the sailors as they pulled upon the ropes.

If Once You Have Slept on an Island

Rachel Field (1894–1942)

If once you have slept on an island
You'll never be quite the same;
You may look as you looked the day before
And go by the same old name,

You may bustle about in street and shop
You may sit at home and sew,
But you'll see blue water and wheeling gulls
Wherever your feet may go.

You may chat with the neighbors of this and that
And close to your fire keep,
But you'll hear ship whistle and lighthouse bell
And tides beat through your sleep.

Oh! you won't know why and you can't say how
Such a change upon you came,
But – once you have slept on an island,
You'll never be quite the same!

The View To and From the Island

From *The House on the Island, 1938* | Grace Pettman (1870–1952)

13 June

Far out in the Channel, Roma could see the islands. One seemed merely a flat sandbank, the second bearing a couple of white-washed houses, and a lighthouse. Farther off, an islet smaller than either of the others, was covered with a dense woodland down to the water's edge, on all sides save one. A large house stood back from a space which had been left clear of trees in order to give an uninterrupted view of sea and coastline.

. . . . . .

Roma went out of doors, and down to the beach beside the lapping water, looking across at Queen's Holme. Was it possible it was only a few hours before she had been there, at school, and now – ?

She walked right round the island on the strip of shell sand that bordered it. Then she made her way back by one of the paths through the thick growing trees. The sun was near to setting now, and the long dark shadows filled the woodlands with gloom.

. . . . . .

The summer sun sank over the western sea, … a sudden hush fell over everything, and the birds ceased their evening chorus of song. The chill breeze that comes after sunset blew over the water.

Meeting at Night

Robert Browning (1812–1889)

I

The grey sea and the long black land;
And the yellow half-moon large and low;
And the startled little waves that leap
In fiery ringlets from their sleep,
As I gain the cove with pushing prow,
And quench its speed in the slushy sand.

II

Then a mile of warm sea-scented beach;
Three fields to cross till a farm appears;
A tap at the pane, the quick sharp scratch
And blue spurt of a lighted match,
And a voice less loud, thro' its joys and fears,
Than the two hearts beating each to each!

14 June

To Lie on the Beach

From *The Ragged Trousered Philanthropists, 1914*

Robert Tressell (1870–1911)

15 June

Discussing the overtime of former years:

Most of them spoke of those bygone times with poignant regret, but there were a few – generally fellows who had been contaminated by contact with Socialists or whose characters had been warped and degraded by the perusal of Socialist literature – who said that they did not desire to work overtime at all – ten hours a day were quite enough for them – in fact they would rather do only eight. What they wanted, they said, was not more work, but more grub, more clothes, more leisure, more pleasure and better homes. They wanted to be able to go for country walks or bicycle rides, to go out fishing or to go to the seaside and bathe and lie on the beach and so forth. But these were only a very few; there were not many so selfish as this. The majority desired nothing but to be allowed to work, and as for their children, why, 'what was good enough for themselves oughter be good enough for the kids'.

They often said that such things as leisure, culture, pleasure and the benefits of civilization were never intended for 'the likes of us'.

No Tides

From *Letters written during a short residence in Sweden, Norway and Denmark, 1796* | Mary Wollstonecraft (1759–1797)

Letter VI

The sea was boisterous; but, as I had an experienced pilot, I did not apprehend any danger. Sometimes I was told, boats are driven far out and lost. However, I seldom calculate chances so nicely – sufficient for the day is the obvious evil!

We had to steer amongst islands and huge rocks, rarely losing sight of the shore, though it now and then appeared only a mist that bordered the water's edge. The pilot assured me that the numerous harbours on the Norway coast were very safe, and the pilot-boats were always on the watch. The Swedish side is very dangerous, I am also informed; and the help of experience is not often at hand, to enable strange vessels to steer clear of the rocks, which lurk below the water, close to the shore.

There are no tides here, nor in the Cattegate, and, what appeared to me a consequence, no sandy beach. Perhaps this observation has been made before; but it did not occur to me till I saw the waves continually beating against the bare rocks, without ever receding to leave a sediment to harden.

Sonnet LXXV

From *Amoretti* | Edmund Spenser (c. 1552–1599)

One day I wrote her name upon the strand,
    But came the waves and washed it away:
    Again I wrote it with a second hand,
    But came the tide, and made my pains his prey.
Vain man, said she, that dost in vain assay,
    A mortal thing so to immortalize
    For I myself shall like to this decay,
    And eke my name be wiped out likewise.
Not so, (quod I) let baser things devise
    To die in dust, but you shall live by fame:
    My verse your vertues rare shall eternize,
    And in the heavens write your glorious name:
Where whereas Death shall all the world subdue,
    Our love shall live, and later life renew.

A Rocky Coast

From *Nature Rambles, 1930* | Edward Step (1855–1931)

To many of us, the summer holiday means a visit to the seaside. It will be well for us, having a strong taste for natural beauty, if we are not condemned to spend the time in one of those 'popular resorts' where the townsfolk pride themselves upon having buried Nature under a mile or two of concrete promenades. In such places, it is well to turn our backs upon the sea, and go inland for our rambles.

If, however, we can get to one of the quiet coast villages that are still at some distance from the railway and the motor-road, we shall find Nature at the door-step; and the days of our visit will be all too short to allow us to see much of what is to be seen. If we have a choice in the matter, a rocky coast is to be preferred, for there we shall find rock-pools without number, and here and there little coves with sandy beaches, which will afford great variety in the wild life teeming around us.

A Hard Journey

From *Under the Foeman's Flag, 1896* | Robert Leighton (1858–1934)

Between Dunkirk and Calais there are but a few miles of sea, and a swift-sailing sloop such as the *Pride of Wapping* might with a favourable breeze cover the distance in a single day. But that memorable summer of 1588 was one of almost ceaseless storms, and our passage, although so very short in point of distance, was, in its accomplishment, long and tedious, and not without peril. Such backing and filling, such veering and tacking, such rolling and pitching, such helpless laboring against the head winds and mountainous waves, I wish not to see again.

19 June

Seaside Etiquette

John Agard (1949–)

The whites
sun themselves
on the pebbles.

The blacks
ensconce themselves
in the shade.

Some put this down
to genetics
I like to think
it's seaside etiquette –

a way of ensuring
an equal share
of summer's bliss
for every epidermis.

O to bask in the sun
O to bask in the shade.
Beaches means decisions.
There's that rug to be laid.

The Force of the Sea

From *The Story of My Heart, 1883* | Richard Jefferies (1848–1887)

21 June

There, alone, I went down to the sea. I stood where the foam came to my feet, and looked out over the sunlit waters. The great earth bearing the richness of the harvest, and its hills golden with corn, was at my back; its strength and firmness under me. The great sun shone above, the wide sea was before me, the wind came sweet and strong from the waves. The life of the earth and the sea, the glow of the sun filled me; I touched the surge with my hand, I lifted my face to the sun, I opened my lips to the wind. I prayed aloud in the roar of the waves – my soul was strong as the sea and prayed with the sea's might. Give me fulness of life like to the sea and the sun, to the earth and the air; give me fulness of physical life, mind equal and beyond their fulness; give me a greatness and perfection of soul higher than all things; give me my inexpressible desire which swells in me like a tide – give it to me with all the force of the sea.

Ralph to Mary

Verses 1–2 | Amy Levy (1861–1889)

Love, you have led me to the strand,
    Here, where the stilly, sunset sea,
    Ever receding silently,
Lays bare a shining stretch of sand;

Which, as we tread, in waving line,
    Sinks softly 'neath our moving feet;
    And looking down our glances meet,
Two mirrored figures – yours and mine.

The Journey to Boulogne

From *Travels Through France and Italy, 1766*

Tobias Smollett (1721–1771)

Letter I, Boulogne sur mer, June 23, 1763

The first thing I did when I arrived at Dover this last time, was to send for the master of a packet-boat, and agree with him to carry us to Boulogne at once, by which means I saved the expence of travelling by land from Calais to this last place, a journey of four-and-twenty miles. The hire of a vessel from Dover to Boulogne is precisely the same as from Dover to Calais, five guineas; but this skipper demanded eight, and, as I did not know the fare, I agreed to give him six. We embarked between six and seven in the evening, and found ourselves in a most wretched hovel, on board what is called a Folkstone cutter. The cabin was so small that a dog could hardly turn in it, and the beds put me in mind of the holes described in some catacombs, in which the bodies of the dead were deposited, being thrust in with the feet foremost; there was no getting into them but end-ways, and indeed they seemed so dirty, that nothing but extreme necessity could have obliged me to use them. We sat up all night in a most uncomfortable situation, tossed about by the sea, cold, arid cramped and weary, and languishing for want of sleep. At three in the morning the master came down, and told us we were just off the harbour of Boulogne; but the wind blowing off shore, he could not possibly enter, and therefore advised us to go ashore in the boat. I went upon deck to view the coast, when he pointed to the place where he said Boulogne stood, declaring at the same time we were within a short mile of the harbour's mouth. The morning was cold and raw, and I knew myself extremely subject to catch cold; nevertheless we were all so impatient to be ashore, that I resolved to take his advice.

Sailing to Greenland

From *Michel the Giant: An African in Greenland, 1981* |

Tété-Michel Kpomassie (1941–)

Translated by James Kirkup (1918–2009)

We were a handful of human beings far from land, imprisoned in a ship that plunged and reared and was dwarfed by mountainous waves. The thought of sinking nagged at us all, though no one mentioned it. None of my previous voyages had reduced me to such dark despair.

The 'night' of Wednesday, June 23, was extraordinary: a night of wild commotion. Objects kept tumbling over with tremendous crashes and luggage ploughed from one end of the cabin to the other, while the whole vessel creaked and groaned. Next morning the sea suddenly became as smooth as a millpond. The air turned so cold that it started to cramp my breathing: we were approaching the barrier ice.

The Sound of the Sea

H. W. Longfellow (1807–1882)

The sea awoke at midnight from its sleep,
　　And round the pebbly beaches far and wide
　　I heard the first wave of the rising tide
　　Rush onward with uninterrupted sweep;
A voice out of the silence of the deep,
　　A sound mysteriously multiplied
　　As of a cataract from the mountain's side,
　　Or roar of winds upon a wooded steep.
So comes to us at times, from the unknown
　　And inaccessible solitudes of being,
　　The rushing of the sea-tides of the soul;
And inspirations, that we deem our own,
　　Are some divine foreshadowing and foreseeing
　　Of things beyond our reason or control.

The Lido

From *Italian Hours, 1909* | Henry James (1843–1916)

May in Venice is better than April, but June is best of all. Then the days are hot, but not too hot, and the nights are more beautiful than the days. Then Venice is rosier than ever in the morning and more golden than ever as the day descends. She seems to expand and evaporate, to multiply all her reflections and iridescences. Then the life of her people and the strangeness of her constitution become a perpetual comedy, or at least a perpetual drama. Then the gondola is your sole habitation, and you spend days between sea and sky. You go to the Lido, though the Lido has been spoiled. When I first saw it, in 1869, it was a very natural place, and there was but a rough lane across the little island from the landing-place to the beach. There was a bathing-place in those days, and a restaurant, which was very bad, but where in the warm evenings your dinner did n't much matter as you sat letting it cool on the wooden terrace that stretched out into the sea. To-day the Lido is a part of united Italy and has been made the victim of villainous improvements. A little cockney village has sprung up on its rural bosom and a third-rate boulevard leads from Santa Elisabetta to the Adriatic. There are bitumen walks and gas-lamps, lodging-houses, shops and a *teatro diurno*. The bathing-establishment is bigger than before, and the restaurant as well; but it is a compensation perhaps that the cuisine is no better. Such as it is, however, you won't scorn occasionally to partake of it on the breezy platform under which bathers dart and splash, and which looks out to where the fishing-boats, with sails of orange and crimson, wander along the darkening horizon. The beach at the Lido is still lonely and beautiful, and you can easily walk away from the cockney village.

Salt Pools

From *The Beauties of Scenery, 1943* | Vaughan Cornish (1862–1948)

On the north coast of Devonshire, where the range of tide is great, the furrowed rocks exposed at low tide retain pools of salt water lined with seaweed of beautiful colours, with sea anemones waving their arms, and shells lying on the sandy floor. These still, salt pools should be viewed from a recumbent position and with the eyes shielded from the landscape. Then they are realized as gems of scenery. Every object receives a glaze and lustre from the clear water which neither rock nor vegetation displays on land.

The Unchanging

Sara Teasdale (1884–1933)

Sun-swept beaches with a light wind blowing
From the immense blue circle of the sea,
And the soft thunder where long waves whiten –
These were the same for Sappho as for me.

Two thousand years – much has gone by forever,
Change takes the gods and ships and speech of men –
But here on the beaches that time passes over
The heart aches now as then.

The Last Night

From *The Great Gatsby, 1925* | F. Scott Fitzgerald (1896–1940)

29 June

Then I wandered down to the beach and sprawled out on the sand.

Most of the big shore places were closed now and there were hardly any lights except the shadowy, moving glow of a ferryboat across the Sound. And as the moon rose higher the inessential houses began to melt away until gradually I became aware of the old island here that flowered once for Dutch sailors' eyes – a fresh, green breast of the new world. Its vanished trees, the trees that had made way for Gatsby's house, had once pandered in whispers to the last and greatest of all human dreams; for a transitory enchanted moment man must have held his breath in the presence of this continent, compelled into an aesthetic contemplation he neither understood nor desired, face to face for the last time in history with something commensurate to his capacity for wonder.

Pirates

From *Peter Pan, 1904, Peter and Wendy, 1911* |

J. M. Barrie (1860–1937)

We hear them before they are seen, and it is always the same dreadful song:

> ‘Avast belay, yo ho, heave to,
>   A-pirating we go,
> And if we’re parted by a shot
>   We’re sure to meet below!’

A more villainous-looking lot never hung in a row on Execution Dock.

JULY

I Think We're Ship-wrecked

Seaside Reading: Voyages

The voyages here vary from delightful to frankly terrifying. Most are about much more than simply travelling from A to B. All inspired me and convinced me that I am definitely an armchair sailor.

Sir Francis Chichester, *The Lonely Sea and the Sky, 1964*
Gipsy Moth Circles the World, 1967
Horatio Clare, *Down to the Sea in Ships, 2014*
Josie Dew, *Saddled at Sea, 2006*
Thor Heyerdahl, *The Kon-Tiki Expedition, 1948*
Philip Marsden, *The Summer Isles, 2019*
Eric Newby, *On the Shores of the Mediterranean, 1984*
Peter Nichols, *A Voyage for Madmen, 2001*
Adam Nicolson, *Seamanship, 2004*
Jonathan Raban, *Coasting, 1986*
Tim Severin, *The Brendan Voyage, 1982* and following voyages to 1994
Tiziano Terzani, *A Fortune-teller Told Me, 1997*
(This book is about not flying, rather than specifically travelling by sea, but the chapter 'Hurrah for Ships!', amongst others, earns it a place here.)
Paul Theroux, *The Kingdom by the Sea, 1983*
Gavin Young, *Slow Boats to China, 1981*
Slow Boats Home, 1985

Swimming

From *The Summer Book, 1972, 1975* | Tove Jansson (1914–2001)

Translated by Thomas Teal

'I want to go swimming,' the child said. She waited for opposition, but none came. So she took off her clothes, slowly and nervously. She glanced at her grandmother – you can't depend on people who just let things happen. She put her legs in the water.

'It's cold,' she said.

'Of course it's cold,' the old woman said, her thoughts somewhere else. 'What did you expect?'

The child slid in up to her waist and waited anxiously.

'Swim,' her grandmother said. 'You can swim.'

It's deep, Sophia thought. She forgets I've never swum in deep water unless somebody was with me. And she climbed out again and sat down on the rock.

Seaside

Rupert Brooke (1887–1915)

Swiftly out from the friendly lilt of the band,
The crowd's good laughter, the loved eyes of men,
I am drawn nightward; I must turn again
Where, down beyond the low untrodden strand,
There curves and glimmers outward to the unknown
The old unquiet ocean. All the shade
Is rife with magic and movement. I stray alone
Here on the edge of silence, half afraid,

Waiting a sign. In the deep heart of me
The sullen waters swell towards the moon,
And all my tides set seaward.
From inland
Leaps a gay fragment of some mocking tune,
That tinkles and laughs and fades along the sand,
And dies between the seawall and the sea.

Boy turned Mermaid

From *The Vicar of Morwenstow; Being a Life of Robert Stephen Hawker, 1876* | S. Baring-Gould (1834–1924)

Robert Hawker (1803–1875)

At full moon in the July of 1825 or 1826, he swam or rowed out to a rock at some little distance from the shore, plaited seaweed into a wig, which he threw over his head, so that it hung in lank streamers half-way down his back, enveloped his legs in an oilskin wrap, and, otherwise naked, sat on the rock, flashing the moonbeams about from a hand-mirror, and sang and screamed till attention was arrested. Some people passing along the cliff heard and saw him, and ran into Bude, saying that a mermaid with a fish's tail was sitting on a rock, combing her hair, and singing.

A number of people ran out on the rocks and along the beach, and listened awestruck to the singing and disconsolate wailing of the mermaid. Presently she dived off the rock, and disappeared.

Next night crowds of people assembled to look out for the mermaid; and in due time she reappeared, and sent the moon flashing in their faces from her glass. Telescopes were brought to bear on her; but she sang on unmoved, braiding her tresses, and uttering remarkable sounds, unlike the singing of mortal throats which have been practised in do-re-mi.

This went on for several nights; the crowd growing greater, people arriving from Stratton, Kilkhampton, and all the villages round, till Robert Hawker got very hoarse with his nightly singing, and rather tired of sitting so long in the cold. He therefore wound up the performance one night with an unmistakable 'God save the King,' then plunged into the waves, and the mermaid never again revisited the 'sounding shores of Bude.'

The Common Tern

From *British Birds in their Haunts, 1862* | Rev C. A. Johns (1811–1874)

5 July

Very frequently a single Tern may be observed pursuing its course in a line with the breakers on a sandy shore at the distance perhaps of from fifty to a hundred yards from the beach. Its beak is pointed downwards, and the bird is evidently on the look-out for prey. Suddenly it descends perpendicularly into the water, making a perceptible splash, but scarcely disappearing. In an instant it has recovered the use of its wings and ascends again, swallowing some small fish meanwhile if it has been successful, but in any case continuing its course as before. I do not recollect ever to have seen a Tern sit on the water to devour its prey when fishing among the breakers. Often, too, as one is walking along the shore, or sailing in a boat, when the sea is calm, a cruising party of Terns comes in sight. Their flight now is less direct than in the instance just mentioned, as they 'beat' the fishing-ground after the fashion of spaniels, still, however, making way ahead. Suddenly one of the party arrests its flight, hovers for a few seconds like a Hawk, and descends as if shot, making a splash as before. If unsuccessful it rises at once, but if it has captured the object on which it swooped, it remains floating on the water until it has relieved itself of its incumbrance by the summary process of swallowing it. I do not know a prettier sight than a party of Terns thus occupied. They are by no means shy, frequently flying quite over the boat, and uttering from time to time a short scream, which, though not melodious, is more in keeping with the scene than a mellow song would be.

Similes

Mimi Khalvati (1944–)

The yacht lies like an elegant equation in the mind.
Last night it lay on black velvet like a glasswing butterfly,

wings folded, two tall masts. The straightness of the horizon
never ceases to be astonishing, putting one in a daze –

only a slight swell in the water to prove that we are not
in a painted vestibule, that this is not an annunciation.

And here's the yellow ferry which reminds me of
Elizabeth Bishop's desk; my table, metallic, sunflecked,

of Hockney's swimming pools. Everything is always
like something else. Each makes love to the other.

You are like me, they say. Blue paint has spattered
the whitewash, speckled the flagstones – the eye jumps

from blue to blue, island to island, raisin to raisin in a cake.
Archie hated raisins in cake, peas in rice. His beard

was salt and pepper, white at the time of death. To have
one terrible disease gives you no immunity against another.

Fashionable Bathing

From *Domestic Manners of the Americans, 1832* |

Fanny Trollope (1779–1863)

7 July

Many of the best families had left the city for different watering-places, and others were daily following. Long Branch is a fashionable bathing place on the Jersey shore, to which many resort, both from this place and from New York; the description given of the manner of bathing appeared to me rather extraordinary, but the account was confirmed by so many different people, that I could not doubt its correctness. The shore, it seems, is too bold to admit of bathing machines, and the ladies have, therefore, recourse to another mode of ensuring the enjoyment of a sea-bath with safety. The accommodation at Long Branch is almost entirely at large boarding-houses, where all the company live at a *table d'hôte*. It is customary for ladies on arriving to look round among the married gentlemen, the first time they meet at table, and to select the one her fancy leads her to prefer as a protector in her purposed visits to the realms of Neptune; she makes her request, which is always graciously received, that he would lead her to taste the briny wave; but another fair one must select the same protector, else the arrangement cannot be complete, as custom does not authorise *tête à tête* immersion.

Crime

From *Murder!* 1927 | Arnold Bennett (1867–1931)

Lomax Harder leant over the left arm of the sea-wall of the man-made port of Quangate. Not another soul was there. Night had fallen. The lighthouse at the extremity of the right arm was occulting. The lights – some red, some green, many white – of ships at sea passed in both directions in endless processions. Waves plashed gently against the vast masonry of the wall. The wind, blowing steadily from the north-west, was not cold. Harder, looking about – though he knew he was absolutely alone, took his revolver from his overcoat pocket and stealthily dropped it into the sea. Then he turned round and gazed across the small harbour at the mysterious amphitheatre of the lighted town, and heard public clocks and religious clocks striking the hour.

He was a murderer, but why should he not successfully escape detection?

The Nautilus: A Fairy Boat Song

Verses I-II | Louisa May Alcott (1832–1888)

9 July

Launch our boat from the yellow sand,
Say farewell to the blooming land,
Furl airy wings, fold the mantles blue,
Drink one last cup of honey dew;
For we must leave our fairy home
On a moonlight voyage through the foam.
Spread the silken sail
To the summer gale,
Low singing across the sea;
Float away, float away,
Through foam and spray,
As if o'er flowery lea!

Oh! fear no storm nor cloudy frown,
Though mightier ships than ours go down:
Our helmsman laughs at the wildest gale,
As he drops anchor and furls his sail;
For He who guides the sparrow's wing,
Whose love upholds the frailest thing,
Has given a spell,
To protect the shell
Through the wave's tumultuous flow,
When tempest-tost,
Unwrecked, unlost
It sinks to calmer depths below.

An Inexplicable Light

From *Vingt mille lieues sous les mers, 1870*
Twenty Thousand Leagues under the Sea, 1876

Jules Verne (1828–1905)

Translated by Henry Frith (1840–1917)

Ned Land cried out:

'Hallo, there! There is our enemy, away on the weather beam!'

At this announcement the whole crew ran towards the harpooner – commodore, officers, mates, sailors and boys; even the engineers left the engine-room, and the stokers the furnaces. The order to 'stop her' was given, and the frigate now only glided through the waters by her own momentum.

The darkness was profound; and the Canadian must have had very good eyes. And I wondered what he had seen, and how he had been able to see it. My heart was beating fast.

But Ned Land had not been mistaken, and we all perceived the object he indicated with his outstretched hand.

Two cables' length from the *Abraham Lincoln*, and on the starboard quarter, the sea seemed to be illuminated from below. It was not a common phosphorescence, and could not be mistaken for it. The monster, some fathoms beneath the surface, gave forth this intense light, which had been referred to in the reports of many captains. This wonderful irradiation must have been produced by some tremendously powerful illuminating agent. The luminous part described an immense elongated oval, in the centre of which was condensed a focus of unbearable brilliancy, which radiated by successive gradations.

'It is nothing but an agglomeration of phosphorescent molecules,' cried one of the officers.

'No, sir,' I replied firmly, 'neither the pholades nor salpæ produce such a powerful light. This brilliancy is essentially electric. But look – look – it moves, it advances – it retreats – it is rushing towards us!'

A general cry arose.

'Silence,' cried Farragut. 'Put the helm up – hard! Turn astern!'

White Egrets: 53

Derek Walcott (1930–2017)

The hulls of white yachts riding the orange water
of the marina at dusk, and, under their bowsprits the chuckle
of the chain in the stained sea; try to get there
before a green light winks from the mast and the foc's'le
blazes with glare, while dusk hangs in suspension
with crosstrees and ropes and a lilac-livid sky
with its beer stein of cloud froth touched by the sun,
as stars come out to watch the evening die.
In this orange hour the light reads like Dante,
three lines at a time, their symmetrical tension,
quiet bars rippling from the Paradiso
as a dinghy writes lines made by the scanty
metre of its oar strokes, and we, so
mesmerized can barely talk. Happier
than any man now is the one who sits drinking
wine with his lifelong companion under the winking
stars and the steady arc lamp at the end of the pier.

Flower Girls

Verse 1 | Lucy Larcom (1824–1893)

O my little seaside girl,
    What is in your garden growing?
'Rock-weeds and tangle-grass,
    With the slow tide coming, going;
Samphire and marsh-rosemary
    All along the wet shore creeping;
Sandwort, beach-peas, pimpernel,
    Out of nooks and corners peeping.'

Running into Africa

From *The Story of Dr Dolittle, 1920* | Hugh Lofting (1886–1947)

The Doctor said, 'Very soon we should be able to see the shores of Africa.'

And about half an hour later, sure enough, they thought they could see something in front that might be land. But it began to get darker and darker and they couldn't be sure.

Then a great storm came up, with thunder and lightning. The wind howled; the rain came down in torrents; and the waves got so high they splashed right over the boat.

Presently there was a big BANG! The ship stopped and rolled over on its side.

'What's happened?' asked the Doctor, coming up from downstairs.

'I'm not sure,' said the parrot; 'but I think we're ship-wrecked. Tell the duck to get out and see.'

So Dab-Dab dived right down under the waves. And when she came up she said they had struck a rock; there was a big hole in the bottom of the ship; the water was coming in; and they were sinking fast.

'We must have run into Africa,' said the Doctor. 'Dear me, dear me! – Well – we must all swim to land.'

But Chee-Chee and Gub-Gub did not know how to swim.

'Get the rope!' said Polynesia. 'I told you it would come in handy. Where's that duck? Come here, Dab-Dab. Take this end of the rope, fly to the shore and tie it on to a palm-tree; and we'll hold the other end on the ship here. Then those that can't swim must climb along the rope till they reach the land. That's what you call a "life-line."'

So they all got safely to the shore – some swimming, some flying; and those that climbed along the rope brought the Doctor's trunk and hand-bag with them.

But the ship was no good any more – with the big hole in the bottom; and presently the rough sea beat it to pieces on the rocks and the timbers floated away.

Then they all took shelter in a nice dry cave they found, high up in the cliffs, till the storm was over.

Bermudas

Lines 1–20 | Andrew Marvell (1621–1678)

Where the remote Bermudas ride
In th' Ocean's bosome unespy'd,
From a small Boat, that row'd along,
The listning Winds receiv'd this Song.
    What should we do but sing his Praise
That led us through the watry Maze
Unto an Isle so long unknown,
And yet far kinder than our own?
Where he the huge Sea-Monsters wracks,
That lift the Deep upon their Backs,
He lands us on a grassy Stage,
Safe from the Storms and Prelat's rage.
He gave us this eternal Spring
Which here enamells every thing,
And sends the Fowls to us in care,
On daily Visits through the Air.
He hangs in shades the Orange bright,
Like golden Lamps in a green Night;
And does in the Pomegranates close
Jewels more rich than Ormus shows.

The Whale: an Island

From *Codex Exoniensis: The Whale* |

Anon, translated by Benjamin Thorpe (1782–1870)

Like is its aspect
to *a* rough stone,
it, as it were, roves
by *the* sea-shore,
by sand-hills surrounded,
of sea-aits greatest:
so that imagine
wavefarers,
that on some island they
gaze with *their* eyes.
and then fasten
the high-prow'd ships
to that false land
with anchor-ropes,
settle *their* sea-horses
at *the* sea's end,
and then on to that island
mount,
bold of spirit:
the vessels stand
fast by *the* shore,
by *the* stream encircled:
then encamp,
weary in mind,
the seafarers,
(*they* of peril dream not)
on that island.

15 July

A Sea Trip

From *Three Men in a Boat: To say nothing of the Dog!* 1889 |

Jerome K. Jerome (1859–1927)

16 July

If you want rest and change, you can't beat a sea trip.

I objected to the sea trip strongly. A sea trip does you good when you are going to have a couple of months of it, but, for a week, it is wicked.

You start on Monday with the idea implanted in your bosom that you are going to enjoy yourself. You wave an airy adieu to the boys on shore, light your biggest pipe, and swagger about the deck as if you were Captain Cook, Sir Francis Drake, and Christopher Columbus all rolled into one. On Tuesday, you wish you hadn't come. On Wednesday, Thursday, and Friday, you wish you were dead. On Saturday, you are able to swallow a little beef tea, and to sit up on deck, and answer with a wan, sweet smile when kind-hearted people ask you how you feel now. On Sunday, you begin to walk about again, and take solid food. And on Monday morning, as, with your bag and umbrella in your hand, you stand by the gunwale, waiting to step ashore, you begin to thoroughly like it.

I remember my brother-in-law going for a short sea trip once, for the benefit of his health. He took a return berth from London to Liverpool; and when he got to Liverpool, the only thing he was anxious about was to sell that return ticket.

Sea Shell

Amy Lowell (1874–1925)

Sea Shell, Sea Shell,
Sing me a song, O Please!
A song of ships, and sailor men,
And parrots, and tropical trees,

Of islands lost in the Spanish Main
Which no man ever may find again,
Of fishes and corals under the waves,
And seahorses stabled in great green caves.

Sea Shell, Sea Shell,
Sing of the things you know so well.

The Puffin

From *The Deep Sea, 1896* | Edward Step (1855–1931)

The Puffin (*Fratercula arctica*) is identified readily, wherever seen, by its conspicuous compressed orange beak of great depth from top to bottom. This gives it a humorous aspect that belongs to itself alone; but it is useful to it also, for it makes a very efficient cracking instrument wherewith certain of the thinner shelled bivalves may be utilized for the Puffin's food.

One Great Ride

From *Under the Wave at Waimea, 2021* | Paul Theroux (1941–)

Flattened on his board, sledding down the steepness of the wave-washed sand, he entered the water paddling, using the riptide at the right-hand side of the bay to help him into the huge incoming swell and the density of foam. He ducked under three large waves and, still paddling, got himself beyond the break, where five other surfers in the lineup were riding their boards.

. . . . . .

Those young surfers he had met at the party last night – were any of them in the lineup now? He scanned the faces of the surfers near him, and as he did two of them pushed off and were engulfed, tumbled, fighting to balance. Another wave in the set rose behind him, and beyond it, as he adjusted, a likelier wave. A surfer ahead of him slipped sideways, out of sight, like a naked man tumbling from a building, and Sharkey propelled himself into the wave lifting his board, and when the nose of his board protruded into its lip, he jumped and squared his feet for balance and crouched and rode it, skidding slantwise on the curling face, into the moving trough.

His wave was wicked froth spilling over him as it barreled, and he angled his board to right across its face, the dark water below him ripping like a muscle of blue. Then he was streaking down a steep hillside that was carrying him forward and fast in a precipitous skid. It took all the strength he had in his legs to stay upright and to keep the board jammed against the moving slope of gleaming water, and just as he thought he was free of it, a shadow fell over him, the peak of the wave toppling him into a swallowing barrel and speeding him sideways. He shot through it, enclosed by a glittering narrowing cone. He rode it until it swelled and subsided under him, and he was released as the wave broke utterly and flattened and washed and pooled against a wave draining down the beach, allowing Sharkey to float almost to shore. He dropped off his board and pushed it onward to avoid a wave now breaking behind him and threatening to swamp him.

Out of the surf zone, he fell to his knees. All his strength was gone in the effort and exhilaration of that one great ride. He carried his board up a dry sand mound on the beach and gasped with delight.

A Western Voyage

James Elroy Flecker (1884–1915)

My friend the Sun – like all my friends
  Inconstant, lovely, far away –
Is out, and bright, and condescends
  To glory in our holiday.

A furious march with him I'll go
  And race him in the Western train,
And wake the hills of long ago
  And swim the Devon sea again.

I have done foolishly to tread
  The footway of the false moonbeams,
To light my lamp and call the dead
  And read their long black printed dreams.

I have done foolishly to dwell
  With Fear upon her desert isle,
To take my shadowgraph to Hell,
  And then to hope the shades would smile.

And since the light must fail me soon
  (But faster, faster, Western train!)
Proud meadows of the afternoon,
  I have remembered you again.

And I'll go seek through moor and dale
  A flower that wastrel winds caress;
The bud is red and the leaves pale,
  The name of it Forgetfulness.

Then like the old and happy hills
    With frozen veins and fires outrun,
I'll wait the day when darkness kills
    My brother and good friend, the Sun.

Becalmed

From *The Rime of the Ancient Mariner* |

Samuel Taylor Coleridge (1772–1834)

Part II, lines 107-134

Down dropt the breeze, the sails dropt down,
'Twas sad as sad could be;
And we did speak only to break
The silence of the sea!

All in a hot and copper sky,
The bloody Sun, at noon,
Right up above the mast did stand,
No bigger than the Moon.

Day after day, day after day,
We stuck, nor breath nor motion;
As idle as a painted ship
Upon a painted ocean.

Water, water, every where,
And all the boards did shrink;
Water, water, every where,
Nor any drop to drink.

The very deep did rot: O Christ!
That ever this should be!
Yea, slimy things did crawl with legs
Upon the slimy sea.

About, about, in reel and rout
The death-fires danced at night;
The water, like a witch's oils,
Burnt green, and blue and white.

A Cup and a Clamshell

From *Land's End*, 2002 | Michael Cunningham (1952–)

There is a short interval on clear summer evenings in Provincetown, after the sun has set, when the sky is deep blue but the hulls of the boats in the harbour retain a last vestige of light that is visible nowhere else. They become briefly phosphorescent in a dim blue world. Last summer as I stood on the beach by the harbour, watching the boats, I found a coffee cup in the shallows. It's not unusual to find bits of crockery on this beach (Provincetown's harbour, being shaped like an enormous ladle, catches much of what the tides stir landward from the waters that surround Cape Cod), but a whole cup is rare. It was not, I'm sorry to say, the perfect little white china cup that poetry demands. It was in fact a cheap thing, made in the seventies I suppose, a graceless shallow oval, plastic (hence its practical but unflattering ability to survive intact), covered with garish orange and yellow daisies; the official flowers of the insistent, high-gloss optimism I remember from my adolescence, as talk of revolution dimmed and we all started, simply, to dance. It wasn't much of a cup, though it would outlast many of humankind's more vulnerable attempts to embody the notion of hope in everyday objects. It had gotten onto the beach in one piece, while its lovelier counterparts, concoctions of clay and powdered bone, white as moons, lay in fragments on the ocean floor. This cup contained a prim little clamshell, pewter-colored, with a tiny flourish of violet at its broken hinge, and a scattering of iridescent, mica-ish grit, like tea leaves, at its shallow bottom. I held it up, as if I expected to drink from it, as the boats put out their light.

The Corsair

Canto I | George Gordon, Lord Byron (1788–1824)

'O'er the glad waters of the dark blue sea,
Our thoughts as boundless, and our soul's as free
Far as the breeze can bear, the billows foam,
Survey our empire, and behold our home!
These are our realms, no limits to their sway –
Our flag the sceptre all who meet obey.
Ours the wild life in tumult still to range
From toil to rest, and joy in every change.
Oh, who can tell? not thou, luxurious slave!
Whose soul would sicken o'er the heaving wave;
Not thou, vain lord of wantonness and ease!
whom slumber soothes not – pleasure cannot please –
Oh, who can tell, save he whose heart hath tried,
And danced in triumph o'er the waters wide,
The exulting sense – the pulse's maddening play,
That thrills the wanderer of that trackless way?
That for itself can woo the approaching fight,
And turn what some deem danger to delight;
That seeks what cravens shun with more than zeal,
And where the feebler faint – an only feel –
Feel – to the rising bosom's inmost core,
Its hope awaken and Its spirit soar?
No dread of death if with us die our foes –
Save that it seems even duller than repose:
Come when it will – we snatch the life of life –
When lost – what recks it by disease or strife?
Let him who crawls enamour'd of decay,
Cling to his couch, and sicken years away:
Heave his thick breath, and shake his palsied head;
Ours - the fresh turf; and not the feverish bed.
While gasp by gasp he falters forth his soul,
Ours with one pang – one bound – escapes control.

His corse may boast its urn and narrow cave,
And they who loath'd his life may gild his grave:
Ours are the tears, though few, sincerely shed,
When Ocean shrouds and sepulchres our dead.
For us, even banquets fond regret supply
In the red cup that crowns our memory;
And the brief epitaph in danger's day,
When those who win at length divide the prey,
And cry, Remembrance saddening o'er each brow,
How had the brave who fell exulted *now*!'

The Beach End Buoy

From *We Didn't Mean to Go to Sea, 1937* | Arthur Ransome (1884–1967)

Something large loomed out of the fog astern. It was a big red painted cage, like an enormous parrot cage with a pointed top, built on a round raft. On top of the cage was a lantern, and, as they watched, they saw a thin line of white leap up the lantern, vanish and leap again. It was a buoy. In the cage was something big and black … the bell.

'Clang!'

'It's coming jolly fast,' shouted Roger. 'Look at the wash round its bows.'

'It's going to burn into us,' cried Titty.

'It isn't the buoy that's moving,' said John. 'It's us.'

They swept past it, missing it by only a yard. The heavy hammer swung against the bell when they were almost near enough to touch the buoy. The melancholy 'Clang!' boomed in their ears. They read the big white letters painted on the side of the cage … 'BEACH END.' A moment later the buoy had faded away into the fog, and the next 'Clang' sounded out of nothingness.

'Oh, John!' gasped Susan. 'That was the Beach End buoy. We're out at sea.'

Sea-Bathers

D. H. Lawrence (1885–1930)

Oh the handsome bluey-brown bodies, they might just as well be
   gutta percha,
and the reddened limbs red indiarubber tubing, inflated,
and the half-hidden private parts just a little brass tap, rubinetto,
turned on for different purposes.
They call it health, it looks like nullity.

Only here and there a pair of eyes, haunted, looks out as if asking:
where then is life?

Diving

From *The Summer Book, 1972, 1975* | Tove Jansson (1914–2001)

Translated by Thomas Teal

'I can dive,' Sophia said. 'Do you know what it feels like when you dive?'

'Of course I do,' her grandmother said. 'You let go of everything and get ready and just dive. You can feel the seaweed against your legs. It's brown, and the water's clear, lighter towards the top, with lots of bubbles. And you glide. You hold your breath and glide and turn and come up, let yourself rise and breathe out. And then you float. Just float.'

'And all the time with your eyes open,' Sophia said.

'Naturally. People don't dive with their eyes shut.'

'Do you believe I can dive without me showing you?' the child asked.

'Yes, of course,' Grandmother said.

Dover Beach

Matthew Arnold (1822–1888)

The sea is calm to-night.
The tide is full, the moon lies fair
Upon the straits; – on the French coast the light
Gleams and is gone; the cliffs of England stand,
Glimmering and vast, out in the tranquil bay.
Come to the window, sweet is the night air!
Only, from the ling line of spray
Where the sea meets the moon-blanch'd land,
Listen! you hear the grating roar
Of pebbles which the waves draw back, and fling,
At their return, up the high strand,
Begin, and cease, and then again begin,
With tremulous cadence slow, and bring
The eternal note of sadness in.

Sophocles long ago
Heard it on the Ægæan, and it brought
Into his mind the turbid ebb and flow
Of human misery; we
Find also in the sound a thought,
Hearing it by this distant northern sea.

The Sea of Faith
Was once, at the full, and round earth's shore
Lay like the folds of a bright girdle furl'd.
But now I only hear
Its melancholy, long, withdrawing roar,
Retreating, to the breath
Of the night-wind, down the vast edges drear
And naked shingles of this world.

Ah, love, let us be true
To one another! for the world, which seems
To lie before us like a land of dreams,
So various, so beautiful, so new,
Hath really neither joy, nor love, nor light,
Nor certitude, nor peace, nor help for pain;
And we are here as on a darkling plain
Swept with confused alarms of struggle and flight,
Where ignorant armies clash by night.

The First Sunrise in the South Seas

From *In the South Seas, 1896* | Robert Louis Stevenson (1850–1894)

28 July

The first experience can never be repeated. The first love, the first sunrise, the first South Sea island, are memories apart and touched a virginity of sense. On the 28th of July 1888 the moon was an hour down by four in the morning. In the east a radiating centre of brightness told of the day; and beneath, on the skyline, the morning bank was already building, black as ink. We have all read of the swiftness of the day's coming and departure in low latitudes; it is a point on which the scientific and sentimental tourist are at one, and has inspired some tasteful poetry. The period certainly varies with the season; but here is one case exactly noted. Although the dawn was thus preparing by four, the sun was not up till six; and it was half-past five before we could distinguish our expected islands from the clouds on the horizon. Eight degrees south, and the day two hours a-coming. The interval was passed on deck in the silence of expectation, the customary thrill of landfall heightened by the strangeness of the shores that we were then approaching. Slowly they took shape in the attenuating darkness. Ua-huna, piling up to a truncated summit, appeared the first upon the starboard bow; almost abeam arose our destination, Nuka-hiva, whelmed in cloud; and betwixt and to the southward, the first rays of the sun displayed the needles of Ua-pu. These pricked about the line of the horizon; like the pinnacles of some ornate and monstrous church, they stood there, in the sparkling brightness of the morning, the fit signboard of a world of wonders.

Clymping and Selsey

From *Hills and the Sea, 1906* | Hilaire Belloc (1870–1953)

The sea, being governed by a pagan god, made war at once, and began eating up all those fields which had specially been consecrated to the Church, civilization, common sense, and human happiness. It is still doing so, and I know an old man who can remember a forty-acre field all along by Clymping having been eaten up by the sea; and out along past Rustington there is, about a quarter of a mile from the shore, a rock, called the Church Rock, the remains of a church which quite a little time ago people used for all the ordinary purposes of a church.

The sea then began to eat up Selsey. Before the Conquest – though I cannot remember exactly when – the whole town had gone, and they had to remove the cathedral to Chichester. In Henry VIII's time there was still a park left out of the old estates, a park with trees in it; but this also the sea has eaten up; and here it is that I come to the Looe Stream. The Looe stream is a little dell that used to run through the park, and which to-day, right out at sea, furnishes the only gate by which ships can pass through the great maze of banks and rocks which go right out to sea from Selsey Bill, miles and miles, and are called the Owers.

Sea Love

Charlotte Mew (1869–1928)

Tide be runnin' the great world over:
    'Twas only last June month I mind that we
Was thinkin' the toss and the call in the breast of the lover
    So everlastin' as the sea.

Here's the same little fishes that sputter and swim,
    Wi' the moon's old glim on the grey, wet sand;
An' him no more to me nor me to him
    Than the wind goin' over my hand.

Castle Boterel

From *A Pair of Blue Eyes, 1873* | Thomas Hardy (1840–1928)

The place is pre-eminently (for one person at least) the region of dream and mystery. The ghostly birds, the pall-like sea, the frothy wind, the eternal soliloquy of the waters, the bloom of dark purple cast, that seems to exhale from the shoreward precipices, in themselves lend to the scene an atmosphere like the twilight of a night vision.

One enormous sea-bord cliff* in particular figures in the narrative; and for some forgotten reason or other this cliff was described in the story as being without a name. Accuracy would require the statement to be that a remarkable cliff which resembles in many points the cliff of the description bears a name that no event has made famous.

*Beeny Cliff

AUGUST

I Gathered Shells

Seaside Reading: Non Fiction

This is the longest of my three lists and contains the greatest breadth of subjects. Here you will find maritime history, shipwrecks, lighthouse keepers, marine biology, climate change, rock pools, beaches, people who loved the sea and those who battled and loathed it. It travels from a single cove on the Cornish coast to the depths of the deepest ocean. There are also some books that would fit as well on the Journeys page. They are listed alphabetically by the author as I couldn't work out a better way to divide them.

Lamorna Ash, *Dark, Salt, Clear, 2020*
David Attenborough and Colin Buttfield, *Ocean: Earth's Last Wilderness, 2025*
Meg Clothier, *The Shipping Forecast, 2024*
Charles Clover, *Rewilding the Sea: How to Save our Oceans, 2022*
Jacques-Yves Cousteau, *The Silent World, 1953*
Nick Crane, *Coast: Our Island Story, 2010*
Helen Czerski, *Blue Machine: How the Ocean Shapes our World, 2023*
Kathryn Ferry, *Beach Huts and Bathing Machines, 2009*
David Grann, *The Wager: A Tale of Shipwreck, Mutiny and Murder, 2023*
James Hamilton-Paterson, *Seven Tenths: The Sea and its Thresholds, 1992*
Philip Hoare, *The Sea Inside, 2013,*
Risingtidefallingstar, 2017,
The Sea, 2022
Barry Lopez, *Arctic Dreams, 1986*
Beth Lynch, *The Cove: A Cornish Haunting, 2024*
Ruth Maning-Sanders, *Seaside England, 1951*
Philip Marsden, *The Levelling Sea, 2012*
Andrew Martin, *To the Sea by Train, 2025*
Tom Nancollas, *Seashaken Houses, 2018*
Adam Nicolson, *The Sea Room, 2001,*
The Sea is Not Made of Water/Life Between the Tides, 2021
Nathaniel Philbrick, *In the Heart of the Sea, 2000*
Tim Winton, *Land's Edge: A Coastal Memoir, 1993*
Lisa Woollett, *Lost to the Sea, 2024*

Driving Home

Rachel Rooney (1962–)

I hold this shell against my ear.
Inside, a wave that sucks the shore,
music drifting from the pier,
a tapping spade, a seagull's call.

Listen, sea-shell. Can you hear
my heart sink slowly with the sun,
the rolling of a salty tear
and an engine's sleepy hum?

Clothing for the Seaside

From *The Diary of a Nobody, 1892* | George Grossmith (1847–1912) and Wheedon Grossmith (1854–1919)

August 1. – Ordered a new pair of trousers at Edwards's, and told them not to cut them so loose over the boot; the last pair being so loose and also tight at the knee, looked like a sailor's, and I heard Pitt, that objectionable youth at the office, call out 'Hornpipe' as I passed his desk. Carrie has ordered of Miss Jibbons a pink Garibaldi and blue-serge skirt, which I always think looks so pretty at the seaside. In the evening she trimmed herself a little sailor-hat, while I read to her the *Exchange and Mart*. We had a good laugh over my trying on the hat when she had finished it; Carrie saying it looked so funny with my beard, and how the people would have roared if I went on the stage like it.

August 2. – Mrs. Beck wrote to say we could have our usual rooms at Broadstairs. That's off our mind. Bought a coloured shirt and a pair of tan-coloured boots, which I see many of the swell clerks wearing in the City, and hear are all the 'go'.

August 3. – A beautiful day. Looking forward to to-morrow. Carrie bought a parasol about five feet long. I told her it was ridiculous. She said: 'Mrs. James, of Sutton, has one twice as long so'; the matter dropped. I bought a capital hat for hot weather at the seaside. I don't know what it is called, but it is the shape of the helmet worn in India, only made of straw. Got three new ties, two coloured handkerchiefs, and a pair of navy-blue socks at Pope Brothers.

The Flowing Tide

From *English Rispetti* | Augusta Webster (1837–1894)

The slow green wave comes curling from the bay
 And leaps in spray along the sunny marge,
And steals a little more and more away,
 And drowns the dulse, and lifts the stranded barge.
Leave me, strong tide, my smooth and yellow shore;
But the clear waters deepen more and more:
 Leave me my pathway of the sands, strong tide;
 Yet are the waves more fair than all they hide.

Revere Beach

From *A Swimming Lesson: Essence, 1993* | Jewelle L. Gomez (1948–)

At nine years old I didn't realize my grandmother, Lydia, and I were doing an extraordinary thing by packing a picnic lunch and riding the elevated line from Roxbury to Revere Beach. It seemed part of the natural rhythm of summer to me. I didn't notice how the subway cars emptied of most of their Black passengers as the train left Boston's urban center and made its way into the Italian and Irish suburban neighbourhoods to the north. It didn't seem odd that all of the Black families stayed in one section of the beach and never ventured onto the boardwalk to the concession stands or the rides except in groups.

I do remember Black women perched cautiously on their blankets, tugging desperately at bathing suits rising too high in the rear and complaining about their hair 'going back'. Not my grandmother, though. She glowed with an unashamed athleticism as she waded out, just inside the reach of the waves, and moved along the riptide parallel to the shore. Once submerged, she would load me onto her back and begin her long tireless strokes. With the waves partially covering us, I followed her rhythm with my short, chubby arms, taking my cues from the powerful movement of her back muscles. We did this again and again until I'd fall off, and she'd catch me and set me upright in the strong New England surf. I was thrilled by the wildness of the ocean and my grandmother's fearless relationship to it. I loved the way she never consulted her mirror after her swim, but always looked as if she had been born to the sea, a kind of aquatic heiress.

The Wind

From *Ozma of Oz, 1907* | L. Frank Baum (1856–1919)

The wind blew hard and joggled the water of the ocean, sending ripples across its surface. Then the wind pushed the edges of the ripples until they became waves, and shoved the waves around until they became billows. The billows rolled dreadfully high: higher even than the tops of houses. Some of them, indeed, rolled as high as the tops of tall trees, and seemed like mountains; and the gulfs between the great billows were like deep valleys.

All this mad dashing and splashing of the waters of the big ocean, which the mischievous wind caused without any good reason whatever, resulted in a terrible storm, and a storm on the ocean is liable to cut many queer pranks and do a lot of damage.

The Sea-Limits

D. G. Rossetti (1828–1882)

Consider the sea's listless chime:
  Time's self it is, made audible, –
  The murmur of the earth's own shell.
Secret continuance sublime
  Is the sea's end: our sight may pass
  No furlong further. Since time was,
This sound hath told the lapse of time.

No quiet, which is death's, – it hath
  The mournfulness of ancient life,
  Enduring always at dull strife.
As the world's heart of rest and wrath,
  Its painful pulse is in the sands.
  Last utterly, the whole sky stands,
Grey and not known, along its path.

Listen alone beside the sea,
  Listen alone among the woods;
  Those voices of twin solitudes
Shall have one sound alike to thee:
  Hark where the murmurs of thronged men
  Surge and sink back and surge again, –
Still the one voice of wave and tree.

Gather a shell from the strown beach
  And listen at its lips: they sigh
  The same desire and mystery,
The echo of the whole sea's speech.
  And all mankind is thus at heart
  Not anything but what thou art:
And Earth, Sea, Man, are all in each.

The Strange Ship

From *Dracula, 1897* | Bram Stoker (1847–1912)

Cutting from *The Dailygraph,* 8 August
(*Pasted in Mina Murray's Journal.*)
Before long the searchlight discovered some distance away a schooner with all sails set, apparently the same vessel which had been noticed earlier in the evening. The wind had by this time backed to the east, and there was a shudder amongst the watchers on the cliff as they realized the terrible danger in which she now was. Between her and the port lay the great flat reef on which so many good ships have from time to time suffered, and, with the wind blowing from its present quarter, it would be quite impossible that she should fetch the entrance of the harbour. It was now nearly the hour of high tide, but the waves were so great that in their troughs the shallows of the shore were almost visible, and the schooner, with all sails set, was rushing with such speed that, in the words of one old salt, 'she must fetch up somewhere, if it was only in hell.' Then came another rush of sea-fog, greater than any hitherto – a mass of dank mist, which seemed to close on all things like a grey pall, and left available to men only the organ of hearing, for the roar of the tempest, and the crash of the thunder, and the booming of the mighty billows came through the damp oblivion even louder than before. The rays of the searchlight were kept fixed on the harbour mouth across the East Pier, where the shock was expected, and men waited breathless. The wind suddenly shifted to the north-east, and the remnant of the sea-fog melted in the blast; and then, *mirabile dictu*, between the piers, leaping from wave to wave as it rushed at headlong speed, swept the strange schooner before the blast, with all sail set, and gained the safety of the harbour. The searchlight followed her, and a shudder ran through all who saw her, for lashed to the helm was a corpse, with drooping head, which swung horribly to and fro at each motion of the ship. No other form could be seen on deck at all. A great awe came on all as they realised that the ship, as if by a miracle, had found the harbour, unsteered save by the hand of a dead man!

Ocean, an Ode

Verses 1–2 | Edward Young (1683–1765)

Sweet rural scene!
Of flocks and green!
At careless ease my limbs are spread;
All nature still
But yonder rill;
And listening pines not o'er my head:

In prospect wide,
The boundless tide!
Waves cease to foam, and winds to roar;
Without a breeze,
The curling seas
Dance on, in measure, to the shore.

A Sunny Southern Shore

From *The Phoenix and the Carpet, 1904* | E. Nesbit (1858–1924)

The greenest of green slopes led up to glorious groves where palm-trees and all the tropical flowers and fruits that you read of in *Westward Ho!* and *Fair Play* were growing in rich profusion. Between the green, green slope and the blue, blue sea lay a stretch of sand that looked like a carpet of jewelled cloth of gold, for it was not greyish as our northern sand is, but yellow and changing – opal-coloured like sunshine and rainbows. And at the very moment when the wild, whirling, blinding, deafening, tumbling upside-downness of the carpet-moving stopped, the children had the happiness of seeing three large live turtles waddle down to the edge of the sea and disappear in the water. And it was hotter than you can possibly imagine, unless you think of ovens on a baking-day.

At the Sea-Side

Robert Louis Stevenson (1850–1894)

When I was down beside the sea
A wooden spade they gave to me
          To dig the sandy shore.
My holes were empty like a cup.
In every hole the sea came up,
          Till it could come no more.

The Dead Sea

From *The Innocents Abroad, 1869* | Mark Twain (1835–1910)

The Dead Sea is small. Its waters are very clear, and it has a pebbly bottom and is shallow for some distance out from the shores. It yields quantities of asphaltum; fragments of it lie all about its banks; this stuff gives the place something of an unpleasant smell.

. . . . . .

It was a funny bath. We could not sink. One could stretch himself at full length on his back, with his arms on his breast, and all of his body above a line drawn from the corner of his jaw past the middle of his side, the middle of his leg and through his ancle bone, would remain out of water. He could lift his head clear out, if he chose. No position can be retained long; you lose your balance and whirl over, first on your back and then on your face, and so on. You can lie comfortably, on your back, with your head out, and your legs out from your knees down, by steadying yourself with your hands. You can sit, with your knees drawn up to your chin and your arms clasped around them, but you are bound to turn over presently, because you are top-heavy in that position. You can stand up straight in water that is over your head, and from the middle of your breast upward you will not be wet. But you can not remain so. The water will soon float your feet to the surface. You can not swim on your back and make any progress of any consequence, because your feet stick away above the surface, and there is nothing to propel yourself with but your heels. If you swim on your face, you kick up the water like a stern-wheel boat. You make no headway. A horse is so top-heavy that he can neither swim nor stand up in the Dead Sea. He turns over on his side at once. Some of us bathed for more than an hour, and then came out coated with salt till we shone like icicles.

Peace

(Sidmouth) | Radclyffe Hall (1880–1943)

Evening upon the calm sweet sea,
A little wind asleep,
Dim sails that drift as tranquilly
As dreams in slumber deep.
A seagull on the water's breast
Folds up his wings of white;
As peaceful and as much at rest
As is my heart to-night.

The Birth of the Moon

From *The Sea Around Us, 1951* | Rachel Carson (1907–1964)

The birth of the moon probably helped shape other regions of the world ocean besides the Pacific. When part of the crust was torn away, strains must have been set up in the remaining granite envelope. Perhaps the granite mass cracked open on the side opposite the moon scar. Perhaps, as the earth spun on its axis and rushed on its orbit through space, the cracks widened and the masses of granite began to drift apart, moving over a tarry, slowly hardening layer of basalt. Gradually the outer portions of the basalt layer became solid and the wandering continents came to rest, frozen into place with oceans between them. In spite of theories to the contrary, the weight of geologic evidence seems to be that the locations of the major ocean basins and the major continental land masses are today much the same as they have been since a very early period of the earth's history.

Samphire at Boulogne

From *Travels Through France and Italy, 1766*

Tobias Smollett (1721–1771)

Letter III, Boulogne, August 15, 1763

The ooze, impregnated with sea salt, produces, on this side of the harbour, an incredible quantity of the finest *samphire* I ever saw. The French call it *passe-pierre*; and I suspect its English name is a corruption of *sang-pierre*. It is generally found on the faces of bare rocks that overhang the sea, by the spray of which it is nourished. As it grew upon a naked rock, without any appearance of soil, it might be naturally enough called *sang du pierre*, or *sang-pierre*, blood of the rock; and hence the name *samphire*.

The Rugged Shore

From *Odyssey, 8–7th century* BCE, *Book Five, lines 537–558*

Homer (8th century BCE)

Translated by George Chapman (c. 1559–1634)

'O,' said Ulysses then, 'now Jupiter
Hath giv'n me sight of an unhop'd – for shore,
Though I have wrought these seas so long, so sore –
Of rest yet no place shows the slend'rest prints,
The rugged shore so bristled is with flints,
Against which every way the waves so flock,
And all the shore shows as one eminent rock,
So near which 'tis so deep, that not a sand
Is there for any tired foot to stand,
Nor fly his death-fast-following miseries,
Lest, if he land, upon him foreright flies
A churlish wave, to crush him 'gainst a cliff,
Worse than vain rend'ring all his landing strife.
And should I swim to seek a hav'n elsewhere,
Or land less way-beat, I may justly fear
I shall be taken with a gale again,
And cast a huge way off into the main;
And there the great Earth-shaker (having seen
My so near landing, and again his spleen
Forcing me to him) will some whale send out,
(Of which a horrid number here about
His Amphitrite breeds) to swallow me.'

17 August

The French Coast

From *Willa Cather in Europe, 1956* | Willa Cather (1876–1947)

We crossed from Newhaven to Dieppe on a night when the Channel ran smoothly as glass and the stars stood clear in the midnight sky. Soon after the long lines of the coast-wise lights of England had quite died away, the sky clouded, and except where a pale star here and there struggled through, there was nothing to break the common blackness of the sea and sky. If one stared hard enough and long enough it was possible to divine the horizon line rather than see it. The boat was crowded and the wind blew cold, and the decks were peopled with miserable shivering Latins who had not secured staterooms and crouched under rubber blankets. When we quitted the decks at about one o'clock in the morning, they were scenes of chill and heaviness and discomfort. About three o'clock, however, I heard a rush of feet aft, and, tumbling into my ulster and mufflers, hurried out to see what had occasioned the excitement. Above the roar of the wind and thrash of the water I heard a babble of voices, in which I could only distinguish the word 'France' uttered over and over again with a fire and fervour that was in itself a panegyric. Far to the south there shone a little star of light out of the blackness, that burned from orange to yellow and back to orange again; the first light of the coast of France.

Sea-shells

E. Nesbit (1858–1924)

I gathered shells upon the sand,
  Each shell a little perfect thing,
So frail, yet potent to withstand
  The mountain-waves' wild buffeting.
Through storms no ship could dare to brave
The little shells float lightly, save
All that they might have lost of fine
Shape and soft colour crystalline.

Yet I amid the world's wild surge
  Doubt if my soul can face the strife,
The waves of circumstance that urge
  That slight ship on the rocks of life.
O soul, be brave, for He who saves
The frail shell in the giant waves,
Will bring thy puny bark to land
Safe in the hollow of His hand.

The Suez Canal

From *Maiden Voyage, 1943* | Denton Welch (1915–1948)

Then began the long, silent slipping through the Suez Canal, with the soft desert on either side and the water licking and sucking at the banks as we passed. I stayed on deck in the coolness till late at night, staring at the desert and the dark blue sky. Camels passed in the daytime bearing draped, precarious-looking men who sometimes sang or shouted to us in high keening voices.

Nuptial on Brighton Beach

Grace Nichols (1950–)

As Sea gusts in
in veils of smoky grey
the seagulls descend
over the flaking balustrades –

Noisy bridesmaids
making their way behind
her bridal train of lacy foam
the shuffling guests of rolling stones

With raucous speeches
with feathered cries –
and how they applaud this
wild and windy union of Sea and Sky

Seaside Crowds

From *Sketches by Boz: The Tugges of Ramsgate, 1836* |

Charles Dickens (1812–1870)

21 August

The sun was shining brightly; the sea, dancing to its own music, rolled merrily in; crowds of people promenaded to and fro; young ladies tittered; old ladies talked; nursemaids displayed their charms to the greatest possible advantage; and their little charges ran up and down, and to and fro, and in and out, under the feet, and between the legs, of the assembled concourse, in the most playful and exhilarating manner. There were old gentlemen, trying to make out objects through long telescopes; and young ones, making objects of themselves in open shirt-collars; ladies, carrying about portable chairs, and portable chairs carrying about invalids; parties, waiting on the pier for parties who had come by the steam-boat; and nothing was to be heard but talking, laughing, welcoming, and merriment.

Exultation is the going

Emily Dickinson (1830–1886)

Exultation is the going
Of an inland soul to sea,
Past the houses – past the headlands –
Into deep Eternity –

Bred as we, among the mountains,
Can the sailor understand
The divine intoxication
Of the first league out from land?

Contrary Winds

From *Letters written during a short residence in Sweden, Norway and Denmark, 1796* | Mary Wollstonecraft (1759–1797)

23 August

Letter I

Eleven days of weariness on board a vessel not intended for the accommodation of passengers have so exhausted my spirits, to say nothing of the other causes, with which you are already sufficiently acquainted, that it is with some difficulty I adhere to my determination of giving you my observations, as I travel through new scenes, whilst warmed with the impression they have made on me.

The captain, as I mentioned to you, promised to put me on shore at Arendall or Gothenburg in his way to Elsineur, but contrary winds obliged us to pass both places during the night. In the morning, however, after we had lost sight of the entrance of the latter bay, the vessel was becalmed; and the captain, to oblige me, hanging out a signal for a pilot, bore down towards the shore.

My attention was particularly directed to the lighthouse, and you can scarcely imagine with what anxiety I watched two long hours for a boat to emancipate me; still no one appeared. Every cloud that flitted on the horizon was hailed as a liberator, till approaching nearer, like most of the prospects sketched by hope, it dissolved under the eye into disappointment.

A Perfect Sailing Day

From *The House by the Sea, 1977* | May Sarton (1912–1995)

Yesterday I had my first sail since I came here more than two years ago. It was an absolutely perfect sailing day, brilliant, sunny, just enough wind and not too much. And I, landlubber that I am, was fascinated by all the sailing lore, the atmosphere of kinship between the owners of boats, the whole world it becomes, once one is involved. Heidi, who invited me, began to sail when she was over forty and progressed from small boats to this fine yawl that sleeps four, built for her by Bob Reed of Kennebunkport, the decks of teak, the mast, Sitka spruce, I think she said. *Pixie* is a good steady boat, and it was a grand day on the water! So relaxed and holidayish, I felt I had been away for a week when I got home after nine.

Eerie Waters

E. Pauline Johnson (Tekahionwake) (1861–1913)

A dash of yellow sand,
Wind-scattered and sun-tanned;
Some waves that curl and cream along the margin of the strand;
And, creeping close to these
Long shores that lounge at ease,
Old Erie rocks and ripples to a fresh sou'-western breeze.

A sky of blue and grey;
Some stormy clouds that play
At scurrying up with ragged edge, then laughing blow away,
Just leaving in their trail
Some snatches of a gale;
To whistling summer winds we lift a single daring sail.

O! wind so sweet and swift,
O! danger-freighted gift
Bestowed on Erie with her waves that foam and fall and lift,
We laugh in your wild face,
And break into a race
With flying clouds and tossing gulls that weave and interlace.

Buchan's Buller

From *Journal of a Tour to the Hebrides, 1785*

James Boswell (1740–1795)

We got immediately into the coach, and drove to *Dunbui*, a rock near the shore, quite covered with sea-fowls; then to a circular bason of large extent, surrounded with tremendous rocks. On the quarter next the sea, there is a high arch in the rock, which the force of the tempest has driven out. This place is called *Buchan's Buller*, or the *Buller of Buchan*, and the country people call it the *Pot*. Mr Boyd said it was so called from the French *Bouloir*. It may be more simply traced from *Boiler* in our own language. We walked round this monstrous cauldron. In some places, the rock is very narrow; and on each side there is a sea deep enough for a man of war to ride in; so that it is somewhat horrid to move along. However, there is earth and grass upon the rock, and a kind of road marked out by the print of feet; so that one makes it out pretty safely: yet it alarmed me to see Dr Johnson striding irregularly along. He insisted on taking a boat, and sailing into the Pot. We did so. He was stout, and wonderfully alert. The Buchan-men all shewing their teeth, and speaking with that strange sharp accent which distinguishes them, was to me a matter of curiosity. He was not sensible of the difference of pronunciation in the south and north of Scotland, which I wondered at.

As the entry into the *Buller* is so narrow that oars cannot be used as you go in, the method taken is to row very hard when you come near it, and give the boat such a rapidity of motion that it glides in. Dr Johnson observed what an effect this scene would have had, were we entering into an unknown place. There are caves of considerable depth; I think, one on each side. The boatmen had never entered either of them far enough to know the size. Mr Boyd told us that it is customary for the company at Peterhead-well, to make parties, and come and dine in one of the caves here.

Sand-Between-the Toes

A. A. Milne (1882–1956)

I went down to the shouting sea,
Taking Christopher down with me,
For Nurse had given us sixpence each –
And down we went to the beach.

We had sand in the eyes and the ears and the nose,
And sand in the hair, and sand-between-the-toes.
Whenever a good nor'-wester blows,
Christopher is certain of
Sand-between-the-toes.

The sea was galloping grey and white;
Christopher clutched his sixpence tight;
We clambered over the humping sand –
And Christopher held my hand.

We had sand in the eyes and the ears and the nose,
And sand in the hair, and sand-between-the-toes.
Whenever a good nor'-wester blows,
Christopher is certain of
Sand-between-the-toes.

There was a roaring in the sky;
The sea-gulls cried as they blew by;
We tried to talk, but had to shout –
Nobody else was out.

When we got home, we had sand in the hair,
In the eyes and the ears and everywhere;
Whenever a good nor'-wester blows,
Christopher is found with
Sand-between-the-toes.

The Isthmus of Panama

From *Wonderful Adventures of Mrs Seacole in Many Lands, 1857* | Mary Seacole (1805–c. 1881)

All my readers must know – a glance at the map will show it to those who do not – that between North America and the envied shores of California stretches a little neck of land, insignificant-looking enough on the map, dividing the Atlantic from the Pacific. By crossing this, the travellers from America avoided a long, weary, and dangerous sea voyage round Cape Horn, or an almost impossible journey by land.

But that journey across the Isthmus, insignificant in distance as it was, was by no means an easy one. It seemed as if nature had determined to throw every conceivable obstacle in the way of those who should seek to join the two great oceans of the world. I have read and heard many accounts of old endeavours to effect this important and gigantic work, and how miserably they failed. It was reserved for the men of our age to accomplish what so many had died in attempting, and iron and steam, twin giants, subdued to man's will, have put a girdle over rocks and rivers, so that travellers can glide as smoothly, if not as inexpensively, over the once terrible Isthmus of Darien, as they can from London to Brighton. Not yet, however, does civilization, rule at Panama. The weak sway of the New Granada Republic, despised by lawless men, and respected by none, is powerless to control the refuse of every nation which meet together upon its soil. Whenever they feel inclined now they overpower the law easily; but seven years ago, when I visited the Isthmus of Panama, things were much worse, and a licence existed, compared to which the present lawless state of affairs is enviable.

The Sea

From: *Tales of the Hall, Book IV, The Adventures of Richard*

George Crabbe (1754–1832)

29 August

Pleasant it was to view the sea-gulls strive
Against the storm, or in the ocean dive,
With eager scream, or when they dropping gave
Their closing wings to sail upon the wave:
Then as the winds and waters raged around,
And breaking billows mix'd their deafening sound,
They on the rolling deep securely hung,
And calmly rode the restless waves among.
Nor pleased it less around me to behold,
Far up the beach, the yesty sea-foam roll'd;
Or from the shore upborne, to see on high,
Its frothy flakes in wild confusion fly:
While the salt spray that clashing billows form,
Gave to the taste a feeling of the storm.

On a Cruise Ship

From *The Pillars of Hercules, 1995* | Paul Theroux (1941–)

Gliding along a perfectly flat sea that was blue and unwrinkled under a blue and cloudless sky, a slight breeze, Italy showing as a low smoky shoreline to the east, we passed between Elba and Corsica. The captain made an announcement to this effect, some people looked up and squinted past the rail, then returned to their reading.

. . . . . .

The white ship growled south bathed in full sunshine on the glittering sea, following the low shore of Italy that was never more than a long narrow stripe at the horizon, like the edge of a desert, a streak of glowing dust.

The Lighthouse

From *To the Lighthouse, 1927* | Virginia Woolf (1882–1941)

They were very close to the Lighthouse now. There it loomed up, stark and straight, glaring white and black, and one could see the waves breaking in white splinters like smashed glass upon the rocks. One could see lines and creases in the rocks. One could see the windows clearly; a dab of white on one of them, and a little tuft of green on the rock. A man had come out and looked at them through a glass and gone in again. So it was like that, James thought, the Lighthouse one had seen across the bay all these years; it was a stark tower on a bare rock. It satisfied him.

SEPTEMBER

Tangled Sea-weed

A New Pleasure

From *Letters written during a short residence in Sweden, Norway and Denmark, 1796* | Mary Wollstonecraft (1759–1797)

Letter VIII

Chance likewise led me to discover a new pleasure equally beneficial to my health. I wished to avail myself of my vicinity to the sea and bathe; but it was not possible near the town; there was no convenience. The young woman whom I mentioned to you proposed rowing me across the water amongst the rocks; but as she was pregnant, I insisted on taking one of the oars, and learning to row. It was not difficult, and I do not know a pleasanter exercise. I soon became expert, and my train of thinking kept time, as it were, with the oars, or I suffered the boat to be carried along by the current, indulging a pleasing forgetfulness or fallacious hopes.

. . . . . .

Sometimes, to take up my oar once more, when the sea was calm, I was amused by disturbing the innumerable young star fish which floated just below the surface; I had never observed them before, for they have not a hard shell like those which I have seen on the seashore. They look like thickened water with a white edge, and four purple circles, of different forms, were in the middle, over an incredible number of fibres or white lines. Touching them, the cloudy substance would turn or close, first on one side, then on the other, very gracefully, but when I took one of them up in the ladle, with which I heaved the water out of the boat, it appeared only a colourless jelly.

Recuerdo

Edna St Vincent Millay (1892–1950)

We were very tired, we were very merry –
We had gone back and forth all night on the ferry.
It was bare and bright, and smelled like a stable –
But we looked into a fire, we leaned across a table,
We lay on a hill-top underneath the moon;
And the whistles kept blowing, and the dawn came soon.

We were very tired, we were very merry –
We had gone back and forth all night on the ferry;
And you ate an apple, and I ate a pear,
From a dozen of each we had bought somewhere;
And the sky went wan, and the wind came cold,
And the sun rose dripping, a bucketful of gold.

We were very tired, we were very merry,
We had gone back and forth all night on the ferry.
We hailed, 'Good morrow, mother!' to a shawl-covered head,
And bought a morning paper, which neither of us read;
And she wept, 'God bless you!' for the apples and pears,
And we gave her all our money but our subway fares.

The Effects of the Sea

From *Mapp and Lucia, 1931* | E. F. Benson (1867–1940)

Isabel Poppit continued to inhabit her bungalow by the sea.

. . . . . .

With her skin turned black with all those sun-baths, and her hair spiky with so many sea-baths, Isabel resembled a cross between a kipper and a sea-urchin.

Starting Surfing

From *Barbarian Days: A Surfing Life*, 2015 | William Finnegan (1952–)

Why had I even started surfing? In one picture-book version, the hook had been set on a shining afternoon in Ventura when I was ten. Ventura was on the coast north of Los Angeles. There was a diner on the pier. My family ate there on beach weekends. From our booth by the window, I could see surfers out at a spot known as California Street. They were silhouettes, backlit by low sun, and they danced silently through the glare, their boards like big dark blades, slashing and gliding, swift beneath their feet. California Street was a long cobblestone point, and to me, at ten, the waves that broke along its shelf seemed like they were arriving from some celestial workshop, their glowing hooks and tapering shoulders carved by ocean angels. I wanted to be out there, learning to dance on water. The snug fracas of the family dinner felt vestigial. Even my chiliburger, a special treat, lost its fascination.

The Sea-bird's Cry

Rev. Robert Stephen Hawker, Vicar of Morwenstow (1803–1875)

'Tis harsh to hear, from ledge or peak,
The sunny cormorant's tuneless shriek;
Fierce songs they chant, in pool or cave,
Dark wanderers of the western wave.
Here will the listening landsman pray
For memory's music, far away;
Soft throats that nestling by the rose,
Soothe the glad rivulet as it flows.

Cease, stranger! cease that fruitless word,
Give eve's hushed bough to woodland bird:
Let the winged minstrel's valley-note
'Mid flowers and fragrance, pause and float.
Here must the echoing beak prevail,
To pierce the storm and cleave the gale;
To call, when warring tides shall foam,
The fledgeling of the waters home.

Wild things are here of sea and land,
Stern surges and a haughty strand;
Sea-monsters haunt yon caverned lair,
The mermaid wrings her briny hair.
That cry, those sullen accents sound
Like native echoes of the ground.
Lo! He did all things well Who gave
The sea-bird's voice to such a wave.

A Perfect Birthday

From *Father and Son, 1907* | Edmund Gosse (1849–1928)

Fortunately my Father was able to take us away in the autumn for six weeks by the sea in Wales, the expenses of this tour being paid for by a professional engagement, so that my seventh birthday was spent in an ecstasy of happiness, on golden sands, under a brilliant sky, and in sight of the glorious azure ocean beating in from an infinitude of melting horizons.

The Pattern of Life

From *Sylvia's Lovers, 1863* | Elizabeth Gaskell (1810–1865)

The magnates of Monkshaven were those who had the largest number of ships engaged in the whaling-trade. Something like the following was the course of life with a Monkshaven lad of this class. He was apprenticed as a sailor to one of the great shipowners – to his own father, possibly – along with twenty other boys, or, it might be, even more. During the summer months he and his fellow apprentices made voyages to the Greenland seas, returning with their cargoes in the early autumn; and employing the winter months in watching the preparation of the oil from the blubber in the melting-sheds, and learning navigation from some quaint but experienced teacher, half schoolmaster, half sailor, who seasoned his instructions by stirring narrations of the wild adventures of his youth. The house of the shipowner to whom he was apprenticed was his home and that of his companions during the idle season between October and March. The domestic position of these boys varied according to the premium paid; some took rank with the sons of the family, others were considered as little better than servants. Yet once on board an equality prevailed, in which, if any claimed superiority, it was the bravest and brightest. After a certain number of voyages the Monkshaven lad would rise by degrees to be captain, and as such would have a share in the venture; all these profits, as well as all his savings, would go towards building a whaling vessel of his own, if he was not so fortunate as to be the child of a shipowner.

Emigravit

Helen Hunt Jackson (1830–1885)

With sails full set, the ship her anchor weighs.
Strange names shine out beneath her figure head.
What glad farewells with eager eyes are said!
What cheer for him who goes, and him who stays!
Fair skies, rich lands, new homes, and untried days
Some go to seek: the rest but wait instead
Until the next stanch ship her flag doth raise.
Who knows what myriad colonies there are
Of fairest fields, and rich, undreamed-of gains
Thick planted in the distant shining plains
Which we call sky because they lie so far?
Oh, write of me, not 'Died in bitter pains,'
But 'Emigrated to another star!'

The Atoll Fakarava

From *In the South Seas, 1896* | Robert Louis Stevenson (1850–1894)

9 September

By a little before noon we were running down the coast of our destination, Fakarava: the air very light, the sea near smooth; though still we were accompanied by a continuous murmur from the beach, like the sound of a distant train. The isle is of a huge longitude, the enclosed lagoon thirty miles by ten or twelve, and the coral tow-path, which they call the land, some eighty or ninety miles by (possibly) one furlong. That part by which we sailed was all raised; the underwood excellently green, the topping wood of coco-palms continuous – a mark, if I had known it, of man's intervention. For once more, and once more unconsciously, we were within hail of fellow-creatures, and that vacant beach was but a pistol-shot from the capital city of the archipelago. But the life of an atoll, unless it be enclosed, passes wholly on the shores of the lagoon; it is there the villages are seated, there the canoes ply and are drawn up; and the beach of the ocean is a place accursed and deserted, the fit scene only for wizardry and shipwreck, and in the native belief a haunting ground of murderous spectres.

. . . . . .

We were scarce well headed for the pass before all heads were craned over the rail. For the water, shoaling under our board, became changed in a moment to surprising hues of blue and grey; and in its transparency the coral branched and blossomed, and the fish of the inland sea cruised visibly below us, stained and striped, and even beaked like parrots. I have paid in my time to view many curiosities; never one so curious as that first sight over the ship's rail in the lagoon of Fakarava. But let not the reader be deceived with hope. I have since entered, I suppose, some dozen atolls in different parts of the Pacific, and the experience has never been repeated. That exquisite hue and transparency of submarine day, and these shoals of rainbow fish, have not enraptured me again.

I Go Down to the Shore

Mary Oliver (1935–2019)

I go down to the shore in the morning
and depending on the hour the waves
are rolling in or moving out,
and I say, oh, I am miserable,
what shall –
what should I do? And the sea says
in its lovely voice:
Excuse me, I have work to do.

Late in the Season

From *The Captain of the Pole-Star, 1883* |

Sir Arthur Conan Doyle (1859–1930)

September 11th. – Lat. 81° 40' N.; long. 2° E. Still lying-to amid enormous ice fields. The one which stretches away to the north of us, and to which our ice-anchor is attached, cannot be smaller than an English county. To the right and left unbroken sheets extend to the horizon. This morning the mate reported that there were signs of pack ice to the southward. Should this form of sufficient thickness to bar our return, we shall be in a position of danger, as the food, I hear, is already running somewhat short. It is late in the season, and the nights are beginning to reappear.

This morning I saw a star twinkling just over the fore-yard, the first since the beginning of May. There is considerable discontent among the crew, many of whom are anxious to get back home to be in time for the herring season, when labour always commands a high price upon the Scotch coast.

A shoal of stars in ocean night

Lemn Sissay (1967–)

A shoal of stars in ocean night
Moon adrift with cargo light
Captin yawns, 'Dawn's in sight –
All is well, all is right'

The Bay of Bideford

From *The Cruise of the Tomtit, Household Words, 1855* |

Wilkie Collins (1824–1889)

13 September

About noon we sailed for Clovelly. Our smooth passage across the magnificent Bay of Bideford is the recollection of our happy voyage which I find myself looking back on most lovingly while I now write. No cloud was in the sky. Far away, on the left, sloped inward the winding shore, so clear, so fresh, so divinely tender in its blue and purple hues, that it was the most inexhaustible of luxuries only to look at it. Over the watery horizon, to the right, the autumn sun hung grandly, with the fire-path below, heaving on a sea of lustrous darkest blue. Flocks of wild birds, at rest, floated, chirping on the water all around. The fragrant, steady breeze was just enough to fill our sails. On and on we went, with the bubbling sea-song at our bows to soothe us; on and on, till the blue lustre of the ocean grew darker, till the sun sank redly towards the far waterline, till the sacred evening stillness crept over the sweet air, and hushed it with a foretaste of the coming night. What sight of mystery and enchantment rises before us now? Steep, solemn cliffs, bare in some places – where the dark-red rock has been rent away, and the winding chasms open grimly to the view – but clothed for the most part with trees, which soften their summits into the sky, and sweep all down them, in glorious masses of wood, to the very water's edge.

The Sea-reach of the Thames

From *Heart of Darkness, 1899* | Joseph Conrad (1857–1924)

The *Nellie*, a cruising yawl, swung to her anchor without a flutter of the sails, and was at rest. The flood had made, the wind was nearly calm, and being bound down the river, the only thing for it was to come to and wait for the turn of the tide.

The sea-reach of the Thames stretched before us like the beginning of an interminable waterway. In the offing the sea and the sky were welded together without a joint, and in the luminous space the tanned sails of the barges drifting up with the tide seemed to stand still in red clusters of canvas sharply peaked, with gleams of varnished sprits. A haze rested on the low shores that ran out to sea in vanishing flatness. The air was dark above Gravesend, and farther back still seemed condensed into a mournful gloom, brooding motionless over the biggest, and the greatest, town on earth.

The Ark

From *Noah built the Ark* | James Weldon Johnson (1871–1938)

But Noah was a just and righteous man.
Noah walked and talked with God.
And, one day, God said to Noah,
He said: Noah, build thee an ark.
Build it out of gopher wood.
Build it good and strong.
Pitch it within and pitch it without.
And build it according to the measurements
That I will give to thee.
Build it for you and all your house,
And to save the seeds of life on earth;
For I'm going to send down a mighty flood
To destroy this wicked world.

And Noah commenced to work on the ark.
And he worked for about one hundred years.
And ev'ry day the crowd came round
To make fun of Old Man Noah.
And they laughed and they said: Tell us, old man,
Where do you expect to sail that boat
Up here amongst the hills?

The Great Fish

From *The Old Man and the Sea, 1952* | Ernest Hemingway (1899–1961)

Then he began to pity the great fish that he had hooked. He is wonderful and strange and who knows how old he is, he thought. Never have I had such a strong fish nor one who acted so strangely. Perhaps he is too wise to jump. He could ruin me by jumping or by a wild rush. But perhaps he has been hooked many times before and he knows that this is how he should make his fight. He cannot know that it is only one man against him, nor that it is an old man. But what a great fish he is and what he will bring in the market if the flesh is good. He took the bait like a male and he pulls like a male and his fight has no panic in it. I wonder if he has any plans or if he is just as desperate as I am?

North Sea

Verses 1–3 | Jeffery Day (1896–1918)

Dawn on the drab North Sea! –
colourless, cold, and depressing,
with the sun that we long to see
refraining from his blessing.
To the westward – sombre as doom:
to the eastward – grey and foreboding:
Comes a low, vibrating boom –
the sound of a mine exploding.

Day on the drear North Sea! –
wearisome, drab, and relentless.
The low clouds swiftly flee;
bitter the sky and relentless.
Nothing at all in sight
save the mast of a sunken trawler,
fighting her long, last fight
with the waves that mouth and maul her.

Gale on the bleak North Sea! –
howling a dirge in the rigging.
Slowly and toilfully
through the great, grey breakers digging,
thus we make our way,
hungry, wet, and weary,
soaked with the sleet and spray,
desolate, damp, and dreary.

Swimming

From *The Art of Travel or Shifts and Contrivances Available in Wild Countries, 1855* | Sir Francis Galton (1822–1911)

Landing through Breakers – In landing through a heavy surf, wait for a large wave, and come in on the crest of it; then make every possible exertion to scramble up to some firm holding-place, whence its indraught, when it returns, can be resisted. If drawn back, you will be heavily battered, perhaps maimed, certainly far more exhausted than before, and not a whit nearer to safety. Avoid receiving a breaker in the attitude of scrambling away from it on hands and knees: from such a position, the wave projects a man headforemost with fearful force, and rolls him over and over in its surge. He ought to turn on his back the instant before the breaker is upon him; and then all will go well, and he will be helped on, and not half-killed by it. Men on shore can rescue a man who is being washed to and fro in the surf, by holding together, very firmly, hand-in-hand, and forming a line down to the sea: the foremost man clutches the swimmer as soon as he is washed up to him, and holds him firmly while the wave is retiring. The force of the indraught is enormous, and none but strong men can withstand it.

Chins in the Water

From *The Pillars of Hercules, 1995* | Paul Theroux (1941–)

What threw me was the sameness of the sea. The penetrating blue this winter day and the pale sky and the lapping of water on the shore, continuous and unchanging, the simultaneous calm in eighteen countries, and those aqueous and indistinct borders, made it seem like a small world of nations, cheek by jowl, with their chins in the water. And it was so calm I could imagine myself trespassing, from one to another, in a small boat, or even swimming. So much for the immutable sea.

Calm Morning at Sea

Sara Teasdale (1884–1933)

Midocean like a pale blue morning-glory
    Opened wide, wide;
The ship cut softly through the silken surface;
    We watched white sea-birds ride
Unrocking on the holy virgin water
    Fleckless on every side.

Dead Low-water

From *Our English Watering-Place, 1851* | Charles Dickens (1812–1870)

21 September

Sky, sea, beach, and village, lie as still before us as if they were sitting for the picture. It is dead low-water. A ripple plays among the ripening corn upon the cliff, as if it were faintly trying from recollection to imitate the sea; and the world of butterflies hovering over the crop of radish-seed are as restless in their little way as the gulls are in their larger manner when the wind blows. But the ocean lies winking in the sunlight like a drowsy lion – its glassy waters scarcely curve upon the shore – the fishing-boats in the tiny harbour are all stranded in the mud – our two colliers (our watering-place has a maritime trade employing that amount of shipping) have not an inch of water within a quarter of a mile of them, and turn, exhausted, on their sides, like faint fish of an antediluvian species. Rusty cables and chains, ropes and rings, undermost parts of posts and piles and confused timber-defences against the waves, lie strewn about, in a brown litter of tangled sea-weed and fallen cliff which looks as if a family of giants had been making tea here for ages, and had observed an untidy custom of throwing their tea-leaves on the shore.

The Poetry of the Sea

From *Sailing Alone around the World, 1900* | Joshua Slocum
(1844–disappeared after sailing south from Martha's Vineyard 1909)

The Pacific is perhaps, upon the whole, no more boisterous than other oceans, though I feel quite safe in saying that it is not more pacific except in name. It is often wild enough in one part or another. I once knew a writer who, after saying beautiful things about the sea, passed through a Pacific hurricane, and he became a changed man. But where, after all, would be the poetry of the sea were there no wild waves?

Home-Thoughts from the Sea

Robert Browning (1812–1889)

Nobly, nobly Cape Saint Vincent to the North-West died away;
Sunset ran, one glorious blood-red, reeking into Cadiz Bay;
Bluish mid the burning water, full in face Trafalgar lay;
In the dimmest North-East distance, dawned Gibraltar grand
    and gray;
'Here and here did England help me: how can I help England?' – say,
Whoso turns as I, this evening, turn to God to praise and pray,
While Jove's planet rises yonder, silent over Africa.

Kahu Rides the Whale

From *The Whale Rider, 1987* | Witi Ihimaera (1944–)

[Kahutia Te Rangi or Paikea is the legendary ancestor and whale rider in Māori mythology.]

She was the whale rider. Astride the whale she felt the sting of the surf and rain upon her face. On either side the younger whales were escorting their leader through the surf. They broke through into deeper water.

Her heart was pounding. She saw that now she was surrounded by the whale herd. Every now and then one of the whales would come to rub alongside the ancient leader. Slowly, the herd made its way to the open sea.

She was Kahutia Te Rangi. She felt a shiver running down the whale and, instinctively, she placed her head against its skin and closed her eyes. The whale descended in a shallow dive and the water was like streaming silk. A few seconds later the whale surfaced, gently spouting.

Her face was wet with sea and tears. The whales were gathering speed, leaving the land behind. She took a quick look and saw headlights far away. Then she felt that same shiver again, and again, placed her head against the whale's skin. This time when the whale dived, it stayed underwater longer. But Kahu had made a discovery. Where her face was pressed the whale had opened up a small breathing chamber.

A Port

From *Odyssey, 8–7th century* BCE, *Book Thirteen, lines 142–154* | Homer (8th century BCE)

Translated by George Chapman (c. 1559–1634)

And when heav'n's brightest star, that first doth call
The early morning out, advanc'd her head,
Then near to Ithaca the billow-bred
Phræcian ship approach'd. There is a port,
That th' aged sea-God Phorcys makes his fort,
Whose earth the Ithacensian people own,
In which two rocks inaccessible are grown
Far forth into the sea, whose each strength binds
The boist'rous waves in from the high-flown winds
On both the out-parts so, that all within
The well-built ships, that once their harbour win
In his calm bosom, without anchor rest,
Safe, and unstirr'd.

Farewell

From *Dover to Munich* | C. S. Calverley (1831–1884)

Farewell, farewell! Before our prow
  Leaps in white foam the noisy channel,
A tourist's cap is on my brow,
  My legs are cased in tourists' flannel:

Around me gasp the invalids –
  The quantity to-night is fearful –
I take a brace or so of weeds,
  And feel (as yet) extremely cheerful.

The night wears on: – my thirst I quench
  With one imperial pint of porter;
Then drop upon a casual bench –
  (The bench is short, but I am shorter) –

Place 'neath my head the *harve-sac*
  Which I have stowed my little all in,
And sleep, though moist about the back,
  Serenely in an old tarpaulin.

A Seafaring Costume

From *Mapp and Lucia, 1931* | E. F. Benson (1867–1940)

There was a hint of seafaring about Georgie's costume as befitted one who had lately spent so much time on the pier at Folkestone. He had a very nautical-looking cap, with a black shining brim, a dark-blue double-breasted coat, white trousers and smart canvas shoes: really he might have been supposed to have come up to Tilling in his yacht, and have landed to see the town …A piercing whistle from the other side of the street showed him that his appearance had at once attracted attention, and there was Irene planted with her easel in the middle of the pavement, and painting a row of flayed carcasses that hung in the butcher's shop. Rembrandt had better look out …

'Avast there, Georgie,' she cried. 'Home is the sailor, home from sea.'

The Border of the World

From *The Sea Around Us, 1951* | Rachel Carson (1907–1964)

To the ancient Greeks the ocean was an endless stream that flowed forever around the border of the world, ceaselessly turning upon itself like a wheel, the end of earth, the beginning of heaven. This ocean was boundless; it was infinite. If a person were to venture far out upon it – were such a course thinkable – he would pass through gathering darkness and obscuring fog and would come at last to a dreadful and chaotic blending of sea and sky, a place where whirlpools and yawning abysses waited to draw the traveller down into a dark world from which there was no return.

Fly Away, Fly Away Over the Sea

Christina Rossetti (1830–1894)

Fly away, fly away over the sea,
    Sun-loving swallow, for summer is done;
Come again, come again, come back to me,
    Bringing the summer and bringing the sun.

The Colour of the Sea

From *Cape Cod, 1865* | Henry David Thoreau (1817–1862)

Commonly, in calm weather, for half a mile from the shore, where the bottom tinges it, the sea is green, or greenish, as are some ponds; then blue for many miles, often with purple tinges, bounded in the distance by a light almost silvery stripe; beyond which there is generally a dark-blue rim, like a mountain-ridge in the horizon, as if, like that, it owed its color to the intervening atmosphere. On another day it will be marked with long streaks, alternately smooth and rippled, light-colored and dark, even like our inland meadows in a freshet, and showing which way the wind sets.

OCTOBER

The Seagull Spreads his Wings

A Wide Space of Sea

From *The Voyage Out, 1915* | Virginia Woolf (1882–1941)

All the smoke and the houses had disappeared, and the ship was out in a wide space of sea very fresh and clear though pale in the early light. They had left London sitting on its mud. A very thin line of shadow tapered on the horizon, scarcely thick enough to stand the burden of Paris, which nevertheless rested upon it. They were free of roads, free of mankind, and the same exhilaration at their freedom ran through them all. The ship was making her way steadily through small waves which slapped her and then fizzled like effervescing water, leaving a little border of bubbles and foam on either side. The colourless October sky above was thinly clouded as if by the trail of wood-fire smoke, and the air was wonderfully salt and brisk. Indeed it was too cold to stand still.

Evening by the Sea

Algernon Charles Swinburne (1837–1909)

It was between the night and day,
        The trees looked very weary – one by one
Against the west they seemed to sway,
        And yet were steady. The sad sun
In a sick doubt of colour lay
        Across the water's belt of dun.

On the weak wind scarce flakes of foam
        There floated, hardly bourne at all
From the rent edge of water – some
        Between slack gusts the wind let fall,
The white brine could not overcome
        That pale grass on the southern wall.

That evening one could always hear
        The sharp hiss of the shingle, rent
As each wave settled heavier,
        The same rough way. This noise was blent
With many sounds that hurt the air
        As the salt sea-wind came and went.

The wind wailed once and was not. Then
        The white sea touching its salt edge
Dropped in a slow low sigh: again
        The ripples deepened to the ledge,
Across the beach from marsh and fen
        Came a faint smell of rotten sedge.

2 October

Like a hurt thing that will not die
        The sea lay moaning; waifs of weed
Strove thro' the water painfully
        Or lay flat, like drenched hair indeed,
Rolled over with the pebbles, nigh
        Low places where the rock-fish feed.

The Dardanelles

From *The Pillars of Hercules, 1995* | Paul Theroux (1941–)

The Dardanelles is like a canal, no more than a mile wide in some places, linking the eastern basin of the Mediterranean to the Sea of Marmara, where another canal – the Bosphorus – divides Istanbul, and so on to the Black Sea.

The Dardanelles is also the Hellespont of Leander, who swam back and forth to be with Hero; and of Lord Byron, in homage and in imitation. I had thought of swimming it myself – but it looked uninviting in late October, with four- to five-foot breaking waves, and a heavy chop, with a cold wind blowing from Thrace on the north side.

The Hellespont

From *The Glorious Adventure, 1927* | Richard Halliburton (1900–1939 disappeared while attempting to sail a Chinese junk across the Pacific Ocean from Hong Kong to San Francisco)

To me the Hellespont was not just a narrow strait of cold blue water, discharging the Black Sea and the Sea of Marmora into the Ægean. Far more than that: it was a tremendous symbol, – a symbol of audacity, of challenge; of epic poetry, and heroic adventure.

The nature of the Hellespont's first records seem to have set an example for all the historic events that have clustered about it. Its very naming is a dramatic story. The name of 'Hellespont' ('Dardanelles' on the modern maps) goes back to legendary ages, receiving its title from 'Hele', the King of Thessaly's daughter who fell into the channel from the winged ram with the golden fleece, on whose back she was fleeing from her enemies.

The Cormorant

Emily Lawless (1845–1913)

Now the seagull spreads his wing,
And the puffin seeks the shore,
Home flies every living thing,
Yo, ho! the breakers roar!
        Only the Cormorant, dark and sly,
        Watches the waves with a sea-green eye.

Under his bows the breakers fleet,
All alone, alone went he;
Flying alone through the blinding sleet.
Flying alone through the raging sea.
    Only the Cormorant, dark and sly,
        Watches the waves with a sea-green eye.

Round his bark the billows roar,
Dancing along to a lonely grave;
Death behind, and Death before
Yo, ho! the breakers rave!
    Only the Cormorant, dark and sly,
        Watches the waves with a sea-green eye.

Hark! the waves on their iron floor,
See Kilstiffin's naked brow!
Iron cliff, and iron shore,
Erin's saints preserve him now!
        Only the Cormorant, dark and sly,
        Watches the waves with a sea-green eye.

Hark! was that a drowing cry?
Erin's saints receive his soul!
Nothing now twixt sea and sky
Yo, ho! the breakers roll!
    Only the Cormorant, dark and sly,
    Watches the waves with a sea-green eye.

Land! Land!

From *Westward Ho!* 1855 | Charles Kingsley (1819–1875)

Land! land! land! Yes, there it was, far away to the south and west, beside the setting sun, a long blue bar between the crimson sea and golden sky. Land at last, with fresh streams, and cooling fruits, and free room for cramped and scurvy-weakened limbs. And there, too, might be gold, and gems, and all the wealth of Ind. Who knew? Why not? The old world of fact and prose lay thousands of miles behind them, and before them and around them was the realm of wonder and fable, of boundless hope and possibility. Sick men crawled up out of their stifling hammocks; strong men fell on their knees and gave God thanks; and all eyes and hands were stretched eagerly toward the far blue cloud, fading as the sun sank down, yet rising higher and broader as the ship rushed on before the rich trade-wind, which whispered lovingly round brow and sail, 'I am the faithful friend of those who dare!' 'Blow freshly, freshlier yet, thou good trade-wind, of whom it is written that He makes the winds His angels, ministering breaths to the heirs of His salvation. Blow freshlier yet, and save, if not me from death, yet her from worse than death. Blow on, and land me at her feet, to call the lost lamb home, and die!'

The Sea Serpent

From *Wild Wales, 1862* | George Borrow (1803–1881)

Once in October, in the year 1805, as a small vessel of the Traeth was upon the Menai, sailing very slowly, the weather being very calm, the people on board saw a strange creature like an immense worm swimming after them. It soon overtook them, climbed on board through the tiller-hole, and coiled itself on the deck under the mast – the people at first were dreadfully frightened, but taking courage they attacked it with an oar and drove it overboard; it followed the vessel for some time, but a breeze springing up they lost sight of it.

Voyages II

Hart Crane (1899–1932)

– And yet this great wink of eternity,
Of rimless floods, unfettered leewardings,
Samite sheeted and processioned where
Her undinal vast belly moonward bends,
Laughing the wrapt inflections of our love;

Take this Sea, whose diapason knells
On scrolls of silver snowy sentences,
The sceptred terror of whose sessions rends
As her demeanors motion well or ill,
All but the pieties of lovers' hands.

And onward, as bells off San Salvador
Salute the crocus lustres of the stars,
In these poinsettia meadows of her tides, –
Adagios of islands, O my Prodigal,
Complete the dark confessions her veins spell.

Mark how her turning shoulders wind the hours,
And hasten while her penniless rich palms
Pass superscription of bent foam and wave, –
Hasten, while they are true, – sleep, death, desire,
Close round one instant in one floating flower.

Bind us in time, O Seasons clear, and awe.
O minstrel galleons of Carib fire,
Bequeath us to no earthly shore until
Is answered in the vortex of our grave
The seal's wide spindrift gaze toward paradise.

The Whaling Ship

From *Sylvia's Lovers, 1863* | Elizabeth Gaskell (1810–1865)

There rocked the white-sailed ship, as if she were all alive with eagerness for her anchors to be heaved.

How impatient her crew of beating hearts were for that moment, how those on land sickened at the suspense, may be imagined, when you remember that for six long summer months those sailors had been as if dead from all news of those they loved; shut up in terrible, dreary Arctic seas from the hungry sight of sweethearts and friends, wives and mothers. No one knew what might have happened. The crowd on shore grew silent and solemn before the dread of the possible news of death that might toll in upon their hearts with this uprushing tide. The whalers went out into the Greenland seas full of strong, hopeful men; but the whalers never returned as they sailed forth. On land there are deaths among two or three hundred men to be mourned over in every half-year's space of time. Whose bones had been left to blacken on the gray and terrible icebergs? Who lay still until the sea should give up its dead? Who were those who should come back to Monkshaven never, no, never more?

Many a heart swelled with passionate, unspoken fear, as the first whaler lay off the bar on her return voyage.

Ode to Neptune

Phillis Wheatley (1753–1784)

On Mrs. W–'s Voyage to England.

I.

While raging tempests shake the shore,
While Æolus' thunders round us roar,
And sweep impetuous o'er the plain
Be still, O tyrant of the main;
Nor let thy brow contracted frowns betray,
While my Susannah skims the watery way.

II.

The Power propitious hears the lay,
The blue-eyed daughters of the sea
With sweeter cadence glide along,
And Thames responsive joins the song.
Pleased with their notes Sol sheds benign his ray,
And double radiance decks the face of day.

III.

To court thee to Britannia's arms
Serene the climes and mild the sky,
Her region boasts unnumber'd charms,
Thy welcome smiles in ev'ry eye.
Thy promise, Neptune keep, record my pray'r,
Not give my wishes to the empty air.

A Small Branch Covered with Berries

From *The Journal of Columbus's First Voyage 1492–1493* |

Christopher Columbus (1451–1506)

11 October

Thursday, 11th of October.

The course was W.S.W., and there was more sea than there had been during the whole of the voyage. They saw sandpipers, and a green reed near the ship. Those of the caravel *Pinta* saw a cane and a pole, and they took up another small pole which appeared to have been worked with iron; also another bit of cane, a land-plant, and a small board. The crew of the caravel *Niña* also saw signs of land, and a small branch covered with berries. Everyone breathed afresh and rejoiced at these signs.

On Becoming a Mermaid

Lorna Goodison (1947–)

Watching the underlife idle by,
you think drowning must be easy death
just let go and let the water carry you
away and under.
the current pulls your bathing-plaits loose,
your hair floats out straightened by the water
your legs close together fuse all the length down
your feet now one broad foot
the toes spread into
a fish-tail, fan-like
your sex locked under
mother-of-pearl scales
you're a nixie now, a mermaid
a green tinged fish/fleshed woman/thing
who swims with thrashing movements
and stands upended on the sea floor
breasts full and floating buoyed by the salt
and the space between your arms now always
filled and your sex sealed forever under
mother-of-pearl scale/locks closes finally
on itself like some close-mouthed oyster.

13 October

The Picture

From *The Voyage of the Dawn Treader*, 1952 | C. S. Lewis (1898–1963)

It was a picture of a ship – a ship sailing straight towards you. Her prow was gilded and shaped like the head of a dragon with a wide-open mouth. She had only one mast and one large, square sail which was a rich purple. The sides of the ship – what you could see of them where the gilded wings of the dragon ended – were green. She had just run up to the top of one glorious blue wave, and the nearer slope of that wave came down towards you, with streaks and bubbles on it. She was obviously running fast before a gay wind, list over a little on her port side. (By the way, if you are going to read this story at all, and if you don't know already, you had better get it into your head that the left of the ship when you are looking ahead is *port,* and the right is *starboard*.) All the sunlight fell on her from that side, and the water on that side was full of greens and purples. On the other, it was darker blue from the shadow of the ship.

The Inchcape Rock

Verses 1–4 | Robert Southey (1774–1843)

No stir in the air, no stir in the sea,
The Ship was still as she could be;
Her sails from heaven received no motion,
Her keel was steady in the ocean.

Without either sign or sound of their shock,
The waves flow'd over the Inchcape Rock;
So little they rose, so little they fell,
They did not move the Inchcape Bell.

The worthy Abbot of Aberbrothok
Had placed that bell on the Inchcape Rock;
On a buoy in the storm it floated and swung,
And over the waves its warning rung.

When the Rock was hid by the surge's swell,
The Mariners heard the warning Bell;
And then they knew the perilous Rock,
And blest the Abbot of Aberbrothok.

The Inchcape Bell

From *The Story of my Boyhood and Youth, 1913*

John Muir (1883–1914)

Southey's poem 'The Inchcape Bell'*,
A story of a priest and a pirate. A good priest in order to warn seamen in dark stormy weather hung a big bell on the dangerous Inchcape Rock. The greater the storm and higher the waves, the louder rang the warning bell, until it was cut off and sunk by wicked Ralph the Rover. One fine day, as the story goes, when the bell was ringing gently, the pirate put out to the rock, saying, 'I'll sink that bell and plague the Abbot of Aberbrothok.' So he cut the rope, and down went the bell 'with a gurgling sound; the bubbles rose and burst around,' etc. Then 'Ralph the Rover sailed away; he scoured the seas for many a day; and now, grown rich with plundered store, he steers his course for Scotland's shore.' Then came a terrible storm with cloud darkness and night darkness and high roaring waves, 'Now where we are,' cried the pirate, 'I cannot tell, but I wish I could hear the Inchcape bell.' And the story goes on to tell how the wretched rover 'tore his hair,' and 'curst himself in his despair,' when 'with a shivering shock' the stout ship struck on the Inchcape Rock, and went down with Ralph and his plunder beside the good priest's bell. The story appealed to our love of kind deeds and of wildness and fair play.

[*The Inchcape Bell was a common title for Robert Southey's poem The Inchcape Rock.]

What Shall We Do With a Drunken Sailor?

Traditional sea shanty

What shall we do with the drunken sailor,
What shall we do with the drunken sailor,
What shall we do with the drunken sailor,
Earlye in the morning?

Hooray an' up she rises,
Hooray an' up she rises,
Hooray an' up she rises,
Earlye in the morning.

Shave his belly with a rusty razor
. . . . . .
Put him in a long boat till he's sober
. . . . . .
Keep him there and make him bale her,
. . . . . .
Stick him in a scupper with a hosepipe bottom
. . . . . .
Put him in the bed with the captains daughter

That's what we'll do with the drunken sailor,
That's what we'll do with the drunken sailor,
That's what we'll do with the drunken sailor,
Earlye in the morning.

Hooray an' up she rises,
Hooray an' up she rises,
Hooray an' up she rises,
Earlye in the morning.

Porpoise

From *The Old Man and the Sea, 1952* | Ernest Hemingway (1899–1961)

During the night two porpoise came around the boat and he could hear them rolling and blowing. He could tell the difference between the blowing noise the male made and the sighing blow of the female.

'They are good,' he said. 'They play and make jokes and love one another. They are our brothers like the flying fish.'

The Mariner

E. Pauline Johnson (Tekahionwake) (1861–1913)

'*Wreck and stray and castaway.*' – Swinburne

Once more adrift.
O'er dappling sea and broad lagoon,
O'er frowning cliff and yellow dune,
The long, warm lights of afternoon
Like jewel dustings sift.

Once more awake.
I dreamed an hour of port and quay,
Of anchorage not meant for me;
The sea, the sea, the hungry sea
Came rolling up the break.

Once more afloat.
The billows on my moorings press't
They drove me from my moment's rest,
And now a portless sea I breast,
And shelterless my boat.

Once more away.
The harbor lights are growing dim,
The shore is but a purple rim,
The sea outstretches grey and grim.
Away, away, away!

Once more at sea,
The old, old sea I used to sail,
The battling tide, the blowing gale,
The waves with ceaseless under-wail
The life that used to be.

Born at Sea

From *The Coral Island, 1857* | R. M. Ballantyne (1825–1894)

It was a wild, black night of howling storm, the night in which I was born on the foaming bosom of the broad Atlantic Ocean. My father was a sea-captain; my grandfather was a sea-captain; my great-grandfather had been a marine. Nobody could tell positively what occupation *his* father had followed; but my dear mother used to assert that he had been a midshipman, whose grandfather, on the mother's side, had been an admiral in the royal navy. At any rate we knew that, as far back as our family could be traced, it had been intimately connected with the great watery waste. Indeed this was the case on both sides of the house; for my mother always went to sea with my father on his long voyages, and so spent the greater part of her life upon the water.

Sonnet XII

Written on the Sea Shore – October, 1784 | Charlotte Smith (1749–1806)

On some rude fragment of the rocky shore,
  Where on the fractured cliff the billows break,
  Musing, my solitary seat I take,
And listen to the deep and solemn roar.

O'er the dark waves the winds tempestuous howl;
  The screaming sea-bird quits the troubled sea:
  But the wild gloomy scene has charms for me,
And suits the mournful temper of my soul.

Already shipwrecked by the storms of fate,
  Like the poor mariner methinks I stand,
  Cast on a rock; who sees the distant land
From whence no succour comes – or comes too late.
Faint and more faint are heard his feeble cries,
Till in the rising tide the exhausted sufferer dies.

The Last Crest

From *A Pair of Blue Eyes, 1873* | Thomas Hardy (1840–1928)

The journey was along a road by neutral green hills, upon which hedgerows lay trailing like ropes on a quay. Gaps in these uplands revealed the blue sea, flecked with a few dashes of white and a solitary white sail, the whole brimming up to a keen horizon which lay like a line ruled from hillside to hillside. Then they rolled down a pass, the chocolate-toned rocks forming a wall on both sides, from one of which fell a heavy jagged shade over half the roadway. A spout of fresh water burst from an occasional crevice, and pattering down upon broad green leaves, ran along as a rivulet at the bottom. Unkempt locks of heather overhung the brow of each steep, whence at divers points a bramble swung forth into mid-air, snatching at their head-dresses like a claw.

They mounted the last crest, and the bay which was to be the end of their pilgrimage burst upon them. The ocean blueness deepened its colour as it stretched to the foot of the crags, where it terminated in a fringe of white – silent at this distance, though moving and heaving like a counterpane upon a restless sleeper. The shadowed hollows of the purple and brown rocks would have been called blue had not that tint been so entirely appropriated by the water beside them.

The Uncertainty of Ferries

From *Journal of a Tour to the Hebrides, 1785*

James Boswell (1740–1795)

We then set out for the ferry, by which we were to cross to the main land of Argyleshire. Lochbuy:
We bade adieu to Lochbuy, and to our very kind conductor. Sir Allan M'lean, on the shore of Mull, and then got into the ferry-boat, the bottom of which was strewed with branches of trees or bushes, upon which we sat. We had a good day and a fine passage, and in the evening landed at Oban, where we found a tolerable inn. After having been so long confined at different times in islands, from which it was always uncertain when we could get away, it was comfortable to be now on the main land, and to know that, if in health, we might get to any place in Scotland or England in a certain number of days.

The Tuft of Kelp

Herman Melville (1819–1891)

All dripping in tangles green,
    Cast up by a lonely sea
If purer for that, O Weed,
    Bitterer, too, are ye?

Shipping Forecast

Jana Synková (1968–)

Fair or foul? Wind and rain? Will sunny spells prevail –
or thunderstorms, menace; gales, ascend the Beaufort Scale?
Far from Faeroes, Fisher, Fitzroy (formerly Finisterre),
I drift in and out of sleep; the mesmerizing worlds of Sole,
Biscay, Dogger, conjuring up strange dreams of unfamiliar
deeps; ships and trawlers following these lines uttered at
ungodly hours – these forecasts transmitted in reassuring
tones for fishermen and sailors; clutched at keenly, also
by melancholics, insomniacs, and drowning poets.

But I remember Cromarty; how, in some skipper's boat
we skimmed the Sutors at the entry to the Firth; saw,
up-close, ghosts of decommissioned oil platforms, rusting
in the sea. The boat, lurching with each swell of saltwater,
and we not knowing – *is this rough, or fair going*? – feigning
disregard for that wet which gets under the skin and inside
waterproofed things, as only it can in the Black Isle
or Hebrides. But where also a glimmer of sunlight
on mossy outcrops, or lichened rocks, or on the rare-calm
sea, is worth a hundred days of sun elsewhere.

The Land's End

From *Rambles Beyond Railways, 1851* | Wilkie Collins (1824–1889)

The Land's End! There is something in the very words that stirs us all. It was the name that struck us most, and was best remembered by us, as children, when we learnt our geography. It fills the minds of imaginative people with visions of barrenness and solitude, with dreams of some lonely promontory, far away by itself out in the sea – the sort of place where the last man in England would be most likely to be found waiting for death, at the end of the world! It suggests even to the most prosaically constituted people, ideas of tremendous storms, of flakes of foam flying over the land before the wind, of billows in convulsion, of rocks shaken to their centre, of caves where smugglers lurk in ambush, of wrecks and hurricanes, desolation, danger, and death. It awakens curiosity in the most careless – once hear of it, and you long to see it – tell your friends that you have travelled in Cornwall, and ten thousand chances to one, the first question they ask is: 'Have you been to the Land's End?'

And yet, strange to say, this spot so singled out and set apart by our imaginations as something remarkable and even unique of its kind, is as a matter of fact, not distinguishable from any part of the coast on either side of it, by any local peculiarity whatever. If you desire really and truly to stand on the Land's End itself, you must ask your way to it, or you are in danger of mistaking any one of the numerous promontories on the right hand and the left, for your actual place of destination.

Brighton

From *Clayhanger, 1910* | Arnold Bennett (1867–1931)

When, in an astounding short space of time, he stood in the King's Road at Brighton, it seemed to him that he was in a dream; that he was not really at Brighton, that town which for so many years had been to him naught but a romantic name. Had his adventurousness, his foolhardiness, indeed carried him so far? As for Brighton, it corresponded with no dream. It was vaster than any imagining of it. Edwin had only seen the pleasure cities of the poor and of the middling, such as Blackpool and Llandudno. He had not conceived what wealth would do when it organised itself for the purposes of distraction. The train had prepared him to a certain extent, but not sufficiently. He suddenly saw Brighton in its autumnal pride, Brighton beginning one of its fine week-ends, and he had to admit that the number of rich and idle people in the world surpassed his provincial notions. For miles westwards and miles eastwards, against a formidable background of high, yellow and brown architecture, persons the luxuriousness of any one of whom would have drawn remarks in Bursley, walked or drove or rode in thronging multitudes. Edwin could comprehend lolling by the sea in August, but in late October it seemed unnatural, fantastic. The air was full of the trot of glossy horses and the rattle of bits and the roll of swift wheels, and the fall of elegant soles on endless clean pavements; it was full of the consciousness of being correct and successful.

I started Early – Took my Dog –

Emily Dickinson (1830–1886)

I started Early – Took my Dog –
And visited the Sea –
The Mermaids in the Basement
Came out to look at me –

And Frigates – in the Upper Floor
Extended Hempen Hands –
Presuming Me to be a Mouse –
Aground – upon the Sands –

But no Man moved Me – till the Tide
Went past my simple Shoe –
And past my Apron – and my Belt
And past my Bodice – too –

And made as He would eat me up –
As wholly as a Dew
Upon a Dandelion's Sleeve –
And then – I started – too –

And He – He followed – close behind –
I felt His Silver Heel
Upon my Ankle – Then my Shoes
Would overflow with Pearl –

Until We met the Solid Town –
No One He seemed to know –
And bowing – with a Mighty look –
At me – The Sea withdrew –

Rapid Progress

From *Le tour du monde en quatre-vingts jours, 1872*
Around the World in Eighty Days, 1873 | Jules Verne (1828–1905)
Translated by George Makepeace Towle (1841–1893)

The weather, which had hitherto been fine, changed with the last quarter of the moon. The sea rolled heavily, and the wind at intervals rose almost to a storm, but happily blew from the south-west, and thus aided the steamer's progress. The captain as often as possible put up his sails, and under the double action of steam and sail the vessel made rapid progress along the coasts of Anam and Cochin China.

The Uses of Seaweed

From *England: A Natural History, 2024* | John Lewis-Stempel (1967–)

We also took the Massey 35 tractor and its wood-sided trailer down to the beach to gather seaweed to be used as fertilizer on the land. On other occasions, I remember taking seaweed home to give to my grandmother, Great Aunt Kath's sister and a farmer's wife herself, so she could use it to divine the weather. (Seaweed, hung outside the back door, swelled when rain was due, dried out to signal more clement meteorology. My grandparents also had a morning religious ritual, tapping the barometer in the hall, and checking the pine cones on the windowsill of the small sitting room. Sometimes they fell into outright suspicion and consulted the Met Office forecast. The weather is a big thing in farming.)

The Views from Land

From *The Voyage Out, 1915* | Virginia Woolf (1882–1941)

Very few people [on land] thought about the sea.

They took it for granted that the sea was calm; and there was no need, as there is in many houses when the creeper taps on the bedroom windows, for the couples to murmur before they kiss, 'Think of the ships to-night,' or 'Thank Heaven, I'm not the man in the lighthouse!' For all they imagined, the ships when they vanished on the sky-line dissolved, like snow in water. The grown-up view, indeed, was not much clearer than the view of the little creatures in bathing drawers who were trotting in to the foam all along the coasts of England, and scooping up buckets full of water. They saw white sails or tufts of smoke pass across the horizon, and if you had said that these were waterspouts, or the petals of white sea flowers, they would have agreed.

Columbus Discovers Himself

John Agard (1949–)

Sailing interior seas is a risky enterprise.

Who knows what Other dwells
under the skin's uncharted skies?

What manner of fauna and flora
will the blood's Sargasso deliver?

The brain's treacherous horizon ahoy.
The tierra incognita of self-discovery.

O mapless mariner lost in his inner Indies.

NOVEMBER

The Call of the Sea

Going to Sea

From *Treasure Island, 1883* | Robert Louis Stevenson (1850–1894)

Our way, to my great delight, lay along the quays and beside the great multitude of ships of all sizes and rigs and nations. In one, sailors were singing at their work, in another there were men aloft, high over my head, hanging to threads that seemed no thicker than a spider's. Though I had lived by the shore all my life, I seemed never to have been near the sea till then. The smell of tar and salt was something new. I saw the most wonderful figureheads, that had all been far over the ocean. I saw, besides, many old sailors, with rings in their ears, and whiskers curled in ringlets, and tarry pigtails, and their swaggering, clumsy sea-walk; and if I had seen as many kings or archbishops I could not have been more delighted.

And I was going to sea myself, to sea in a schooner, with a piping boatswain and pig-tailed singing seamen, to sea, bound for an unknown island, and to seek for buried treasures!

While I was still in this delightful dream, we came suddenly in front of a large inn and met Squire Trelawney, all dressed out like a sea-officer, in stout blue cloth, coming out of the door with a smile on his face and a capital imitation of a sailor's walk.

'Here you are,' he cried, 'and the doctor came last night from London. Bravo! The ship's company complete!'

'Oh, sir,' cried I, 'when do we sail?'

'Sail!' says he. 'We sail tomorrow!'

Ariel's Song

From The Tempest, Act I scene ii | William Shakespeare (1564–1616)

Full fathom five thy father lies;
　Of his bones are coral made;
Those are pearls that were his eyes:
　Nothing of him that doth fade,
But doth suffer a sea-change
Into something rich and strange:
Sea-nymphs hourly ring his knell.

Ding-dong.

Hark! now I hear them, – Ding-dong, bell.

Lyme

From *Persuasion, 1817* | Jane Austen (1775–1817)

3 November

After securing accommodations, and ordering a dinner at one of the inns, the next thing to be done was unquestionably to walk directly down to the sea. They were come too late in the year for any amusement or variety which Lyme, as a public place, might offer. The rooms were shut up, the lodgers almost all gone, scarcely any family but of the residents left – and, as there is nothing to admire in the buildings themselves, the remarkable situation of the town, the principal street almost hurrying into the water, the walk to the Cobb, skirting round the pleasant little bay, which, in the season, is animated with bathing machines and company; the Cobb itself, its old wonders and new improvements, with the very beautiful line of cliffs stretching out to the east of the town, are what the stranger's eye will seek; and a very strange stranger it must be, who does not see charms in the immediate environs of Lyme, to make him wish to know it better. The scenes in its neighbourhood, Charmouth, with its high grounds and extensive sweeps of country, and still more, its sweet, retired bay, backed by dark cliffs, where fragments of low rock among the sands, make it the happiest spot for watching the flow of the tide, for sitting in unwearied contemplation.

The Mouth of the Mississippi

From *Domestic Manners of the Americans, 1832* |

Fanny Trollope (1779–1863)

On the 4th of November, 1827, I sailed from London, accompanied by my son and two daughters; and after a favourable, though somewhat tedious voyage, arrived on Christmas-day at the mouth of the Mississippi.

The first indication of our approach to land was the appearance of this mighty river pouring forth its muddy mass of waters, and mingling with the deep blue of the Mexican Gulf. The shores of this river are so utterly flat, that no object upon them is perceptible at sea, and we gazed with pleasure on the muddy ocean that met us, for it told us we were arrived, and seven weeks of sailing had wearied us; yet it was not without a feeling like regret that we passed from the bright blue waves, whose varying aspect had so long furnished our chief amusement, into the murky stream which now received us.

Roll on, thou deep and dark blue ocean

CLXXIX, CLXXXIV, Canto IV, *Childe Harold's Pilgrimage* |

George Gordon, Lord Byron (1788–1824)

Roll on, thou deep and dark blue ocean – roll!
Ten thousand fleets sweep over thee in vain;
Man marks the earth with ruin – his control
Stops with the shore; – upon the watery plain
The wrecks are all thy deed, nor doth remain
A shadow of man's ravage, save his own,
When, for a moment, like a drop of rain,
He sinks into thy depths with bubbling groan,
Without a grave, unknell'd, uncoffin'd, and unknown.

. . . . . .

And I have loved thee, Ocean! and my joy
Of youthful sports was on thy breast to be
Borne, like thy bubbles, onward; from a boy
I wanton'd with thy breakers – they to me
Were a delight; and if the freshening sea
Made them a terror – 'twas a pleasing fear,
For I was as it were a child of thee,
And trusted to thy billows far and near,
And laid my hand upon thy mane – as I do here.

The Tankadere

From *Le Tour du monde en quatre-vingts jours, 1872*
Around the World in Eighty Days, 1873 | Jules Verne (1828–1905)
Translated by George Makepeace Towle (1841–1893)

This voyage of eight hundred miles was a perilous venture on a craft of twenty tons, and at that season of the year. The Chinese seas are usually boisterous, subject to terrible gales of wind, and especially during the equinoxes; and it was now early November.

It would clearly have been to the master's advantage to carry his passengers to Yokohama, since he was paid a certain sum per day; but he would have been rash to attempt such a voyage, and it was imprudent even to attempt to reach Shanghai. But John Bunsby believed in the Tankadere, which rode on the waves like a seagull; and perhaps he was not wrong.

Late in the day they passed through the capricious channels of Hong Kong, and the Tankadere, impelled by favourable winds, conducted herself admirably.

Long Trip

Langston Hughes (1901–1967)

The sea is a wilderness of waves,
A desert of water.
We dip and dive,
Rise and roll,
Hide and are hidden
On the sea.
    Day, night,
    Night, day,
The sea is a desert of waves,
A wilderness of water.

Arion of Methymna

From *The Histories, 426–415 BCE* Book I, chapters 23–24

Herodotus (484–c. 425 BCE)

Translated by George Rawlinson (1812–1902)

23. Arion of Methymna, who as a player on the harp, was second to no man living at that time, and who was, so far as we know, the first to invent the dithyrambic measure, to give it its name, and to recite in it at Corinth, was carried to Tænarum on the back of a dolphin.

24. He had lived for many years at the court of Periander, when a longing came upon him to sail across to Italy and Sicily. Having made rich profits in those parts, he wanted to recross the seas to Corinth. He therefore hired a vessel, the crew of which were Corinthians, thinking that there was no people in whom he could more safely confide; and, going on board, he set sail from Tarentum. The sailors, however, when they reached the open sea, formed a plot to throw him overboard and seize upon his riches. Discovering their design, he fell on his knees, beseeching them to spare his life, and making them welcome to his money. But they refused; and required him either to kill himself outright, if he wished for a grave on the dry land, or without loss of time to leap overboard into the sea. In this strait Arion begged them, since such was their pleasure, to allow him to mount upon the quarter-deck, dressed in his full costume, and there to play and sing, and promising that, as soon as his song was ended, he would destroy himself. Delighted at the prospect of hearing the very best harper in the world, they consented, and withdrew from the stern to the middle of the vessel: while Arion dressed himself in the full costume of his calling, took his harp, and standing on the quarter-deck, chanted the Orthian. His strain ended, he flung himself, fully attired as he was, headlong into the sea. The Corinthians then sailed on to Corinth. As for Arion, a dolphin, they say, took him upon his back and carried him to Tænarum, where he went ashore, and thence proceeded to Corinth in his musician's dress, and told all that had happened to him.

The Visiting Sea

Alice Meynell (1847–1922)

As the inhastening tide doth roll,
Dear and desired, along the whole
  Wide shining strand, and floods the caves,
  – Your love comes filling with happy waves
The open sea-shore of my soul.

But inland from the seaward spaces,
None knows, not even you, the places
  Brimmed, at your coming, out of sight,
  – The little solitudes of delight
This tide constrains in dim embraces.

You see the happy shore, wave-rimmed,
But know not of the quiet dimmed
  Rivers your coming floods and fills,
  The little pools 'mid happier hills,
My silent rivulets, over-brimmed.

What! I have secrets from you?Yes.
But, visiting Sea, your love doth press
  And reach in further than you know,
  And fills all these; and when you go,
There's loneliness in loneliness.

Desolate Beaches

From *Tender is the Night, 1934* | F. Scott Fitzgerald (1896–1940)

In November the waves grew black and dashed over the sea wall onto the shore road – such summer life as had survived disappeared and the beaches were melancholy and desolate under the mistral and rain. Gausse's Hôtel was closed for repairs and enlargement and the scaffolding of the summer Casino at Juan-les-Pins grew larger and more formidable. Going into Cannes or Nice, Dick and Nicole met new people – members of orchestras, restaurateurs, horticultural enthusiasts, shipbuilders – for Dick had bought an old dinghy – and members of the Syndicat d'Initiative. They knew their servants well and gave thought to the children's education. In December, Nicole seemed well-knit again; when a month had passed without tension, without the tight mouth, the unmotivated smile, the unfathomable remark, they went to the Swiss Alps for the Christmas holidays.

Wells-Next-the-Sea

Sophie Hannah (1971–)

I came this little seaside town
And went a pub they call The Crown
Where straight away I happened see
A man who seemed quite partial me.
I proved susceptible his charms
And fell right in his open arms
From time time, every now and ten,
I hope meet up with him again.

Crescent Beach

From *The Promised Land, 1912* | Mary Antin (1881–1949)

Crescent Beach is a name that is printed in very small type on the maps of the environs of Boston, but a life-size strip of sand curves from Winthrop to Lynn; and that is historic ground in the annals of my family. The place is now a popular resort for holiday crowds, and is famous under the name of Revere Beach. When the reunited Antins made their stand there, however, there were no boulevards, no stately bath-houses, no hotels, no gaudy amusement places, no illuminations, no showmen, no tawdry rabble. There was only the bright clean sweep of sand, the summer sea, and the summer sky. At high tide the whole Atlantic rushed in, tossing the seaweeds in his mane; at low tide he rushed out, growling and gnashing his granite teeth. Between tides a baby might play on the beach, digging with pebbles and shells, till it lay asleep on the sand. The whole sun shone by day, troops of stars by night, and the great moon in its season.

Into this grand cycle of the seaside day I came to live and learn and play. A few people came with me, as I have already intimated; but the main thing was that *I* came to live on the edge of the sea – I, who had spent my life inland, believing that the great waters of the world were spread out before me in the Dvina. My idea of the human world had grown enormously during the long journey; my idea of the earth had expanded with every day at sea; my idea of the world outside the earth now budded and swelled during my prolonged experience of the wide and unobstructed heavens.

The Spell of the Sea

From *The House by the Sea, 1977* | May Sarton (1912–1995)

I am living under a powerful spell, the spell of the sea. But in one way it is not as I imagined, for I had imagined that part of the spell would be the influence of the tides, rising and falling. But I do not see the rocks or the shoreline from my windows; I look out to the ocean over a long field, so I am not aware of the tides, after all, nor influenced by their rhythm; instead, I am bathed in the gentleness of this field-ocean landscape.

'With ships the sea was sprinkled far and nigh'

William Wordsworth (1770–1850)

With Ships the sea was sprinkled far and nigh,
Like stars in heaven, and joyously it showed;
Some lying fast at anchor in the road,
Some veering up and down, one knew not why.
A goodly Vessel did I then espy
Come like a giant from a haven broad;
And lustily along the bay she strode,
Her tackling rich, and of apparel high.
The Ship was nought to me, nor I to her,
Yet I pursued her with a Lover's look;
This Ship to all the rest did I prefer:
When will she turn, and whither? She will brook
No tarrying; where She comes the winds must stir:
On went She, and due north her journey took.

The Coast-road between Genoa and Spezzia

From *Pictures from Italy, 1846* | Charles Dickens (1812–1870)

Some of the villages are inhabited, almost exclusively, by fishermen; and it is pleasant to see their great boats hauled up on the beach, making little patches of shade, where they lie asleep, or where the women and children sit romping and looking out to sea, while they mend their nets upon the shore. There is one town, Camoglia, with its little harbour on the sea, hundreds of feet below the road; where families of mariners live, who, time out of mind, have owned coasting-vessels in that place, and have traded to Spain and elsewhere. Seen from the road above, it is like a tiny model on the margin of the dimpled water, shining in the sun. Descended into, by the winding mule-tracks, it is a perfect miniature of a primitive seafaring town; the saltest, roughest, most piratical little place that ever was seen. Great rusty iron rings and mooring-chains, capstans, and fragments of old masts and spars, choke up the way; hardy rough-weather boats, and seamen's clothing, flutter in the little harbour or are drawn out on the sunny stones to dry; on the parapet of the rude pier, a few amphibious-looking fellows lie asleep, with their legs dangling over the wall, as though earth or water were all one to them, and if they slipped in, they would float away, dozing comfortably among the fishes; the church is bright with trophies of the sea, and votive offerings, in commemoration of escape from storm and shipwreck. The dwellings not immediately abutting on the harbour are approached by blind low archways, and by crooked steps, as if in darkness and in difficulty of access they should be like holds of ships, or inconvenient cabins under water; and everywhere, there is a smell of fish, and sea-weed, and old rope.

Maracas Beach Prayer

Roger Robinson (1967–)

With sandy grit, with salt and weeds
each large wave returns to beach.
Make my life this simple, Lord.

The waves consume you where you stand
and feet float up from shallow sand.
Make my life this simple, Lord.

I swim past their crash to gentle seas
and tread still water with my feet.
Make my life this simple, Lord.

Some men pull nets, their veins like streams,
and kids, they kick their ball and scream.
Make my life this simple, Lord.

Of all the gifts you have to give
if this could be a way to live,
make my life this simple, Lord.

Crossing the Atlantic

From *The Story of My Boyhood and Youth*, 1913

John Muir (1838–1914)

1849

In crossing the Atlantic before the days of steamships, or even the American clippers, the voyages made in old-fashioned sailing-vessels were very long. Ours was six weeks and three days. But because we had no lessons to get, that long voyage had not a dull moment for us boys.

Father and sister Sarah, with most of the old folk, stayed below in rough weather, groaning in the miseries of seasickness, many of the passengers wishing they had never ventured in 'the auld rockin' creel,' as they called our bluff-bowed, wave-beating ship, and, when the weather was moderately calm, singing songs in the evenings – 'The Youthful Sailor Frank and Bold,' 'Oh, why left I my home, why did I cross the deep,' etc. But no matter how much the old tub tossed about and battered the waves, we were on deck every day, not in the least seasick, watching the sailors at their rope-hauling and climbing work; joining in their songs, learning the names of the ropes and sails, and helping them as far as they would let us; playing games with other boys in calm weather when the deck was dry, and in stormy weather rejoicing in sympathy with the big curly-topped waves.

A Story of the Sea-Shore

Introduction, lines 1–6 | George MacDonald (1824–1905)

I sought the long clear twilights of my home,
Far in the pale-blue skies and slaty seas,
What time the sunset dies not utterly,
But withered to a ghost-like stealthy gleam,
Round the horizon creeps the short-lived night,
And changes into sunrise in a swoon.

Clean and Pure Water

From *The Deep Sea, 1896* | Edward Step (1855–1931)

The ocean does almost everything for man. Consider this statement well, and you will be astounded at the way in which we are everywhere dependent, directly or indirectly, upon the sea as the great reservoir of the world's water, and as the manufacturer, by means of its myriads of living contents, of new and useful material from the old and worn-out rubbish, the very refuse and filth, that we daily pour into it. In fact, one of the principal occupations of civilized man may be said to consist in making clean water dirty; and one of the greatest operations of Nature is to make the dirty water clean and pure again.

The Waves

Mimi Khalvati (1944–)

Every day the world is beloved by me, the seagull eager
for its perch. I woke this morning to a darkened room,

my soul stabled at the gate. We grow older, quieter,
hearing degrees of movement, distance, and the dead

would listen if they could to the voices of the living
as bedrock listens to the ocean. I listen to the waves,

trying to make them go one, two, one, two, to hear
what Virginia Woolf heard. But she heard it in memory,

darling memory that delineates. One, two, one, two,
and all the variable intervals in between surrendering

to 'the very integer' Alice Oswald rhymed with water,
creating a thumb-hole through which to see the world.

Light fluctuates and my soul fluctuates like a jellyfish
underwater. My hand throws animal shadows on paper

and there, outlined, is a single goat, black and white,
standing on top of the mountain, like a tiny church.

The English Channel

From *Around the World in Seventy-Two Days, Pictorial Weeklies Company, New York, 1890* | Nellie Bly (1864–1922)

There has been so much written and told about the English Channel, that one is inclined to think of it as a stream of horrors. It is also affirmed that even hardy sailors bring up the past when crossing over it, so I naturally felt that my time would come.

All the passengers must have been familiar with the history of the channel, for I saw everyone trying all the known preventives of seasickness. The women assumed reclining positions and the men sought the bar.

I remained on deck and watched the sea-gulls, or what I thought were these useful birds – useful for millinery purposes – and froze my nose. It was bitterly cold, but I found the cold bracing until we anchored at Boulogne, France. Then I had a chill.

Echoes

Walter de la Mare (1873–1956)

The sea laments
The livelong day,
Fringing its wastes of sand;
Cries back the wind from the whispering shore –
No words I understand:
Yet echoes in my heart a voice,
As far, as near, as these –
The wind that weeps,
The solemn surge
Of strange and lonely seas.

Struggling to Survive

From *Robinson Crusoe, 1719* | Daniel Defoe (1660–1731)

23 November

Nothing can describe the confusion of thought which I felt when I sunk into the water; for though I swam very well, yet I could not deliver myself from the waves so as to draw breath, till that wave having driven me, or rather carried me a vast way on towards the shore, and having spent itself, went back, and left me upon the land almost dry, but half dead with the water I took in. I had so much presence of mind, as well as breath left, that seeing myself nearer the mainland than I expected, I got upon my feet, and endeavoured to make on towards the land as fast as I could before another wave should return and take me up again. But I soon found it was impossible to avoid it; for I saw the sea come after me as high as a great hill, and as furious as an enemy, which I had no means or strength to contend with. My business was to hold my breath, and raise myself upon the water if I could; and so by swimming, to preserve my breathing and pilot myself towards the shore if possible; my greatest concern now being that the sea, as it would carry me a great way towards the shore when it came on, might not carry me back again with it when it gave back towards the sea.

The Mariner

G. K. Chesterton (1874–1936)

The violet scent is sacred
  Like dreams of angels bright;
The hawthorn smells of passion
  Told in a moonless night.

But the smell is in my nostrils,
  Through blossoms red or gold,
Of my own green flower unfading,
  A bitter smell and bold.

The lily smells of pardon,
  The rose of mirth; but mine
Smells shrewd of death and honour,
  And the doom of Adam's line.

The heavy scent of wine-shops
  Floats as I pass them by,
But never a cup I quaff from,
  And never a house have I.

Till dropped down forty fathoms,
  I lie eternally;
And drink from God's own goblet
  The green wine of the sea.

The Ferry

From *Adé: A Love Story, 2013* | Rebecca Walker (1969–)

To finally climb aboard the ferry that took us away from the mainland of Kenya was to step into a dream. We were never so glad to leave tar and cement, metal and glass, profane music and men who did not take precautions. The boat was not big, but it was old and looked to us seaworthy, although of course there would have been nothing to do if it had been otherwise. It was painted white and a calming pale green, and once it began to move, groaning loudly as the waters churned beneath us, it did not take long for the coastline to disappear and the chaos of the dock to fade from view.

The Beauty of the Ship

Walt Whitman (1819–1892)

When, staunchly entering port,
After long ventures, hauling up, worn and old,
Batter'd by sea and wind, torn by many a fight,
With the original sails all gone, replaced, or mended,
I only saw, at last, the beauty of the Ship.

The Handsome Sailor

From *Billy Budd, written 1891, published 1924* |

Herman Melville (1819–1891)

In the time before steamships, or then more frequently than now, a stroller along the docks of any considerable sea-port would occasionally have his attention arrested by a group of bronzed mariners, man-of-war's men or merchant-sailors in holiday attire ashore on liberty. In certain instances they would flank, or, like a body-guard quite surround some superior figure of their own class, moving along with them like Aldebaran among the lesser lights of his constellation. That signal object was the 'Handsome Sailor' of the less prosaic time alike of the military and merchant navies. With no perceptible trace of the vainglorious about him, rather with the off-hand unaffectedness of natural regality, he seemed to accept the spontaneous homage of his shipmates.

The Call of the Sea

From *The Cruise of the Amaryllis, 1924* | G H P Muhlhauser (1870–1923)

The call of the sea is a peculiar thing. Why anyone who is not obliged to should submit to the confinement, want of society, privations, broken nights, and general unrest, and discomfort, to say nothing of the frequently occurring periods of anxiety in a small yacht, with its elementary cooking, on long trips, is difficult to explain to those who are not drawn to the sea. Indeed I do not understand it myself, but at any rate it is a clean sport, and harms no one and nothing, while the fact that one is contending with mughtly natural forces, and must depend on one's own efforts to get safely through, gives zest to, and sheds a glow of romance over the undertaking.

Ships that Pass in the Night

Paul Laurence Dunbar (1872–1906)

29 November

Out in the sky the great dark clouds are massing;
  I look far out into the pregnant night,
Where I can hear a solemn booming gun
  And catch the gleaming of a random light,
That tells me that the ship I seek is passing, passing.

My tearful eyes my soul's deep hurt are glassing;
  For I would hail and check that ship of ships.
I stretch my hands imploring, cry aloud,
  My voice falls dead a foot from mine own lips,
And but its ghost doth reach that vessel, passing, passing.

O Earth, O Sky, O Ocean, both surpassing,
  O heart of mine, O soul that dreads the dark!
Is there no hope for me? Is there no way
  That I may sight and check that speeding bark
Which out of sight and sound is passing, passing?

The Islands

From *Gulliver's Travels, 1726* | Jonathan Swift (1667–1745)

When I was at some Distance from the Pyrates, I discovered, by my Pocket-Glass, several Islands to the South-East. I set up my Sail, the Wind being fair, with a design to reach the nearest of those Islands, which I made a Shift to do, in about three Hours. It was all rocky: however I got many Birds' Eggs; and, striking Fire, I kindled some Heath and dry Sea Weed, by which I roasted my Eggs. I ate no other Supper, being resolved to spare my Provisions as much as I could. I passed the Night under the Shelter of a Rock, strewing some Heath under me, and slept pretty well.

The next Day I sailed to another Island, and thence to a third and fourth, sometimes using my Sail, and sometimes my Paddles. But, not to trouble the Reader with a particular Account of my Distresses, let it suffice, that on the 5th day I arrived at the last Island in my Sight, which lay South-South-East to the former.

This Island was at a greater Distance than I expected, and I did not reach it in less than five Hours. I encompassed it almost round, before I could find a convenient Place to land in; which was a small Creek, about three Times the Wideness of my Canoe. I found the Island to be all rocky, only a little intermingled with Tufts of Grass, and sweet smelling Herbs. I took out my small Provisions and after having refreshed myself, I secured the Remainder in a Cave, whereof there were great Numbers. I gathered plenty of Eggs upon the Rocks, and got a Quantity of dry Sea-weed, and parched Grass, which I designed to kindle the next Day, and roast my Eggs as well as I could. (For I had about me my Flint, Steel, Match, and Burning-glass.) I lay all Night in the Cave where I had lodged my Provisions. My Bed was the same dry Grass and Sea-weed which I intended for Fewel. I slept very little, for the Disquiets of my Mind prevailed over my Wearyness, and kept me awake. I considered how impossible it was to preserve my Life in so desolate a Place, and how miserable my End must be.

DECEMBER

New Land at Last to be Seen

The Great Western Ocean

From *Journals, 1805* | Meriwether Lewis (1774–1809) & William Clark (1770–1838)

William Clark: *Sunday December 1st 1805*

The emence Seas and waves which breake on the rocks & Coasts to the S W & N W roars like an emence fall at a distance, and this roaring has continued ever Since our arrival in the neighbourhood of the Sea Coast which has been 24 days Since we arrived in Sight of the Great Western (for I cannot Say Pacific) Ocian as I have not Seen one pacific day Since my arrival in its vicinity, and its waters are forming and petially breake with emence waves on the Sands and rockey Coasts, tempestous and horrible.

The Forsaken Merman

Lines 1–22 | Matthew Arnold (1822–1888)

Come, dear children, let us away;
Down and away below!
Now my brothers call from the bay,
Now the great winds shoreward blow,
Now the salt tides seaward flow;
Now the wild white horses play,
Champ and chafe and toss in the spray.
Children dear, let us away!
This way, this way!

Call her once before you go –
Call once yet!
In a voice that she will know:
'Margaret! Margaret!'
Children's voices should be dear
(Call once more) to a mother's ear;

Children's voices, wild with pain –
Surely she will come again!
Call her once and come away;
This way, this way!
'Mother dear, we cannot stay!
The wild white horses foam and fret.'
Margaret! Margaret!

The Wild Story

From *Under the Wave at Waimea, 2021* | Paul Theroux (1941–)

The one wild story that everyone believed about Joe Sharkey was not true, but this was often the case with big-wave riders. It was told he had eaten magic mushrooms on a day declared Condition Black and dropped down a forty-five-foot wave one midnight under the white light of a full moon at Waimea Bay, the wave freaked with clawed rags of blue foam. He smashed his board on the inside break called Pinballs and, unable to make it to shore against the riptide, he swam five miles up the coast, where he was found in the morning, hallucinating on the sand. More proof that he was a hero; that he surfed like a rat on acid.

His being found on the beach at dawn near Banzai Pipeline was a fact, and he'd taken LSD, not mushrooms. But so much of the rest of his life had been outrageous, and sometimes heroic, glowing with sensuous happiness, that his fellow surfers never questioned whether the wave had been a monster, or if he'd been on it, or broken his board, or swum alone to Pipeline, nor did they accuse him in pidgin of *bulai* – lying. Sharkey had shown himself the equal of the best of them.

By the Sea

Christina Rossetti (1830–1894)

Why does the sea moan evermore?
    Shut out from heaven it makes its moan,
It frets against the boundary shore;
    All earth's full rivers cannot fill
    The sea, that drinking thirsteth still.

Sheer miracles of loveliness
    Lie hid in its unlooked-on bed:
Anemones, salt, passionless,
    Blow flower-like; just enough alive
    To blow and multiply and thrive.

Shells quaint with curve, or spot, or spike,
    Encrusted live things argus-eyed,
All fair alike, yet all unlike,
    Are born without a pang, and die
    Without a pang, and so pass by.

Moonfleet Bay

From *Moonfleet, 1898* | John Meade Falkener (1858–1932)

5 December

Our village lies near the centre of Moonfleet Bay, a great bight twenty miles across, and a death-trap to up-channel sailors in a south-westerly gale. For with that wind blowing strong from south, if you cannot double the *Snout*, you must most surely come ashore; and many a good ship failing to round that point has beat up and down the bay all day, but come to beach in the evening. And once on the beach, the sea has little mercy, for the water is deep right in, and the waves curl over full on the pebbles with a weight no timbers can withstand. Then if poor fellows try to save themselves, there is a deadly *under-tow* or rush back of the water, which sucks them off their legs, and carries them again under the thundering waves. It is that back-suck of the pebbles that you may hear for miles inland, even at Dorchester, on still nights long after the winds that caused it have sunk, and which makes people turn in their beds, and thank God they are not fighting with the sea on Moonfleet beach.

Sea Lullaby

Elinor Wylie (1885–1928)

The old moon is tarnished
With smoke of the flood,
The dead leaves are varnished
With colour like blood.

A treacherous smiler
With teeth white as milk,
A savage beguiler
In sheathings of silk

The sea creeps to pillage,
She leaps on her prey;
A child of the village
Was murdered to-day.

She came up to meet him
In a smooth golden cloak,
She choked him and beat him
to death, for a joke.

Her bright locks were tangled,
She shouted for joy
With one hand she strangled
A strong little boy.

Now in silence she lingers
Beside him all night
To wash her long fingers
In silvery light.

Pack Ice

From *South, 1919* | Ernest Shackleton (1874–1922)

The situation became dangerous that night. We pushed into the pack in the hope of reaching open water beyond, and found ourselves after dark in a pool which was growing smaller and smaller. The ice was grinding around the ship in the heavy swell, and I watched with some anxiety for any indication of a change of wind to the east, since a breeze from that quarter would have driven us towards the land. Worsley and I were on deck all night, dodging the pack. At 3 a.m. we ran south, taking advantage of some openings that had appeared, but met heavy rafted pack-ice, evidently old; some of it had been subjected to severe pressure. Then we steamed north-west and saw open water to the north-east. I put the *Endurance's* head for the opening, and, steaming at full speed, we got clear. Then we went east in the hope of getting better ice, and five hours later, after some dodging, we rounded the pack and were able to set sail once more. This initial tussle with the pack had been exciting at times. Pieces of ice and bergs of all sizes were heaving and jostling against each other in the heavy south-westerly swell. In spite of all our care the *Endurance* struck large lumps stem on, but the engines were stopped in time and no harm was done. The scene and sounds throughout the day were very fine.

The Tempest

Verses I-II | Charles Cotton (1630–1687)

I.

Standing upon the margent of the main,
Whilst the high boiling tide came tumbling in,
I felt my fluctuating thoughts maintain
As great an ocean, and as rude, within;
As full of waves, of depths, and broken grounds,
As that which daily laves her chalky bounds.

II.

Soon could my sad imagination find
A parallel to this half world of flood,
An ocean by my walls of earth confined,
And rivers in the channels of my blood:
Discovering man, unhappy man, to be
Of this great frame Heaven's epitome.

Chisil Bank

From *The Itinerary of John Leland In or About the Years 1535–1543* | John Leland (c. 1503/5–1552)

A litle above Abbates-Byri is the hed or point of the Chisil lying north weste, that from thens streach up 7 miles as a maine narow banke by a right line on to south est, and ther buttith on Portland scant a quarter of a mile above the new castell in Portland.

The nature of this bank of Chisil is such that as often as the wind blowith strene at south est so often the se betith it and losiththe bank [and so] kith thorough it; so that if this winde might most continually blow there this bank should sone be beten away and the se fully enter and devide Portland, making it an isle, as surely in tymes past it hath beene as far as I can by any conjecture gather. But as much as the south est wind dooth bete and breke of this Chisille bank, so much doth the north west wynd again socor, strengith and augmentith it.

Submarines

John Graham Bower / 'Klaxon' (1886–1940)

When the breaking wavelets pass all sparkling to the sky,
When beyond their crests we see the slender masts go by,
When the glimpses alternate in bubbles white and green,
And funnels grey against the sky show clear and fair between,
When the word is passed along – 'Stern and beam and bow' –
'Action stations fore and aft – all torpedoes now!'
When the hissing tubes are still, as if with bated breath
They waited for the word to loose the silver bolts of death,
When the Watch beneath the Sea shall crown the great Desire,
And hear the coughing rush of air that greets the word to fire,
We'll ask no advantage, Lord – but only would we pray
That they may meet this boat of ours upon their outward way.

Salt Water and Fresh Water

From *Autobiography of a Super-Tramp, 1908* |

W. H. Davies (1871–1940)

I have often heard salt water mariners sneer at these fresh water sailors, but, after crossing the Atlantic some eighteen times, and making several passages across the lakes, my opinion is that these vast inland lakes are more dangerous to navigate, and far less safe than the open seas.

Mana of the Sea

D. H. Lawrence (1885–1930)

Do you see the sea, breaking itself to bits against the islands
yet remaining unbroken, the level great sea?

Have I caught from it
the tide in my arms
that runs down to the shallows of my wrists, and breaks
abroad in my hands, like waves among the rocks of substance?

Do the rollers of the sea
roll down my thighs
and over the submerged islets of my knees
with power, sea-power
sea-power
to break against the ground
in the flat, recurrent breakers of my two feet?

And is my body ocean, ocean
whose power runs to the shores along my arms
and breaks in the foamy hands, whole power rolls out
to the white-treading waves of two salt feet?

I am the sea, I am the sea!

Night Fishing

From *The Land's End, 1908* | W. H. Hudson (1841–1922)

13 December

The most interesting hour of the day at St. Ives was in the afternoon or evening, the time depending on the tide, when the men issued from their houses and came lurching down the little crooked stone streets and courts to the cove or harbour to get the boats out for the night's fishing. It is a very small harbour in the corner of the bay – a roughly shaped half-moon with two little stone piers for horns, with just room enough inside to accommodate the fleet of about one hundred and fifty boats. The best spectacle is when they are taken out at or near sunset in fair weather, when the subdued light gives a touch of tenderness and mystery to sea and sky, and the boats, singly, in twos and threes, and in groups of half a dozen, drift out from the harbour and go away in a kind of procession over the sea. The black forms on the moving darkening water and the shapely deep-red sails glowing in the level light have then a beauty, an expression, which comes as a surprise to one unaccustomed to such a scene.

Bay of Biscay ~ a sonnet

Jana Synková (1968–)

The sea was quite calm, swirling grey and green;
No vessels espied, just us and the deep;
Marble-like foam forming in the ship's wake,
As we made towards the Bay of Biscay –
That romantic name, on ancient maps seen;
Sails set forth only in fathomless dreams;
Broadcast on forecasts of radio waves;
Made infamous by old sailors' dread tales.
Now, in odd silence, we paused at that place –
Braced for remorseless nor' westerly winds;
Hoping for glimpse of fin; splash of dolphin:
Some anecdote to impress those back home.
But nothing of note, save the odd seabird's
Shrill cry, scraping across the waxy sky.

15 December

Seasick at the Start

From *Around the World in Seventy-Two Days, Pictorial Weeklies Company, New York, 1890* | Nellie Bly (1864–1922)

The morning was beautiful and the bay never looked lovelier. The ship glided out smoothly and quietly, and the people on deck looked for their chairs and rugs and got into comfortable positions, as if determined to enjoy themselves while they could, for they did not know what moment someone would be enjoying themselves at their expense.

. . . . .

When the pilot went off everybody rushed to the side of the ship to see him go down the little rope ladder. I watched him closely, but he climbed down and into the row boat, that was waiting to carry him to the pilot boat, without giving one glance back to us. It was an old story to him, but I could not help wondering if the ship should go down, whether there would not be some word or glance he would wish he had given.

'You have now started on your trip,' someone said to me. 'As soon as the pilot goes off and the captain assumes command, then, and only then our voyage begins, so now you are really started on your tour around the world.'

Something in his words turned my thoughts to that demon of the sea-seasickness.

Never having taken a sea voyage before, I could expect nothing else than a lively tussle with the disease of the wave.

'Do you get seasick?' I was asked in an interested, friendly way. That was enough; I flew to the railing.

Iceland First Seen

Lines 1–14 | William Morris (1834–1896)

Lo from our loitering ship
a new land at last to be seen;
Toothed rocks down the side of the firth
on the east guard a weary wide lea,
And black slope the hill-sides above,
striped adown with their desolate green:
And a peak rises up on the west
from the meeting of cloud and of sea.
Foursquare from base unto point
like the building of Gods that have been.
The last of that waste of the mountains
all cloud-wreathed and snow-flecked and grey.
And bright with the dawn that began
just now at the ending of day.

The Scar on the Globe

From *The Sea Around Us, 1951* | Rachel Carson (1907–1964)

There is to this day a great scar on the surface of the globe. This scar or depression holds the Pacific Ocean. According to some geophysicists, the floor of the Pacific is composed of basalt, the substance of the earth's middle layer, while all other oceans are floored with a thin layer of granite, which makes up most of the earth's outer layer. We immediately wonder what became of the Pacific's granite covering and the most convenient assumption is that it was torn away when the moon was formed. There is supporting evidence.

The King's Ship

From *The Tempest,* Act I, scene ii | William Shakespeare (1564–1616)

I boarded the king's ship; now on the beak,
Now in the waist, the deck, in every cabin,
I flam'd amazement: sometime I'd divide,
And burn in many places; on the topmast,
The yards and bowsprit, would I flame distinctly,
Then meet and join. Jove's lightnings, the precursors
O' th' dreadful thunder-claps, more momentary
And sight-outrunning were not; the fire and cracks
Of sulphurous roaring the most mighty Neptune
Seem to besiege and make his bold waves tremble,
Yea, his dread trident shake.

The First Suitable Ship

From *A Voyage to the South Pole and Round the World: 1777* |

James Cook (1728–1779)

Upon the whole, I am firmly of opinion, that no ships are so proper for discoveries in distant unknown parts, as those constructed as was the Endeavour, in which I performed my former voyage. For no ships of any other kind can contain stores and provisions sufficient (in proportion to the necessary number of men), considering the length of time it will be necessary they should last. And, even if another kind of ships could stow a sufficiency, yet, on arriving at the parts for discovery, they would still, from the nature of their construction and be *less fit* for the purpose.

Hence it may be concluded, so little progress had been hitherto made in discoveries in the Southern Hemisphere. For all ships which attempted it before the Endeavour, were unfit for it; although the officers employed in them had done the utmost in their power.

It was upon these considerations that the Endeavour was chosen for that voyage. It was to these properties in her, that those on board owed their preservation; and hence we enabled to prosecute discoveries in these seas so much longer than any other ship ever did; or could do. And, although discovery was not the first object of that voyage, I could venture to traverse a far greater space of sea, till then unnavigated, to discover tracks of country in high and low South latitudes, and to persevere longer in exploring and surveying more correctly the extensive coasts of those new-discovered countries, than any former Navigator, perhaps, had done during one voyage.

The Sea People

From *The Little Mermaid, 1837* | Hans Christian Andersen (1805–1875)

Translated by M. R. James (1862–1936)

Far out in the sea the water is as blue as the petals of the loveliest of cornflowers, and as clear as the clearest glass; but it is very deep, deeper than any anchor-cable can reach, and many church towers would have to be put one on top of another to reach from the bottom out of the water. Down there live the sea people.

Now you must not think for a moment that there is only a bare white sandy bottom there; no, no: there the most extraordinary trees and plants grow, which have stems and leaves so supple that they stir at the slightest movement of the water, as if they were alive. All the fish, big and little, flit among the branches, like the birds in the air up here. In the deepest place of all lies the sea king's palace. The walls are of coral, and the tall pointed windows of the clearest possible amber, but the roof is of mussel shells that open and shut themselves as the water moves. It all looks beautiful, for in every one of them lie shining pearls, a single one of which would be the principal ornament in a Queen's crown.

The Sea by Moonlight

David Austin (1926–2018)

21 December

Sleepless I lie
the long night through.

In the distance
the whispering of the sea,
in which we were
but this afternoon –
like two fishes.

No, the sea does not give up.
Her restless body moves,
even in the night,
while the clear-faced moon –
her lover –
sparkles in her belly,
and the land lies still in sleep.

Homer and the Basins

From *The Note-books, 1912* | Samuel Butler (1835–1902)

When I returned from Calais last December, after spending Christmas at Boulogne according to my custom, the sea was rough as I crossed to Dover and, having a cold upon me, I went down into the second-class cabin, cleared the railway books off one of the tables, spread out my papers and continued my translation, or rather analysis, of the *Iliad*. Several people of all ages and sexes were on the sofas and they soon began to be sea-sick. There was no steward, so I got them each a basin and placed it for them as well as I could; then I sat down again at my table in the middle and went on with my translation while they were sick all round me. I had to get the *Iliad* well into my head before I began my lecture on *The Humour of Homer* and I could not afford to throw away a couple of hours, but I doubt whether Homer was ever before translated under such circumstances.

Divested of Sea Phrases

From *A New Voyage Round the World, 1697*

William Dampier (c. 1650–1715)

As to my Stile it cannot be expected, that a Seaman: should affect Politeness, for were I able to do it, yet I think I should be little solicitous about it, in a work of this Nature. I have frequently indeed, divested my self of Sea Phrases, to gratify the Land Reader; for which the Seamen will hardly forgive me: And yet, possibly I shall not seem Complaisant enough to the other; because I still retain the use of so many Sea terms. I confess I have not been at all scrupulous in this matter, either as to the one or the other of these; for I am persuaded, that if what I say be intelligible, it matters not greatly in what words it is expressed.

Nonsense

Mary Coleridge (1861–1907)

I had a boat and the boat had wings;
    And I did dream that we went a flying
Over the heads of queens and kings,
    Over the souls of dead and dying,
Up among the stars and the great white rings,
    And where the Moon on her back is lying.

A Sea-Chest

From *The Last Grain Race, 1956* | Eric Newby (1919–2006)

It was the sort of trunk that stingy murderers use for the disposal of their victims; covered with bright yellow fabric and fitted with imitation brass locks, it gave off a gluey smell and was sticky to the touch.

. . . . . .

'I want a wooden sea-chest, not a trunk. That thing will fall to pieces if it gets wet.'

The manager smirked. He was accustomed to this kind of complaint. 'The sea-chest is a thing of the past,' he said, 'are you expecting the fo'c'sle to be filled with water?'

'As a matter of fact, I am.'

'In that case,' he replied rather stiffly, 'you will no doubt want to take your own precautions. We will wrap these in brown paper.'

On the way back to Hammersmith, from the top of a bus I saw a magnificent trunk in the window of a shop that disposed of railway lost property. The trunk in the East India Dock Road had been an octavo trunk; this was a folio and the next day when I went to see it, I found that it even opened like a book. One side contained numbers of drawers intended for shoes and the other a big space for hanging clothes. It was blacker and grander than I had imagined. A small ticket said: 'This trunk by Louis Vuitton for sale', and underneath, more despairingly, 'Must be disposed of'. I bought it for four pounds, and put my shore-going clothes and my pilot jacket, of which at the time I was inordinately proud, in the space once filled with Paquin dresses. Its small white label, *Louis Vuitton. Paris. Nice. Vichy*, with its false promise of more gracious living supported me through periods of homesickness and depression.

Ulysses

Lines 44–70 | Alfred, Lord Tennyson (1809–1892)

There lies the port; the vessel puffs her sail:
There gloom the dark, broad seas. My mariners,
Souls that have toil'd, and wrought, and thought with me –
That ever with a frolic welcome took
The thunder and the sunshine, and opposed
Free hearts, free foreheads – you and I are old;
Old age hath yet his honour and his toil;
Death closes all: but something ere the end,
Some work of noble note, may yet be done,
Not unbecoming men that strove with Gods.
The lights begin to twinkle from the rocks:
The long day wanes: the slow moon climbs: the deep
Moans round with many voices. Come, my friends,
'T is not too late to seek a newer world.
Push off, and sitting well in order smite
The sounding furrows; for my purpose holds
To sail beyond the sunset, and the baths
Of all the western stars, until I die.
It may be that the gulfs will wash us down:
It may be we shall touch the Happy Isles,
And see the great Achilles, whom we knew.
Tho' much is taken, much abides; and tho'
We are not now that strength which in old days
Moved earth and heaven, that which we are, we are;
One equal temper of heroic hearts,
Made weak by time and fate, but strong in will
To strive, to seek, to find, and not to yield.

Two Lifeboats

From *The Wreck of the Golden Mary: The Wreck, 1856* |

Charles Dickens (1812–1870)

Thus, at that tempestuous time of the year, and in that tempestuous part of the world, we shipwrecked people rose and fell with the waves. It is not my intention to relate (if I can avoid it) such circumstances appertaining to our doleful condition as have been better told in many other narratives of the kind than I can be expected to tell them. I will only note, in so many passing words, that day after day and night after night, we received the sea upon our backs to prevent it from swamping the boat; that one party was always kept baling, and that every hat and cap among us soon got worn out, though patched up fifty times, as the only vessels we had for that service; that another party lay down in the bottom of the boat, while a third rowed; and that we were soon all in boils and blisters and rags.

The other boat was a source of such anxious interest to all of us that I used to wonder whether, if we were saved, the time could ever come when the survivors in this boat of ours could be at all indifferent to the fortunes of the survivors in that. We got out a tow-rope whenever the weather permitted, but that did not often happen, and how we two parties kept within the same horizon, as we did, He, who mercifully permitted it to be so for our consolation, only knows. I never shall forget the looks with which, when the morning light came, we used to gaze about us over the stormy waters, for the other boat. We once parted company for seventy-two hours, and we believed them to have gone down, as they did us. The joy on both sides when we came within view of one another again, had something in a manner divine in it; each was so forgetful of individual suffering, in tears of delight and sympathy for the people in the other boat.

The East Coast

From *The South Country, 1909* | Edward Thomas (1878–1917)

It was now that I first accepted the invitation of a relation who lived on the east coast very near the sea. The sea had a sandy shore bounded by a perpendicular sandy cliff, to the edge of which came rough moorland. The sea washed the foot of the cliff at high tide and swept the yellow sand clean twice a day, wiping away all footprints and leaving a fresh arrangement of blue pebbles glistering in the bitter wind. It was impossible to be more alone than on this sand, and I was contented again. The sea brought back the feelings I had when I lay in the buttercup field – the cemetery – and looked into the sky. Walking over the moor the undulations of the land hid and revealed the sea in an always unexpected way, and often as I turned suddenly I seemed to see the blue sky extended so as to reach nearly to my feet and half-way up it went small brown or white clouds like birds – like ships – in fact they were ships sailing on a sea that mingled with the sky. It seemed a beautiful life, where clouds could not help being finely spun or carved, or pebbles help being delicious to eye and touch.

A Lonely Coast

W. H. Davies (1871–1940)

A lonely coast, where sea-gulls scream for wrecks
    That never come; its desolate sides
Last visited, a hundred years ago,
    By one drowned man who wandered with the tides;
There I went mad, and with those birds I screamed,
    Till, waking, found 'twas only what I dreamed.

Searching for the Ship

From *Stories of the Lifeboat, 1894* | Frank Mundell (1870–1932)

The storm was at its height, and 'the billows frothed like yeast' under the lash of the furious wind. Hardly had the lifeboat left the shelter of the breakwater than a huge wave burst over her, drenching the men to the skin, in spite of their waterproofs and cork jackets, and almost sweeping some of them overboard. At one moment they were tossed upwards, as it seemed to the sky; at another they dropped down into a valley of water with huge green walls on either side. Again and again the spray dashed over them in blinding showers, but no one thought of turning back.

Bravely the stout little tug battled with the waves, and slowly but surely made headway against the storm, dragging the lifeboat after her. As they neared the probable position of the wreck, the men eagerly strained their eyes to gain a sight of the object of their search, but nothing met their gaze save the white waters foaming on the fatal sands. Suddenly, through the flying spray, loomed the hull of a large ship, with the breakers dashing over the bows.

B♭ Major

Percival Everett (1956–)

1
The thrill of it all, setting sail,
years away, might as well deliver
the letters ourselves upon return, icy letters
soaked with, overwhelmed with bold.

2
We project deities onto the night
sky, drawings of mammals in the stars,
sketches of crabs, of scorpions
because they scare us.

3
We are the lot that would be explorers,
if the night wouldn't fall so dark,
if the ice storms would turn in

on themselves, behave as we would behave,
if we had the trades behind us,
understanding our prayers.

Index

Sources

John Agard, 'Seaside Etiquette' and 'Columbus Discovers Himself' from *Alternative Anthem: Selected Poems* with Live DVD (Bloodaxe Books, 2009) Reproduced with permission of Bloodaxe Books. www.bloodaxebooks.com @bloodaxebooks (twitter/facebook) #bloodaxebooks

David Austin, 'The Sea by Moonlight (21 Dec)' from *The Breathing Earth* (Enitharmon Press, 2014). © The Estate of David Austin 2026.

Beryl Bainbridge, extract from *Every Man for Himself* (Duckworth Books, 1996). Reproduced with permission of Johnson & Alcock Ltd.

J M Barrie, extract from *Peter Pan* (Macmillan Collector's Library, 2016).

Patricia Beer, 'The Estuary' from *Collected Poems* (Carcanet Press, 1990).

John Betjeman, 'Winter Seascape' from *Collected Poems* (John Murray, 2006). © John Betjeman 2026. Reprinted by permission of Aitken Alexander Associates Ltd.

Rachel Carson, extracts from *The Sea Around Us* (Paladin, 1951).

Juanita Cox, 'Along the Sea Wall'. © 2019-2026 Juanita Cox All Rights Reserved.

Michael Cunningham, extracts from *Land's End*. Copyright © 2002 by Michael Cunningham. Used by permission of Brandt & Hochman Literary Agents, Inc. All rights reserved. Farrar, Straus & Giroux, an imprint of Macmillan.

Anni Domingo, extracts from Breaking the Maafa Chain (Jacaranda Books Art Music Limited, 2021). Reproduced with permission of the Licensor through PLSclear.

Bernadine Evaristo, extract from 'On Top of the World', published in *New Daughters of Africa* (Penguin, 2019) ed. Margaret Busby.

Percival Everett, 'B Flat Major' from *Sonnets for a Missing Key*. Reprinted by permission of Red Hen Press, copyright © 2024 by Percival Everett.

William Finnegan, extracts from *Barbarian Days: A Surfing Life* (Corsair, 2015), Penguin Random House.

John Fowles, extract from *The French Lieutenant's Woman* (Vintage, 1969). Vintage is an imprint of Penguin Random House UK. Aitken Alexander Associates Ltd.

Jewelle Gomez, extract from 'A Swimming Lesson' published in *New Daughters of Africa* (Penguin, 2019) ed. Margaret Busby. Reprinted by permission of SLL/ Sterling Lord Literistic, Inc, copyright Jewelle Gomez.

Lorna Goodison, 'On Becoming a Mermaid' from *Collected Poems* (Carcanet Press, 2017).Sophie Hannah, 'Wells-Next-the-Sea' from *Marrying the Ugly Millionaire (*Carcanet Press, 2015).

Seamus Heaney, 'Glanmore Sonnets VII' from *100 Poems* (Faber and Faber Ltd, 2022). Reprinted by permission of Farrar, Straus and Giroux. All Rights Reserved.

Ernest Hemingway, extracts from *The Old Man and the Sea* (Jonathan Cape, 1952). Published by Jonathan Cape. Copyright © Hemingway Foreign Rights Trust, 1952. Reprinted by permission of The Random House Group Limited. The Ernest Hemingway Foundation.

Robin Hobb, extracts from *Ship of Magic* (Harper Voyager, 1998). HarperCollins Publishers UK.

Langston Hughes, 'Water-Front Streets' and 'Long Trip' from *Selected Poems* (Serpent's Tail, 2020). Copyright © 1994 by The Estate of Langston Hughes. Reprinted by permission of Harold Ober Associates and International Literary Properties LLC.

Witi Ihimaera, extracts from *The Whale Rider* (Puffin, 1987). Penguin Random House UK and Australia.

Tove Jansson, extracts from *The Summer Book* (Sort Of Books, 2003). © Tove Jansson Estate, Tove Jansson Moomin Characters TM

Jenny Joseph, 'Tides' from *Selected Poems* (Bloodaxe, 1992). Copyright © Jenny Joseph, SELECTED POEMS, Bloodaxe 1992. Reproduced with permission of Johnson & Alcock Ltd.

Mimi Khalvati, 'The Waves' and 'Similes' from *The Weather Wheel* (Carcanet Press, 2014).

Tété-Michel Kpomassie, extracts from *Michel the Giant* (Penguin Classics, 2022). Copyright © Flammarion, 1981 Translation copyright © Harcourt, Inc., and Martin Secker & Warburg, Ltd, 1983 Copyright © Tété-Michel Kpomassie, 2022. Translated by James Kirkup. Reprinted by permission of Penguin Books Limited. Translation used by permission of The Random House Group Limited.

C S Lewis, extracts from *The Voyage of the Dawn Treader* (Geoffrey Bles, 1952). Copyright © 1952 C.S. Lewis Pte. Ltd. Extract reprinted by permission.

John Lewis-Stempel, extracts from *England: A Natural History* © John Lewis-Stempel, Transworld Publishers, 2024. Reproduced by permission of The Soho Agency, Penguin Random House UK.

Norman Lewis, extracts from *A Voyage by Dhow* (Picador, 2003).

John Masefield, 'Sea Fever' and 'Cargoes' from *Collected Poems* (Heinemann, 1938). Reproduced by permission of The Society of Authors.

Eric Newby, extracts from *The Last Grain Race* (WIlliam Collins, 2014). HarperCollins Publishers UK.

Grace Nichols, 'Nuptial on Brighton Beach' from *Passport to Here and There* (Bloodaxe, 2020). copyright © Grace Nichols, 2020. Reproduced with permission from Curtis Brown Group Ltd on behalf of Grace Nichols.

Oluwaseun Olayiwola, 'Beacon' and 'Coast' from *Strange Beach: Poems* (Fitzcarraldo Editions, 2025), Copyright © 2024 by Oluwaseun Olayiwola. Reprinted with the permission of The Permissions Company, LLC on behalf of Counterpoint Press, counterpointpress.com.

Mary Oliver, 'I Go Down to the Shore' from A Thousand Mornings (Corsair, 2018). Reprinted by the permission of The Charlotte Sheedy Literary Agency as agent for the author. Copyright © 2012, 2017 by Mary Oliver with permission of Bill Reichblum.Roger Robinson, 'Maracas Beach Prayer' from A Portable Paradise (Peepal Tree Press, 2019).

Arthur Ransome, extracts from *We Didn't Mean to Go to Sea* (Jonathan Cape, 1937). Penguin Random House UK, The Arthur Ransome Estate.

Rachel Rooney, 'Driving Home' from *The Language of Cat* (Otter-Barry, 2011). © Rachel Rooney, 2011, published by Frances Lincoln Children's Books, David Higham Associates.

May Sarton, extracts from *The House by the Sea* (1977). Reprinted by the permission of Russell & Volkening as agents for the author's estate. Copyright © 1977 by May Sarton. Originally published in *The House by the Sea* (W. W. Norton).

Lemn Sissay, 'A Shoal of Stars in Ocean Night' and 'Mist Surrounds the Ship' from *let the light pour in* (Canongate, 2023). Reproduced with permission of the Licensor through PLSclear.

Stevie Smith, 'Not Waving But Drowning' from The Collected Poems and Drawings of Stevie Smith (Faber and Faber Ltd, 2018). Copyright © 1957 by Stevie Smith. Reprinted with the permission of The Permissions Company, LLC, on behalf of New Directions Publishing Corp., ndbooks.com.

Attillah Springer, extracts from 'Castle in the Sand' published in *New Daughters of Africa* (Penguin, 2019) ed. Margaret Busby.

Jana Synková, 'Shipping Forecast' and 'Bay of Biscay' from Pilgrimage. Reproduced with kind permission of Jana Synková

Paul Theroux, extracts from *The Pillars of Hercules* (Penguin, 1996) and *Under the Wave at Waimea* (Hamish Hamilton, PRH UK, 2021). Excerpts from THE PILLARS OF HERCULES and UNDER THE WAVE AT WAIMEA by Paul Theroux. THE PILLARS OF HERCULES, Copy-right © 2008, Paul Theroux, used by permission of The Wylie Agency (UK) Limited. UNDER THE WAVE AT WAIMEA, Copyright © 2021by Paul Theroux, used by permission of The Wylie Agency (UK) Limited.

Derek Walcott, 'White Egrets: 53' from White Egrets (Faber and Faber Ltd, 2010). Copyright © 2010 by Derek Walcott. Reprinted by permission of Farrar, Straus and Giroux. All Rights Reserved.

Rebecca Walker, extract from 'Adé; A Love Story' published in *New Daughters of Africa* (Penguin, 2019) ed. Margaret Busby.

Batsford is committed to respecting the intellectual property rights of others. We have taken all reasonable efforts to ensure that the reproduction of all contents on these pages is done with the full consent of the copyright owners. If you are aware of unintentional omissions, please contact the company directly so that any necessary corrections may be made for future editions.

Bibliography

These books inspired and educated me in equal measure. I couldn't have compiled this anthology without them.

Patrick Barkham, Coastlines: *The Story of Our Shore, 2015*

Madeleine Bunting, *The Seaside: England's Love Affair, 2023*

Meg and Chris Clothier, *Sea Fever: A Seaside Companion, 2021*

The Oxford Companion to Ships and the Sea, 1976 (edited by Peter Kemp) and later editions

Brian Lavery, *A Short History of Seafaring, 2019*